THE
ADVOCATE'S
DAUGHTER

ALSO BY ANTHONY FRANZE

The Last Justice

THE
ADVOCATE'S
DAUGHTER

ANTHONY FRANZE

MINOTAUR BOOKS
A THOMAS DUNNE BOOK
NEW YORK

THOMAS DUNNE BOOK FOR MINOTAUR BOOKS.
An imprint of St. Martin's Publishing Group.

THE ADVOCATE'S DAUGHTER. Copyright © 2016 by Anthony Franze. All rights reserved. Printed in the United States of America. For information, address St. Martin's Press, 175 Fifth Avenue, New York, N.Y. 10010.

www.thomasdunnebooks.com

www.minotaurbooks.com

Designed by Omar Chapa

Library of Congress Cataloging-in-Publication Data

Names: Franze, Anthony J., author.
Title: The advocate's daughter / Anthony Franze.
Description: First edition. | New York : Minotaur Books, 2016. | "A Thomas Dunne book."
Identifiers: LCCN 2015042573
    ISBN 978-1-250-07165-1 (hardcover)
    ISBN 978-1-4668-8283-6 (e-book)
Subjects: LCSH: United States. Supreme Court—Officials and employees—Fiction. | Murder—Investigation—Fiction. | Family secrets—Fiction. | Political fiction. | GSAFD: Suspense fiction. | Mystery fiction. | Legal stories.
Classification: LCC PS3606.R4228 A67 2016 | DDC 813/.6—dc23
LC record available at http://lccn.loc.gov/2015042573

Our books may be purchased in bulk for promotional, educational, or business use. Please contact your local bookseller or the Macmillan Corporate and Premium Sales Department at (800) 221-7945, extension 5442, or by e-mail at MacmillanSpecialMarkets@macmillan.com.

First Edition: March 2016

10   9   8   7   6   5   4   3   2   1

For Jake, Emma, and Aiden

THE
ADVOCATE'S
DAUGHTER

PROLOGUE

Misawa, Japan
Thirty Years Ago

It all started with a bottle of Nikka whiskey and a cold stare.

Sean set the bottle on the counter and smiled at the old woman who glowered at him from behind the register. The liquor store was quiet but for the buzz of fluorescent lamps, which cast a flickering haze over the narrow aisles and faded cardboard signs scrawled in Japanese.

Sean didn't know if she could tell that he was only fourteen years old. Maybe his height, six feet, and perhaps cultural differences would make it difficult for the woman to discern an American's age. But he glanced at Kenny, who'd sauntered over with another bottle. Short, floppy mess of hair, mouth full of braces. The old lady had to realize they were teenagers. And the disdain in her eyes—a wrinkled look of disgust—said that she not only knew, but hoped the boys would drink every drop, pass out, and choke on their own vomit. That's how it was outside the military base. The locals hated them. Sean's dad said it was because Americans corrupted and polluted everywhere they went. The community surrounding a base was always filled with two things, his dad would say: bars and whores. He would know.

Sean dug out the money from the front pocket of his jeans and handed the ball of sweaty bills to the woman. She smoothed them on the counter, mumbling something to herself. She packed the bottles in a single brown sack.

"*Domo,*" Sean said. He scooped up the sack and headed toward the door, Kenny trailing after him.

The woman said nothing.

Another storekeeper, probably the old lady's husband, narrowed his eyes as Sean marched past him toward the door.

"Hey, get your fucking hands off me." It was Kenny's voice.

Sean spun around and saw the old man gripping Kenny's arm. Kenny wrenched it free and kept moving.

"*Thief!*" the storekeeper bellowed in a thick accent. "*Thief!*"

The woman joined in, screaming words Sean couldn't understand.

Kenny sprinted out of the store, and Sean instinctively tore after him.

"*Thief! Thief!*"

The boys raced past a blur of pachinko parlors and bars on the shuttered main drag. Kenny disappeared around the corner up ahead. Sean kept running, the sting of sweat dripping into his eyes, the sack a clumsy bundle in his arms. He veered right, following Kenny, but his friend was nowhere in sight. Sean risked a quick look over his shoulder. The storekeeper hadn't kept up, but Sean didn't slow down until he heard a loud whisper from an alleyway.

"Seany boy."

Sean ran over to his friend. Kenny was bent over, a hand on each thigh, breathing raggedly. Kenny looked up and flashed a smile.

"What the hell?" Sean's voice was labored, his chest heaving up and down. "You stole something? Why? . . . We had money."

"They had it coming—treating us like that, thinking we'd steal something from their shitty store."

"We usually *do* steal something from their shitty store."

"Yeah, but it's the principle of the thing." Kenny pulled a flask-sized bottle from the front of his jeans. "It's their own fault." He untwisted the bottle's cap and took a swig, followed by a quiver. "You know how hard it is to run with this in your underwear? My dick nearly broke off."

Sean smiled in spite of himself. "Small loss."

They left the alley and walked a maze of side streets to another alleyway, this one lined with vacant buildings. Sean stopped in front of a boarded-up former nightclub sprayed with graffiti: their clubhouse. He pried at the door until it gave way and the two ambled inside. The smell of damp and rot filled the air. They walked to the stairwell, went up to the second floor, and out onto the crumbling terrace. There was an explosion of flapping wings as crows squawked away into the sky. They sat on a two-foot ledge, feet hanging over the side.

Sean opened a bottle, took a long pull, and passed it to his friend. The sun was setting as they stared out over the alleyway. There was a bar wedged between two abandoned buildings. The place had no customers out front and was as run-down as the clubhouse, but muffled music seeped out from the cracks in its walls. Behind the bar, Misawa Air Base's tall perimeter wall. Beyond the wall, an overgrown lot.

"You think he's coming?" Sean asked.

Kenny shrugged. He took another drink and wiped his mouth with the back of his hand. He then pointed his chin to the alley below. "Here comes the dipshit now."

Sean was about to call out to Juan, but Kenny shushed him. As Juan approached the clubhouse door, Kenny held out the bottle, set his aim, and let it fall.

The glass shattered noisily on the pavement and Juan jumped back with a yelp.

Kenny burst into laughter. "You look like you about pissed yourself, you dumb Mexican," he called down.

Juan glared up at them. He was a skinny kid, and he seemed even scrawnier than usual from this height. He muttered something and went inside the clubhouse, soon joining them on the ledge.

As darkness crawled across the alleyway the boys finished another bottle. A light affixed to the bar clicked on.

"Shit," Juan said. "What time is it? I gotta be home by eight."

"Eight? Is *Sesame Street* on or something?" Kenny said.

"You know my dad," Juan said.

Sean looked at his watch and then stood and brushed off his jeans. The booze had kicked in, and he clutched the railing to steady himself. "Let's get the hell out of here."

The three stumbled their way out of the clubhouse. As Sean turned to jam the clubhouse door shut, a voice sliced into the night air. *"You!"*

Sean whirled around. At the mouth of the alley, a silhouette. The figure stalked toward them and came under the bar's yellow light: the old man from the liquor store.

The storekeeper charged at Kenny, grabbing him by the shirt and ramming him into the clubhouse wall.

"Get the fuck off me, old man!"

The storekeeper's face was flushed and he shouted, a slur of Japanese, spittle hitting Kenny's face. Sean grabbed the storekeeper's arm, but the man—strong for his age and size and smelling of whiskey himself—pushed Sean away. As the old man fended off Sean, Kenny managed to break free. He barreled into the man. The storekeeper stumbled backward but got hold of Kenny's shirt, and the two fell hard to the pavement.

Sean looked around for help, but there was only Juan who just stood there, frozen.

Kenny tried to get up, but the storekeeper pulled him to the ground, eventually pinning Kenny down, straddling him. The old man raised a fist, but hesitated, as if just realizing he was about to punch a teenage kid in the face. Before the storekeeper could decide, Kenny kneed the man in the groin. The storekeeper doubled over. Kenny shoved him away, leapt to his feet, and kicked the man in the side. Rolling away, the storekeeper drew a sharp breath and moaned.

Sean ran over and hoisted the storekeeper up by the arm. He called for Juan to help and, after a long moment, Juan took hold of the old man's other arm. The storekeeper was on his feet now. He struggled, trying to rip his arms free. That's when Kenny ran up to him. Sean thought Kenny was going to spit in the storekeeper's face.

But then he heard it. An indescribable groan.

The storekeeper's body stiffened, and there was a gasp. Before Sean could react, Kenny made several quick jabs and pulled his hand away. The storekeeper's body went limp and slumped to the ground. Kenny's right hand—clutching a blade—was red with blood.

Sean and Juan stood there, stunned. Kenny closed the knife, jammed it into his pocket, and yelled at them to run. They raced across the alley, down a narrow path, to the back of the bar. Scrambling up some trash bins, they climbed over the base's ten-foot perimeter wall. Sean went last, his shirt catching on the barbed wire as he dropped to the ground.

Juan sat in the grass, his back against the cinder blocks. "He's dead." Tears streamed down his face. "He's dead."

"Shut up. We don't know that," Sean said. But he did.

Juan hugged his skinny arms around his knees and began rocking back and forth. "He's dead . . ."

Kenny took out the knife, unfolded it, and wiped the blade on the grass. "If he's dead," Kenny said, "he had it coming."

For the rest of Sean's brief time in Japan, he never spoke to Kenny or Juan again. He left them and that ugly night behind. The world was a bigger place back then—no Internet, no Facebook, no Twitter. And for thirty years, Sean had no idea what had become of them, no reason to believe that their secret would come to light.

Until he was about to be nominated for a seat on the U.S. Supreme Court.

CHAPTER 1

Washington, D.C., Suburbs
Present Day

There should have been a sign. A feeling. Some sense of impending doom. But Sean Serrat's day started like any other.

"Daddy, guess what?"

Sean always felt a tiny rush of emotion when his children called him *Daddy,* a word that was fading to extinction in his home.

"Daddy," Jack repeated. Sean glanced at his son, who was perched on a stool at the granite kitchen counter shoveling Cheerios into his mouth. Sunshine cut through the window and a shadow fell across the seven-year-old's round face. Jack's teenage brother, Ryan, sat next to him crunching a bagel.

"What is it, buddy?" Sean stood near the stove, bowl in one hand, spoon in the other, trying not to drip on his tie.

"I told my friend, Dean, about our family Money Jar."

"Yeah?"

"I told him that some families have Swear Jars where you have to put money in if you say a bad word. But *we* have a Money Jar that has money in it and you say bad words into the jar." Jack cupped his orange juice glass over his mouth and demonstrated with a muffled, "Butt, poop, ass."

Ryan blurted a laugh, spattering flecks of bagel over the countertop.

Sean tried to hold back a smile. "I don't think you should tell your friends about the Money Jar," he said. "And maybe let's not tell Mommy about—"

"Don't tell Mommy what?" Emily said, strolling into the kitchen. She wore black yoga pants and a T-shirt and her skin glistened from her morning jog. The boys snickered and Sean reached for the coffee pot and poured Emily a cup.

Emily's eyes narrowed. "What are you boys up to?"

"Us? Up to something?" Sean said, handing her the coffee.

Emily gave a sideways look: *Silly boys.* She smelled the coffee, smiled, and took a sip. "You look so handsome," she said. She set the mug on the counter and adjusted the knot on Sean's tie. "The new suit looks great. Are you excited for your first day?"

Sean gave a fleeting smile, trying to look sufficiently enthusiastic, something he knew his wife would see through. The job change had been Emily's idea. No, her demand.

"Hey Dad," Ryan said, "what's with the suit? I thought you were gonna be the boss, so doesn't that mean you can just wear jeans or whatever you want?"

"It's a big law firm, kiddo, and I'm not the boss. And anyway, I don't take fashion advice from eighth-graders who need a haircut and can't keep their pants pulled up."

"Seriously, go with jeans," Ryan said. "Set the tone. Show a little confidence."

"Leave Dad alone," Emily said. "He's going to be the talk of the ladies at the office." She clasped Sean's chin in her hand and pressed his cheeks together. "How often do you think a tall, dark, and handsome man walks into that stuffy law firm?" She tippy-toed and gave Sean a soft kiss.

"Guys, please." Ryan lifted a hand to shield his eyes.

Sean grabbed his wife's bottom to torture his fourteen-year-old.

Ryan shuddered. "Really, stop."

"You and Jack go get your backpacks together for school," Sean said. "Unless you want us to make out a little first." He wrapped his arm around Emily's waist and pulled her to him.

"I'm out," Ryan said. Hands on his temples like horse blinders, he marched out of the kitchen. His little brother imitated the move and followed after him.

"You said you might see Abby today?" Emily asked.

"Yeah. I'm going to a reception this afternoon at Georgetown for Justice Malburg's retirement. Jonathan told me she'd be there."

"Did Jon say how she's doing?" Emily opened the refrigerator door. Its face was a collage of family photographs and Jack's artwork held in place with magnets. Under one of the magnets, a bumper sticker: STAND UP FOR WHAT'S RIGHT, EVEN IF YOU'RE STANDING ALONE.

"He says Abby's the star research assistant of all his students."

"Tell her to call me. And that she'd *better* come to dinner tonight. She missed last week, and tonight's a celebration."

Sean nodded. "That reminds me," he said, "did she talk with you yesterday?"

"No, why?"

"I missed her call when I was at Brooks Brothers. She left me a voice mail that she wanted to talk about something, but with all the running around to get ready for today, I forgot to call back."

"Did she sound okay?" Emily asked. Her smile lines were always more pronounced when she was worried. "I haven't heard from her in a couple days."

"It didn't sound urgent. And she didn't call back, so I'm sure she's fine. I'll see what she needs today at Georgetown."

Distorted music whined from the kitchen counter. "Who Knew" by Pink. Last summer Abby had changed her mother's ringtone as a joke, and Emily never figured out how to switch it back. Abby and Emily both now walked around with Pink blaring from their phones whenever someone called.

"Maybe that's her." Emily scanned the iPhone, then tapped on the screen, sending the call to voice mail. "Just Margo," she said with a frown.

"Abby's fine. I'll tell her to give you a call."

Sean kissed his wife and called out good-byes to his sons. On the walk to the subway he thumbed a text to Abby. She didn't reply.

CHAPTER 2

Sean made his way down the escalator into the concrete arches and dim light of the Metro. The station smelled of smoldering rubber, and his tie blew over his shoulder in the push of air from a train entering the platform. He waved his SmarTrip card over the scanner at the gate and stepped into the train car just before the unforgiving doors clamped shut.

The orange vinyl seats were filled, and Sean gripped the metal handrail, trying not to lose his footing as the train jerked and jostled. He looked about the subway car. It was the usual cast: college students hypnotized by their phones, tourists wearing flip-flops and studying their travel guidebooks, and government workers with laminated security badges dangling from cords around their necks, the quintessential Washington status symbol. He caught one of the government types stealing a look at him. The man's gaze dropped back to the *Washington Post*. Sean wondered if the guy recognized him from the story in that morning's paper. Sean had already received several e-mails from friends about the piece: *Nice photo—smile much? Don't forget us little people. Mr. Big Shot,* and the like. The story, and others like it over the past two weeks, speculated that Sean had resigned from the solicitor general's office in anticipation that the president would soon nominate him to the Supreme Court; that Sean needed some daylight between himself and the controversial abortion and privacy cases that the office would handle next term. As is often the case in Washington, the truth was more pedestrian. The two Fs: family and finances. Heading the appellate group at a large law firm meant he'd have dozens of junior lawyers at his disposal—a large staff would allow him to be home more for the boys. And the firm paid ten times what he made at the solicitor general's office, ending his constant worries about surviving in overpriced D.C. on a government salary.

For most lawyers, the prospect of being on the short list for a Supreme Court nomination would be thrilling, an actor's Oscar nomination. For Sean, though, the newspaper story was unsettling. Not because of the job. After years of representing the federal government before the Supreme Court, he could do the job. History had shown that several justices had been dummies, and they'd gotten by. It was the attention. A nomination meant public scrutiny. A vetting. Which meant a deep look into his past. And that was something he didn't want or need.

The train pulled into Dupont Circle. Sean stepped aside to let an elderly woman totter out. It was then that he felt a hard shoulder bump from behind. It wasn't a brush-by—it had some energy to it. Purposeful. He watched the man with greasy hair and flannel shirt push roughly out of the subway car into the crowd on the platform. As the train doors started to close, the man twisted around and looked Sean in the eyes.

"They know, Sean," he said. "They know."

Sean did a double take. *Did he just say my name?* The train pulled away from the station, and Sean watched through the window as the man vanished into the sea of commuters. Sean must've misheard. Then it dawned on him. That damn story in the *Post*. But the guy said, *They know*. All the attention was making him paranoid.

The train hit Sean's stop at Farragut North, and he walked the two blocks to the Harrington & Caine building. In the lobby, he paused for a moment and took it all in. A glass and steel atrium spiraled up twelve stories, each floor occupied by more than a hundred lawyers. Three women in headset mikes sat behind a sleek reception table. Copies of *The Wall Street Journal* were neatly folded

beside leather chairs in the waiting area. The setting was a stark
contrast to the ornate fifth floor of the Justice Department building where Sean had spent most of his career. No portraits, no crown
moldings, no American flags or other pretentious symbols of the
Office of the Solicitor General and its important work representing the United States before the Supreme Court. Harrington &
Caine had a modern, ruthless design. A fitting metaphor, Sean
thought, for his move from the self-important government sphere
to the rainmaking-obsessed planet of Big Law.

As Sean checked in at the front desk, his phone vibrated and
he read the text message from Emily:

> Good luck today! I love you!
> p.s. still no word from Abby :(

CHAPTER 3

The morning at Harrington & Caine was a haze of computer training, tax and benefit forms, and lots of people whose names Sean would never remember. By early afternoon, he was eager to see some familiar faces at the reception for Justice Malburg.

He took a cab to First Street and walked to the Georgetown Law campus. A small fleet of black Cadillacs were parked along First, which Sean assumed was the security detail for the Supreme Court justices attending the event. A clock tower stood under a cloudless April sky, cutting a narrow shadow over the only patch of grass on the urban campus.

"Sean," Cecilia Lowenstein called to him in her husky voice. She gave him a cheek-to-cheek kiss. He'd once told her that he hated the faux European greeting, but that only encouraged Cecilia. Sean scanned the queue at the entrance of the Hotung International building. The line was filled with Washington's upper echelon: the Supreme Court Bar. A group of insufferable blowhards. Intellectual elitists. Terrible dressers. *His* people.

"Well, if it isn't the 'modest superstar' I've read so much about," Cecilia said, flapping a copy of the *Washington Post*.

Sean frowned and shook his head. "Let's not . . ."

"You're no fun." Cecilia adjusted her skirt and wobbled slightly in heels that seemed taller than she could handle. "So how's your first day in private practice? Realized how much it sucks yet?"

"They're still just showing me where the restrooms are and how to turn on my computer, so I haven't had to deal with billable hours yet."

"Ugh, don't get me started about billables. We were spoiled at OSG." Cecilia, like most of the Supreme Court community, spoke in abbreviations and acronyms. It wasn't the Office of the Solicitor General, it was OSG. It wasn't Justice Robert Reeves Anderson, it was RRA. A case wasn't dismissed as improvidently granted, it was DIG-ed. There was the GVR (granted, vacated, and remanded) and the CVSG (the court calling for the views of the solicitor general), and the list went on. An ivory tower version of annoying teenage text-speak.

Cecilia scrutinized the line ahead of them. "Most of these schmucks charge a thousand bucks an hour for lower court appeals, but will take the Supreme Court cases for free just so they can get oral arguments. With the justices hearing fewer and fewer cases every term, times are tough, my friend. And your law firm's gonna be so starstruck the first year that they won't give you grief that you're not pulling in much money, but that'll change."

Sean had heard this a million times from Cecilia, who'd left OSG two years ago to head the appellate group at Beacher & Bishop. She was right that getting Supreme Court cases in private practice wasn't easy. At OSG, they were part of a small band of elite government lawyers whose sole job was to represent the United States government in cases before the Supreme Court. The office was so influential with the nine justices that the solicitor general often was called "The Tenth Justice." They didn't have to go out and hustle for work; the cases came to them. The court accepted only about seventy out of seven thousand petitions requesting review each term, so in private practice the competition for a piece of that 1 percent was fierce. It was an open secret that when the court granted *certiorari* in a case, even the most prominent Supreme Court lawyers would engage in the distasteful practice of cold calling or e-mailing the parties offering to take the case for free. Still, it gave Sean solace that despite her gloom and doom, Cecilia already had racked up seven arguments while in private practice.

"Thanks for the pep talk," Sean said wearily. "I can always count on you, Cel."

"So, you really don't want to talk about this?" Cecilia flapped the newspaper again.

Sean rolled his eyes.

"You know I hate modesty," Cecilia said.

"I'm hardly being modest. We all know who's getting the nomination." Sean's gaze cut to Senator Mason James, who was at the front of the line.

Cecilia wrinkled her nose. "Maybe you're right. Those dumb shits on the Hill are determined to get one of their own on the court—even if it means a schemer like James. But clients will still be impressed, so you should take advantage of the attention." All nine of the current justices had been federal judges at the time of their appointment, something a block of senators had criticized as a departure from history that left the court too detached from the policy implications of its decisions. Senator James, the former attorney general of Virginia and a brilliant legal mind, offered the best of all worlds, they said. But Sean considered James as nothing more than a politician.

At the entrance, the dean of the law school and Professor Jonathan Tweed greeted guests.

Cecilia scowled at the sight of Professor Tweed. "Your buddy seems to be relishing the attention as usual."

"Can you be nice today?"

Cecilia didn't respond. When they reached the receiving line, she skipped by Tweed and greeted the dean with a hug.

Tweed gripped Sean's hand. "I see some things never change," Tweed said, shooting a glance at Cecilia.

Sean shrugged.

"No wait, I take that back," Tweed said. "Things *do* change. I thought you'd never sell out and join the private sector."

"Maybe if law schools didn't pay professors so much, we parents wouldn't have to change jobs to afford the tuition."

"You obviously haven't seen *my* pay stub," Tweed replied.

Sean grinned and then eyed the bandage that ran from Tweed's left temple to the middle of his cheek. "I hope the other guy looks worse."

"If only my life was so exciting," Tweed said. "Biking accident— hit some gravel in Rock Creek Park. I was on a date, so it was a little embarrassing."

"Hard to keep up with the nineteen-year-olds, I guess," Sean said.

"Don't be ridiculous," Tweed said, scanning for who was in earshot. "She was twenty."

Sean emitted a small, dry laugh.

Tweed said, "I'll come by and chat in a bit. And, hey, you're in private practice now, so you need to actually say hello to people and be friendly."

"Is Abby here?" Sean asked.

"I haven't seen her. But you don't think she'd miss out on being the envy of her classmates, do you?" Tweed pointed up. Windows lined the second-floor atrium overlooking the reception area. Law students were pressed against the glass gawking at the assemblage of legal elite.

Sean smiled. "I suppose she wouldn't. If you see her before I do, please send her my way."

Tweed nodded, already shaking hands with the next person in line.

"Get you a drink?" Cecilia asked. She plucked a cracker with olive tapenade from a silver tray offered by a server. Sean looked about the room. All clans accounted for. The former solicitor generals, the legal giants who got the best Supreme Court cases in private practice, mingled near the bar. At the boundaries, huddled in groups of three or four, the current staff of OSG. They talked in whispers and studiously displayed their non-alcoholic drinks. And at the center of the room, the VIPs: the dean, Supreme Court justices, members of Congress. Circling them were the nakedly ambitious. Sean saw Senator James chatting with Justice Scheuerman.

The senator let out a big laugh at whatever the justice had said. Sean was sure it wasn't *that* funny.

Cecilia clutched Sean's arm. "There's Justice Carr, let's say hello."

"I'd really rather just wait for the program to start." Carr was the newest member of the high court, confirmed just a few months ago. He was the only member of The Nine whom Sean had never met. From what he knew, though, Thaddeus Dupont Carr—"T.D." or "Touch Down" to friends—was one of those guys you loved to hate. College football star (thus the nickname), editor of the *Stanford Law Review,* and the youngest judge appointed to the Ninth Circuit until he breezed through the Supreme Court confirmation process.

"Come on, you'll like him. He's got a dry sense of humor, like you," Cecilia said. "You're coming."

Cecilia soon had Justice Carr laughing. She was famously profane and didn't censor herself for anyone, Supreme Court justices included. Carr finally turned to Sean and said, "I don't envy you."

Sean gave an apologetic smile and said, "Oh, Cecilia's harmless, you just have to get used to her lack of a filter." He'd spent a career apologizing for Cecilia.

The justice chortled. "No, I meant this morning's story in the *Post.* I remember when the press was speculating about my nomination. Reporters actually dug through the trash cans at my house."

Sean furrowed his brow. "Seriously?"

"Dead serious," Justice Carr said. "Be careful."

Sean nodded, not sure how to respond. After a few seconds, he opted for changing the subject. "My daughter met you recently."

"Oh yeah?"

"She's a law student here. Jon Tweed brought a group of his students to the court in January. Abby said your talk was 'inspirational.' Her word."

The justice laughed. "Oh, to be young and so easily fooled."

Senator James brushed by. Justice Carr's eyes traced James's path.

"Want some free advice?" Carr asked.

"From you?" Sean said. "Of course."

"When I was being considered for the nomination, someone wisely told me to always keep an eye on the competition."

Sean nodded.

"But in your case," Carr tilted his head toward Senator James, "you might want to get a food taster."

Cecilia was right. Sean was starting to like Justice Carr.

CHAPTER 4

There was a tap of a microphone and the rumble in the room dissipated. The dean stood on a platform in the reception area of Hotung. He was a bald, thin man in his fifties and behind him sat eighty-year-old Chief Justice Malburg. She was in a large wing chair that seemed to swallow her up. After some opening remarks, the dean turned the microphone over to Jonathan Tweed, the school's Supreme Court scholar-in-residence.

Tweed's eyes swept over the crowd. "We are here today," he said after a long moment, "to honor Chief Justice Malburg for her tremendous contributions to the court and to our law." Applause filled the hall. Tweed turned to Malburg, his hands clapping, encouraging the extended show of appreciation for the popular justice.

"But before we begin," Tweed said after another long pause, "the dean has given me the honor of announcing the creation of a new award—the Malburg Advocacy Award—that the Law Center will present each year to the lawyer who best exemplifies the gold standard in advocacy and professionalism we have long admired in the chief." Tweed's glance cut through the crowd, landing on Sean. "This year, it is my great pleasure to present the first Malburg Award to an old and dear friend of mine."

Oh no.

Tweed smirked.

Don't fucking do it, Jon.

"It is my honor," Tweed said, stretching out the words and still smirking, "to present the first annual Malburg Award to Sean Serrat."

At this, the room grew loud. Sean felt his face flush and he gave a modest shake of the head.

Tweed continued, "Few lawyers ever have the chance to argue even one case before the Supreme Court. Sean's argued a remarkable *fifty-two* cases, each time representing our government with humility and dignity. Now, everyone knows that the Office of the Solicitor General lost a great advocate when Sean left to join the private sector, but I say the office also lost something else: a little piece of its heart." Tweed sipped from a glass of water and gave the crowd a contemplative look. "Before I became a law professor, I spent a decade at OSG and I'll never forget my first day on the job there. I was welcomed by this deputy SG who, frankly, scared the hell out of me." Tweed grinned and the crowd tittered.

"He was tall and intimidating and had this piercing gaze. He corrected me twice for mispronouncing his name. 'It's sur-rot, not sur-*rat*, I'm not a rodent,' he said." More laughter. "He *was* kind enough, however, to warn me that I might want to stay late that night since tradition was for the president to call and welcome all new members of the office." Tweed paused again. "How nice of him, I thought. And sure enough, at seven-thirty I got a call: 'Would I hold for the president? Well, of course, yes.' I did what I think most people do when they get a call from the president of the United States and I stood up. Ten minutes passed and I said, 'Okay, that's understandable, the president is probably finishing up negotiations with China or something.' Another ten minutes. 'Okay, I'll wait.' Then another ten. That's when I heard something outside my office door. Muffled laughter. I set down the phone and opened the door. And there was Sean Serrat and five of my new colleagues. They'd made the prank call and had a betting pool on how long I would stay on hold. Sean won."

The room boomed with laughter. Sean accepted the award without remarks, just a mock bow.

As the rumble of applause faded, Tweed stared out at the audience. He dropped the grin and his expression turned serious. "Of course, the most important reason we are here today is to honor Chief Justice Malburg. I'm sometimes asked about my most memorable argument at the court. Inevitably I think of the chief. I like to say that I made three oral arguments for every case: the one I planned to make, the one I made, and the one on the car ride home I *wished* I'd made. Those rides home usually left me thinking of all the great responses I *should* have given to Chief Justice Malburg. She usually left me feeling even more battered than I look today." Tweed gestured to his bandage and the audience laughed again.

Tweed introduced Stanton Jones, a veteran Supreme Court advocate and president of the Washington National Opera. Jones presented Chief Justice Malburg, an avid opera fan, with a signed poster from the Richard Strauss opera *Ariadne auf Naxos*. And then two women from the National Opera performed for the elderly justice.

During the beautiful serenade, Sean's eyes searched the room for his daughter. No Abby.

CHAPTER 5

Sean slipped into the backseat of the cab and gave the driver the address for his new office. The sedan smelled of whatever the cabbie had for lunch. Something with onions. Sean took out his phone and called Emily.

"Hey there," he said when she answered. "Did you track down Abby? She wasn't at the reception."

"She wasn't there? She's not responding to my texts. I'm getting worried."

"I'm sure she just got caught up with school. Finals are coming up. You know how she—"

"Hold on," Emily cut in, "I'm getting another call—it might be her."

Traffic was heavy, and the cab was at a standstill. Phone pressed to his ear, Sean rolled down the window for some air. He loosened his tie and gazed absently out onto the street. It was then that he had the feeling that he was being watched. Eyes on him. The cabdriver wasn't looking at him in the rearview, so he glanced out the window again. He saw a man standing on the corner near the security gate at the front of Georgetown's campus. The man stood facing Sean, arms crossed. He wore sunglasses, so Sean couldn't see his eyes. But he seemed to be staring defiantly into the cab. He had stringy hair that touched his shoulders and he wore a flannel shirt. What's with all the flannel in the spring? Sean thought about the guy from the train that morning who—

"Sean, it was Ryan's school." Emily's voice jarred his attention away from the man. "I need to go pick him up. He's in trouble again."

Sean diverted the cab to take him home. By the time he'd arrived, Emily had already retrieved Ryan from the middle school. She met Sean at the front door of their colonial.

Sean blew out a loud sigh. "Where is he?"

Emily pointed a finger upstairs. Sean could hear the distortion and moody baritone of Alice in Chains drifting from Ryan's room.

"I thought we were past all this," Sean said.

"Me too." Emily handed Sean a sheet of paper. "The principal said a girl's mother came in. She'd found these Facebook messages Ryan sent to her daughter."

Sean glanced at the paper:

SirRyan 8:53pm
Sup

Allison Moss 8:53pm
Gtg in a minute. Mom calling 4 me

SirRyan 8:54pm
kk. you still want the weed?

Allison Moss 8:54pm
you got some???

SirRyan 8:54pm
Ya. you still want it?

Allison Moss 8:54pm
U sure u got it? Or is this like last time

SirRyan 8:54pm
Got from Chipotle guy, man in red

Allison Moss 8:54pm
Huh?

SirRyan 8:54pm
Guy at Chipotle who sells; wears red clothes and red hat.

Allison Moss 8:54pm
You 4 real?

SirRyan 8:55pm
You want it or not. 20 bks

Allison Moss 8:55pm
Will see if I can get the $. gtg

SirRyan 8:55pm
kk. bring to my locker after gym

"Idiot," Sean said. After all their talks—the lectures about how things on the Internet stay forever, about drugs, the therapy sessions—here they were again. *You still want the weed?*

"What does he say about all this?" Sean asked.

"Deny, deny, deny," Emily said. "I actually didn't want to get into it until he had a chance to calm down."

"We need to search his room and go through his phone and Facebook," Sean said. His instincts, born of his own years as a teenager, were that Ryan was guilty until proven innocent. He may defend the Constitution at work, but that didn't mean it applied at home.

"No," Emily said, "we need to *talk* with him."

Ryan had no better defense lawyer than his mother. Other than Sean's workaholic tendencies, the only point of contention in their marriage was Ryan. And the two issues were interrelated. Emily never said so directly, but she blamed Sean for Ryan's acting out. If he'd just been home more. She also thought that Sean was too hard on their son. Maybe he was.

Sean decided to turn down the temperature a notch. "*Talk* to him? I haven't read a lot of parenting books, but I'm pretty sure I was taught to cram it all down inside and then wash away the festering resentment with cheap booze."

Emily's eyes turned to slits, but she couldn't conceal the slightest tight-lipped smile. "Remember," she said before they opened Ryan's door, "he's only fourteen and one mistake isn't going to ruin his life."

"It only takes one mistake . . ." Sean's voice trailed off. He knew too well how one mistake could change everything. But he also knew it wasn't worth pursuing the line of argument further.

Emily tapped on Ryan's door, and they went inside.

Their son's domain had remnants of Little Boy Ryan—*Diary of a Wimpy Kid* books, a Pikachu stuffed animal, soccer trophies covered in dust. Those relics gave way to the world of Teenage Ryan: electric guitar, dumbbells, scattered clothes. Axl Rose grimaced at Sean from a vintage Guns N' Roses poster over the bed. Sean often joked that, when it came to music, his son was born a few decades too late. Ryan was stretched out on the bed, face buried in a pillow. Sean pressed a button on the iPod docking station, and the music went quiet.

Ryan lifted his head. "I'm sorry, okay," he said. His hair was matted, face blotchy red, tear-streaked, another reminder of Ryan as a little boy. Not the stranger who appeared two years ago when, as the doctors explained it, puberty struck early and kicked his ADHD impulse control problems into overdrive.

"I don't know why I sent the messages," Ryan said. "I never did weed. And I swear I never sold any."

Emily sat on the bed beside him and rubbed his back. "We just don't understand why you'd write those things? And why you'd sneak on the Internet when you've worked so hard to earn back everyone's trust?"

The "why" questions dominated the next twenty minutes. Sean knew they'd never get a satisfying answer. But Emily, as always, said all the right things—things Sean was too angry or too impatient or too stubborn to say. She told Ryan to get cleaned up for dinner. He would *not* be ruining the celebration of Dad's new job.

"Do we have to tell Abby about this at dinner?" Ryan asked.

"Tonight's about Dad," Emily said. Another lawyerly technique, answering him without answering him. She would have been a great litigator had she decided to go into practice rather than stay home with the kids. Emily gestured to Sean that it was time to leave Ryan's room. You had to pace yourself with teenagers, she always said.

As they padded downstairs, Sean said, "If this is middle school, what's high school gonna be like?"

Emily didn't reply, she just sighed.

"I'm still searching his room," Sean said.

"I know you are, Sean," Emily said, exasperated. "I know."

CHAPTER 6

The search of Ryan's room had yielded nothing so far. Sean would have to leave the computer and Facebook investigation to his more technology-proficient wife. For now, he had only a few minutes before Emily and the boys returned from the store or whatever errand Emily had come up with to pacify Sean's pathetic need to play detective. He leaned against Ryan's doorframe, staring into the room. He tried to channel his inner teen. Where would he have hidden pot or booze or *Playboy*s or something incriminating?

He turned and looked about the hallway, assessing the fingerprint smudges and dings and nicks, staple décor in any home with boys. He opened the hall linen closet. Just towels and toilet paper and clean sheets. He eyed the attic door on the ceiling. More finger smudges, near the latch. *Hmm.* He reached up and hooked his finger around the ringlet latch and pulled down. The hinged door opened, the springs creaking and groaning. The door had a ladder, a folded-up contraption, attached to it. He brushed away some spiderwebs and unfolded the ladder and climbed into the mouth of the attic.

It was dark and the air warm. Musty. Sean adjusted his eyes to the dark and found the switch. A single exposed bulb flickered on and Sean surveyed the boxes, old furniture, and rolled-up carpet remnants in the dim light.

He stood, careful not to hit his head against the triangle of the roof. A bump on the head could be fatal since the roof was not insulated; rusty nails that secured the exterior shingles poked through the wood. Another one of the joys of owning a historic home, and a reminder of how little a million dollars got you in an affluent D.C. suburb.

He walked carefully down the small pathway lined with junk. He really needed to clean the attic. He decided it would make a good punishment for Ryan's latest debacle. He scouted about, not seeing any contraband. He spotted the small coffin-like boxes for Abby's American Girl dolls. He remembered when she was about twelve and packed them up for storage and how a quadrant of his heart had disintegrated in his chest. Deciding the entire search was wrongheaded, he turned back toward the shaft of light coming from the hole in the floor.

Along the path, a dimpled old box caught his eye. Scrawled on its side in black Sharpie was the word JAPAN. He thought he'd long ago buried that box deep in the bowels of the attic. He crouched down and opened the box's flaps. On top were a few Japanese comic books, some wooden nunchucks, and a throwing star, the types of precious cultural artifacts only a fourteen-year-old could fully appreciate. Under it all, a pile of vinyl albums. His collection from when he was a kid. He flipped through them. AC/DC, Quiet Riot, Van Halen, and some embarrassing ones, Night Ranger, Duran Duran. He pulled out one of his old favorites, Def Leppard's *Pyromania*. The soundtrack of his youth. He wiped a hand across the cover, clearing away the dust.

A chill fell over him. Just a few days ago he'd heard "Rock of Ages" on the radio and it had thrust him back to that night. In fact, Japan had crossed his mind more than once in recent days—the familiar pit in his stomach, the faintest shortness of breath. It had been so long since he'd thought about it, dwelled on it, that he sometimes wondered if it was all a bad dream. An old movie he'd seen that he had latched on to in his memories as real. But it was real. All too real. The memories had resurfaced with such vigor, he assumed, because of all the attention he was getting about the possible Supreme Court nomination. Paranoia.

He realized that he was kneading the palm of his left hand with his thumb, feeling the ridges of the scar. The three of them had each cut into their palms to seal their blood oath. They'd used the same blade that killed the storekeeper and swore to never speak a word of that night for the rest of their lives. Sean reflected on the melodrama of it (to say nothing of the unsanitariness of using the same blade). Then the questions that had long haunted him fired through his brain: Why did Kenny do it? And why hadn't Sean seen it coming? He could've stopped him. And why, when Sean had immediately broken his oath and gone to his father for help, had his dad chosen to bury it all?

Sean pulled out the disc from the Def Leppard sleeve and blew on the black vinyl. He debated whether to look inside the sleeve to see if the item was still there. He told himself not to. But he slid his hand inside the cardboard and felt for it. The paper touched his fingertips, and he took in a deep breath before sliding it out. He flattened the newspaper clipping on the top of the cardboard box. It was wrinkled and yellowed and written in a language he couldn't read. It was incredibly stupid to keep it, but he just could never quite part with it. The newspaper photo of the Japanese storekeeper stared up at him. He heard his father's voice. *You will tell no one. Ever. This is about more than just you, Sean.* Another voice pulled him out of it.

"Whatcha doin'?" Jack's head popped up from the hole in the floor, eyes wide, mouth agape. The gopher from *Caddy Shack*. An attic is a magical place for a seven-year-old.

Sean fumbled to shove the newspaper clipping back into the album sleeve.

"Hey, buddy," Sean said. "Be careful on the ladder there."

"Mom said it's time to get ready for dinner."

"Okay, I'll be down in a minute."

"Can I come in? I'll be careful. I'll—"

"Sorry, pal. Too dangerous. Lots of nails sticking out and it's dark up here."

"Aw, man. That's what Abby said too." Jack frowned.

"Abby was up here?"

"Yep."

"When was that?"

"The other day."

"What was she doing?"

"I dunno. She was looking at that box there." Jack pointed to the JAPAN box. "She was digging through the same stuff you're looking at."

CHAPTER 7

At ten-thirty, Sean walked up the stairs and found Emily in the bathroom. She was leaning over the sink washing her face. Her nightgown didn't quite reach the back of her thighs. Even after all these years, the sight of the curve of her bottom caused Sean to stir.

"I tried calling her again," Sean said. He unbuttoned his shirt. "It went straight to voice mail." Abby had not shown up at the restaurant for dinner either.

"I'm worried about her," Emily said.

"She's probably just on a studying binge," Sean said.

Emily shook her head as she brushed her teeth. "No," she gurgled, toothpaste foaming at the corners of her mouth. She dabbed her lips with a towel. "She knew this was a celebration dinner. And she never ignores my text messages. It's not like her, Sean."

"Maybe that's what she was calling me about yesterday, to say she couldn't make it."

"I really wish you would have taken her call."

"It's not like I was dodging her. I just missed the call. Kind of like you do nine out of ten times when I call your cell."

"Aren't you worried?" Emily said, ignoring the jab.

Sean let out a low breath. "What do you want me to do? I can drive to her apartment. But you remember what happened last time."

"You'll never let that go."

"It was embarrassing for her, and for me. If she's got a boy there again, I just—"

"Fine, I'll go," Emily said. She marched to the bedroom. By the time Sean caught up with her, Emily had already pulled open a dresser drawer and thrown a pair of jeans on the bed.

"I'm not letting you drive to Capitol Hill at this hour," he said. "I'll go."

Emily continued getting dressed.

Sean said, "You have a long day tomorrow. We've still got to go through Ryan's Facebook messages, and you've got a shitty meeting ahead with Ryan and Dr. Julie. You get some sleep and I'll go check on her."

"I won't be sleeping until I know where she is, so it doesn't matter if—"

"Em, please. I don't mind going. I could actually use the fresh air. Can you try to call her again?"

He saw signs of retreat in Emily's face, so he started changing from his dress shirt and suit pants into a T-shirt and jeans.

Emily frowned as she took the iPhone from her ear. "Still no answer," she said. "Maybe I should call Malik?"

"I thought she'd stopped seeing him? Do you even have his number?" Malik was a Supreme Court law clerk and six years older than Abby. The age difference hadn't bothered Sean so much as the kid's ambition and cockiness, not uncommon traits of the court's clerks.

"They still date. I don't have his number, though. Do you think someone at OSG would have it?"

Sean looked at his watch. "What am I supposed to do, call the SG or the Supreme Court and ask for the contact information for a law clerk because my adult daughter hasn't checked in with me in the last day?" Sean watched his wife's face harden.

"Em, I'm sorry. Let me go to her apartment. I'm sure she's just studying and unplugged to escape distractions. You know how she is. While I'm gone maybe you can track down Malik's number from one of Abby's friends."

Emily didn't respond. Her eyes were fixed on the iPhone, index finger tapping and sliding. Sean went downstairs, dug up the spare key to Abby's apartment from the kitchen junk drawer, and walked out the side door to the SUV. Was he worried? He tried not to be. But as every parent knows, apprehension comes with the job. It's a lifetime of disquieting moments—those few seconds you lose sight of them at the neighborhood swimming pool, when they don't arrive home from school at their usual time, when they grow up and don't check in. So, yeah, like thousands of other times, he was worried.

CHAPTER 8

Sean drove on winding Rock Creek Parkway, which mercifully had no traffic. It was dark and he kept telling himself to slow down since deer were common on this stretch of national parkland, which ran from his neighborhood in Chevy Chase, Maryland, to downtown D.C. As he slowed, a bottle on the passenger seat rolled forward and clunked onto the floor. Eyes fixed on the road, he reached down and placed it back on the seat. The bottle was filled with a gold liquid that looked like bourbon and had a ribbon tied around its neck. He hadn't noticed the bottle earlier that night. On the face of the bottle, a note card was taped over its label that read CONGRATULATIONS ON THE NEW JOB! No signature. He was no liquor connoisseur, but he assumed it was expensive stuff.

He pressed the SUV's voice recognition button and said, "Call home."

Emily picked up on the first ring.

"It's me," Sean said. "I'm almost to her place. Any luck reaching anyone?"

Emily's voice bellowed from the speakers over Sean's head. "I just found Michelle's number and texted her. No word yet. And still nothing from Abby."

"Try not to worry. I know it's hard, but I'm sure she's okay. I'll be at her place in about five minutes. I love you."

"I love you too. I'm sorry I was crabby. I'm just really worried."

"I know." He added, "You can make it up to me when I get home, after we find her." Emily clicked off without responding.

He curled around the road past the Washington Monument—"the giant pencil" as Abby called it when she was a little girl—and onto Pennsylvania Avenue. His gaze fixed on the Capitol dome, a glowing beacon ahead.

Sean turned onto Abby's street, which was lined with historic town houses. With no spots open in front of Abby's place, he had to double-park. He jumped out of the SUV, startling a woman walking her dog. He nodded hello, hurried along the brick path, then trekked down the stairwell that led to Abby's English basement apartment.

No front light on. He'd have a word with Abby about that. The door had a window, covered in metal bars on the outside, a curtain inside. He cupped his hand and peered into the glass, but he couldn't see inside. He knocked and waited a moment before sliding the key into the lock.

The door creaked open. It was pitch black. Sean felt along the wall until he found a light switch, and clicked it on. Panic swept through him. Abby's apartment had been ransacked.

CHAPTER 9

Sean clutched his phone. *Pick up. Please pick up.* On the fifth ring, a groggy voice.

"Hel-lo."

"Frank, it's Sean Serrat, I'm so sorry to call you at this hour but it's an emergency." He and Frank Pacini were more neighbors than friends, but they always enjoyed one another's company at neighborhood barbecues. And their daughters were close in age and friendly, if not friends. Their professional careers also crossed paths. Pacini, the deputy director of the FBI, would sometimes accompany agents to OSG if the government was working on a criminal appeal that was important to the Bureau. Sean had thought of calling 911, but he still didn't think, or want to think, something had really happened to Abby. And besides, who wouldn't choose a top FBI official over a D.C. cop on the night shift?

"Sean, of course, no problem, what's going on?"

Sean could hear Pacini shushing his wife, Ginger, in the background.

"It's Abby. She's missing. We haven't heard from her, which is unusual. She missed a family celebration dinner tonight, so Emily had me come to her apartment on the Hill. I'm inside right now. Abby's not here and the place has been trashed."

"Are you sure it's not just a mess? My daughter's dorm room used to look like—"

"I'm certain," Sean said. He examined the living room of his daughter's narrow basement apartment. A lamp was broken and a desk nearby had all the drawers pulled out. The galley kitchen, which was just a sink and refrigerator separated from the living area by a small counter, had pots, pans, and shattered dishes littered on the floor.

"Have you called the District police, Sean? There's jurisdictional issues I'll need to—"

"I've only called you. I want someone who knows Abby and who'll give a shit."

A sigh blew into the phone's receiver. "How long's she been missing?"

"It's not the amount of time I'm worried about, Frank. It's her apartment. Someone's broken in and she's not responding to calls or texts. Please, I want someone here I trust. I'm asking you as a friend—as a father—to please come." Sean tried to steady his breathing.

Pacini was quiet. After a long pause, he said, "Okay, Sean. Give me the address. And don't touch anything until I arrive."

CHAPTER 10

It was thirty minutes before Sean heard the knock on Abby's door. As Pacini instructed, he hadn't touched anything, but he had carefully roamed, visually inspecting the apartment. The bedroom and bathroom, like the rest of the place, were torn apart.

Pacini scanned the living room and agreed that it wasn't simply a student's clutter. "I don't think we need to panic," Pacini said. "She could've just gone out of town with friends, and someone noticed her apartment was vacant and broke in. When's the last time you spoke with her?"

Sean thought about this. "Actually talked? About a week ago. She called me yesterday afternoon, but I missed the call."

"Was she planning any trips or has she taken off in the past? My daughter's pulled that crap and scared the hell out of us just like this."

"You've met Abby. It's the end of the semester at law school and she's obsessive about her grades, so she wouldn't take off. She also doesn't own a car. And you know Emily. Abby wouldn't dare make her mother worry like this."

Pacini walked into the living room, his steps purposeful, each foot landing so he didn't move any debris. He was wearing what Ryan would call "dad jeans" and a polo.

"We need to call in the District police. I'm not sure if Abby's apartment is within the jurisdiction of the Capitol Police, but I'll reach out to my contacts there too. Don't worry, I'll stay involved as long as I can. And I'll get some agents from the Bureau here tonight. The field office is only five minutes away."

"Thank you, Frank."

Pacini nodded. "I need a recent photo of Abby."

Sean clicked on his smartphone and pulled up a photo of his daughter. It was a close-up, her face freckled from the sun, taken last summer at the beach.

"And I need her mobile phone number and carrier," Pacini added. "We may be able to track her phone."

Pacini pulled out his own mobile. Before dialing he said, "I think she's gonna turn up fine, Sean, but I have to ask you some questions because the people I'm gonna call will ask."

Sean nodded.

"Has Abby been having any problems with anyone? A boyfriend, neighbor, or anyone?"

"Not that I know of."

"Anything out of the ordinary with Abby lately? Drinking too much or—"

Sean cut him off with a sharp shake of the head.

Pacini hesitated. "Have *you* had any problems with anyone? Threats?"

"Me? Why would I get threats? And what would that have to do with Abby?"

"The newspaper stories about your possible nomination to the Supreme Court."

It hadn't occurred to Sean that Abby's disappearance could be related to him. "No one in the public knows who I am. Hell, more people can identify Judge Judy than a justice on the Supreme Court, much less someone who *might* be a nominee. No threats, nothing like that." His mind drifted to the man on the subway, but he dismissed it quickly.

"I'm gonna keep that avenue open," Pacini said. "Not because I believe there's anything to it. But because it gives my agents a plausible jurisdictional hook."

Pacini began making calls, and Sean left the apartment to get some air. Outside, the moon gave the street a silver glow. Headlights approached and part of him expected Abby to pull up in a friend's car and yell at him for being a ridiculous, smothering father. But when the sedan stopped in front of Abby's apartment, two men in blue windbreakers climbed out. Pacini's team. Sean opened the SUV's door, deciding it was time to make the call he dreaded. Emily.

CHAPTER 11

From the overhead speakers, Emily's sobbing filled the SUV as Sean tried to sound convincing that Abby would be okay. But he had a lump like a fist lodged in his throat. There was a knock on the window.

"Hold on, Em, Frank needs something."

He fumbled for the automatic window button, then the glass hummed down. Pacini had dark circles under his eyes and a look of concern.

"My guys have captured a signal on Abby's phone. Does she know anyone who lives on Lexington Place? It's not too far from here."

"I don't know," Sean said.

Emily's disembodied voice said, "I think that's where Malik lives."

"Are you sure?" Sean said.

"I picked her up there once. I could've sworn it was on Lexington."

"Who's Malik?" Pacini asked.

Emily's voice: "A boy she's seeing."

Pacini's face seemed to relax. His stare narrowed. "You hadn't already checked with her boyfriend before calling me?"

"He's not really her boyfriend," Sean said, realizing how this must look to Pacini, who'd been dragged out of bed in the middle of the night.

"The signal doesn't give us an exact address, just a location on the street," Pacini said. "A lot of the places on the Hill are connected row houses, so it may be hard to pinpoint the exact location of the phone. Do you know this kid's address?"

Sean shook his head and Emily was quiet. Pacini pulled out his phone, but was interrupted.

Emily's voice again: "Turn on the navigation system," she said. "There's a button that lists all the locations entered in the system. When I picked up Abby from Malik's place, I think I put in his address. Maybe it's still in there."

Sean powered-on the navigation system. The screen on the dashboard showed a list of addresses and he scrolled down. There it was: 833 LEXINGTON PLACE, NE.

"What are you doing?" Pacini asked as the SUV's engine roared on.

"I'm going to find my daughter."

Pacini looked at him, then over to Abby's apartment. Agents were standing on the stoop talking to the residents who lived in the town house above Abby's basement apartment. "Let me come with you, at least."

Sean clicked the unlock button, and Pacini climbed into the SUV. Before he'd buckled his seatbelt, Sean was speeding down the narrow streets of Capitol Hill.

"Slow down a little," Pacini said as the wheels screeched around Stanton Park. A blue line on the navigation screen pointed around the park and left on Sixth Street. Sean took a fast left, then a right, and jerked to a stop in front of a row house on Lexington. A woman's monotone voice from the navigation system said, "You. Have. Reached. Your. Destination."

Sean jumped out of the SUV and ran to the front door. He rang the bell several times and then started pounding. The curtains on a side window opened a slit, closed, then he heard the click of locks.

"Can I help you?" The man at the door was black, in his late twenties. He wore a white tank and workout shorts. He looked at Sean, then Pacini, then Sean again.

"Mr. Serrat? . . . Is everything okay?"

"Abby's missing," Sean said. "Malik, is she here?"

"Missing?" Malik Montgomery said. A bewildered look. "She's not here."

Sean peered over Malik's shoulder into the row house. Noticing, Malik said, "You're welcome to come in."

Sean pushed inside, Pacini right behind him. The row house, with rich hardwood, high ceilings, and expensive-looking furniture, didn't fit with the salary of a young judicial clerk. Sean recalled Emily saying that Malik was from money.

"Mr. Serrat, you're more than welcome to look around," Malik said, trailing behind. "But she's not here."

Sean turned to Malik. He stared deep into the young man's eyes. "Then why's her phone here?"

"Her phone?" Malik said. "What do you mean? Her phone's not here."

Sean didn't respond and instead pulled out his own mobile and dialed Abby's number. He put the phone to his ear, confirmed ringing, then pulled it away. He treaded down the hallway, tilting his head slightly, listening. Malik started to speak, and Sean held up his hand, shushing him.

A faint reverberation, music. Sean stepped toward the sound. He opened the door to a bedroom.

"Is this your room?" he asked Malik.

"No. It's the guest bedroom."

Sean crouched, ear toward the floor. More tinny music, muffled. The bed. He looked under it. There was no phone, but the music grew louder. Another sinking feeling. He put both hands under the mattress and flipped it off of the box springs.

And there it was. An iPhone in a shiny black case, ringtone blaring.

"Who Knew" by Pink.

CHAPTER 12

Sean launched himself at Malik Montgomery, grabbing him by the shirt and pinning him against the wall. A picture crashed to the floor, its frame cracking and glass shattering across the hardwood.

"Where's Abby?" His voice was guttural, desperate.

"I don't know, I swear, Mr. Serrat." Malik was breathing heavily, his eyes wide.

Pacini put his hand on Sean's forearm, but Sean yanked it free. The room grew hot and Pacini's voice seemed far away.

"Sean, you need to calm down," Pacini said. "This isn't helping."

Sean just stood there with Malik pinned. Malik didn't resist.

"Sean!"

Pacini's bark finally snapped Sean out of it. Sean's senses were on overload. He was surprised at his own response. He released the grip on Malik's shirt. Malik just stood there, a shell-shocked expression on his face.

Pacini gestured to a chair angled in the corner of the room. Malik silently took a seat. Sean's heart was thumping now. He started to speak, but Pacini raised a hand to quiet him.

In an even tone Pacini said, "Malik, we need to ask you a few questions."

Malik sat rigidly in the chair and gave a nod. He seemed to be collecting himself.

"First, you understand you have the right to remain silent and to have a lawyer present?"

That prompted a puzzled look from Malik. "You're Mirandizing me? Seriously?"

"Do you understand your rights? You're willing to talk without a lawyer present?"

"Of course, don't be ridiculous."

Pacini's eyes swept over Malik, like he was assessing not just the man's words but also his body language. Then: "When did you last see Abby?"

"Yesterday," Malik said. "We went to dinner. Sonoma on Pennsylvania Avenue."

"Anyone see you there?"

"We didn't see anyone we know, if that's what you mean. But the waiter should remember us. And I have the credit card receipt probably."

"What time was that?"

"I got there around eight, and Abby met me there about five minutes later."

"And what time did you leave?"

Malik put a hand on his chin. "We left no later than nine o'clock."

"And Abby came back to your place?" Pacini baited.

"No, actually, she didn't," Malik said, a slight edge to his voice now. "She said she was going to the library to study."

"You and Abby have anything to drink at dinner?"

Malik gave an exasperated sigh. "We each had a glass of wine."

"So after a night out of dinner and wine, she just went to the library and you came home?"

"Look, man, I'm not one of the poor dumb black kids you're used to dealing with, so cut the shit."

"It was just a question," Pacini said. "Why are you getting so upset?"

"I'm upset because you barge into my house in the middle of the night, my friend is missing, and you're wasting your time accusing me of something when you should be out trying to find her."

Pacini washed a hand over his face. "Okay, Malik, so you go to dinner. You said you were there for less than an hour. That's a pretty fast meal for a place like Sonoma."

"We actually had a fight, which is why I think the waiter might remember us." Malik's shoulders slumped, as though he realized how it sounded the second the words came out of his mouth.

"A fight?"

"She said she didn't want to see me anymore."

Pacini held Malik's gaze. "She broke up with you?"

Malik chewed on his lip. He nodded.

"That make you angry?"

"It didn't make me happy, but—" Malik stopped himself. "But we weren't very serious so it's not like I'm, like, devastated or anything."

"Did she say why she wanted to break up?"

"She showed up kinda agitated. Said she had too much going on in her life right now. She needed a break."

"What was going on in her life?"

Malik shrugged. "I don't know. When she asked to meet for dinner, I kind of knew she was going to end it, but she never would admit the real reason why."

"The *real* reason? You thought there was something else?"

"Yeah," Malik said. "She's been doing disappearing acts, gone at night—I'm not an idiot. And I've heard some rumors."

"What kind of rumors?"

"That she's seeing somebody."

"Do you know who that somebody is?"

"I don't know. I asked her and she got angry. She wanted to know who was gossiping about her and all that."

"Who told you she was seeing someone else?"

"One of the other clerks. He was giving me shit about it. He'd heard it from this girl at Georgetown or something."

"Did Abby say anything about leaving town or going somewhere with this other guy?"

"No. Once I brought up this other dude she got *pissed*. She stormed out of the place."

"She just got up and left you there?" Pacini asked.

"Yeah, it was embarrassing."

Sean could no longer restrain himself: "If she just left you there, how'd you know she went to the library after dinner?"

Malik blew out another long sigh. "I didn't want to leave it that way. It was stupid. I got my car from the valet and caught up with her on the street. She said sorry for storming out. Said she just has a lot of shit happening in her life"—his gaze flicked to Sean—"family shit."

"Did she say what it was?" Pacini asked.

Malik shook his head.

Pacini looked to Sean. "No idea," Sean said.

Pacini turned back to Malik. "So she has you drop her at the library. What library, the one at the law school?"

"No, the Supreme Court's library. She likes to get away from the drama of campus. And the court's library is really quiet. Hardly anyone even uses the library—everything's online now. I'm a law clerk and I'd never even been in the library until Abby took me there."

"I've been to the downtown D.C. public library and it's pretty crowded," Pacini said.

Sean interjected, "The court's library isn't public." Sean was no stranger to the Supreme Court building, and the kid was right, the basketball court on the top floor got more use than the court's library. It must have been ten years since Sean had set foot in there. He knew Abby liked it, though. She'd told him she loved imagining all the justices of the past working by candlelight.

"If it's not public, how'd Abby get access?" Pacini asked.

Malik said, "I thought her dad got her a pass." His gaze shifted to Sean.

"I didn't. She's Jonathan Tweed's research assistant. I think she said he got her a pass." Sean looked at Pacini. "Jon's a professor at Georgetown and an old friend of mine."

Pacini moved closer to Malik. "The last place you saw her was the Supreme Court?"

"I dropped her off right out front of the building. I waited until I saw her go around to the side entrance."

"If that's right, how did her phone get in your house?"

"I have absolutely no idea."

"You didn't hear it ringing?"

"No."

"Have you had anyone in your place since you had dinner with Abby?"

Malik shook his head again. "Just you two."

"Any ideas how the phone got here?"

Malik looked at Pacini then stared intently into Sean's eyes. "No idea. I swear."

CHAPTER 13

Sean bumped a tire over the curb in front of the Supreme Court building. Pacini had called ahead, and the chief of the Supreme Court Police was waiting for them on the oval plaza. While Pacini spoke to the chief, Sean stayed in the SUV and called Emily. He'd missed three of her calls. He was surprised that she sounded calm. Ryan had woken up, she said. Sean realized that she was putting on a front for their son.

"Just tell him it's my new job," Sean said. "I don't want him worried."

"That makes sense. Don't work too late," Emily said. He imagined how hard she must be struggling to look and sound normal. He heard her say, "Everything's okay. Just a work situation. You really need to get up to bed." Then something muffled, then "Goodnight, sweetie."

"Is he gone?" Sean asked.

"Yes," Emily whispered. "Michelle texted me and said she hadn't seen Abby since class on Friday. What did Malik say?"

Sean noticed that Pacini and the police chief were stealing glances into the SUV. "We're still looking for her, but I can't talk now. Frank is waiting on me. I'll call you soon. I love you." He clicked off. Nothing good would have come from telling Emily about finding Abby's phone or that all of Abby's texts, e-mails, and call logs had been wiped from the device. Or that agents had taken Malik in for questioning. Sean swung open the door and climbed out.

"Sean, this is Carl Martinez, the chief of the Supreme Court's squad," Pacini said. The chief was a buttoned-up Hispanic guy in his fifties, or maybe even sixties. It was hard to tell because he was one of those fit ex-military types, though he had a tired face—deep lines and serious bags under the eyes. He gave Sean's hand a firm shake.

Although the Supreme Court community was like Mayberry (everybody knew everybody else), Sean had never met the chief. The court's police force had more than one hundred officers and Sean vaguely recalled hearing that the former chief had retired recently.

"I've heard a lot about you," the chief said. "Sorry to meet under these circumstances."

"I can't thank you enough for coming in tonight."

"I live nearby and it's no problem at all," the chief said. "I've spoken with the officers on duty last night. They don't remember seeing your daughter, but there were a lot of people in the building for a function. The good news is that we have cameras, so we can check the video."

Chief Martinez walked Sean and Pacini to the right of the plaza. The white marble steps that led up to the massive portico seemed to emanate light even at night. They went in through the southwest door, dumped their pockets into little baskets, and stepped through the metal detectors. The lone officer manning the entrance didn't make eye contact with Sean.

The chief then guided them to his office. The long hallway was dimly lit and the chief's shoes clacked on the polished marble floor. In his years roaming the building, Sean had never been inside the police office.

On the walk, Martinez and Pacini engaged in small talk. The weather, the court's recent renovations, how the new job was going for the chief, the do-you-know-so-and-so game cops play. When they seemed to sense that their forced nonchalance wasn't making Sean feel less anxious, they turned the chatter in his direction.

"I was an MP early in my career and once served under your father," the chief said. "He was quite a guy."

Quite a guy. A phrase that could mean so many different things. Everyone who'd ever served in the Armed Forces seemed to have once crossed paths with "the General." Sean made no reply.

The three entered the police office causing the lights, which were set on motion detectors, to click on, a domino of fluorescents. The reception area had a display cabinet filled with police-uniform hats from different countries with a tall, bell-like London Bobby helmet displayed prominently at the center of the collection.

Martinez steered them down another hallway to an interior office. He tapped on the door and escorted them inside. They were met with a nod from a man who sat at a long desk, facing several security monitors. A stack of what Sean assumed were digital recorders were built into the wall. Each device had masking tape on its face with locations—GREAT HALL, CAFETERIA, GIFT SHOP, E. CONF. RM., W. CONF. RM.—written in black Sharpie.

The chief said, "Tom, this is Deputy Director Pacini from the Bureau and you may know Sean Serrat."

The man, who was all shoulders and neck, stood. He hitched up his trousers and shook hands with Sean, then Pacini. Sean didn't recognize him either, but pretended they'd met before.

Chief Martinez said, "Can you pull up the video for last night, the southwest entrance?"

The officer nodded and started pecking his thick fingers on his computer.

"We had a full house last night," the chief said. "A reception from 7:30 until about 9:30, so we can pull the guest list and see if anyone saw your daughter."

"Here we go," the officer said, his gaze fixed on a monitor. The southwest entrance fluttered on the screen and the officer spun a knob that made the images scroll in fast-motion. The bottom right of the screen had a digital clock, which clicked forward rapidly. Men and women in suits put their bags on the conveyer and emptied their pockets. At 19:25, the clock showed a large group entering the court, each going through the same security procedures: keys, change, phones, in the small baskets, large bags on the belt through the X-ray machine. It was basically like an airport. When the clock rolled to 20:20, the screen showed only the doors with an officer occasionally coming into the frame. The clock wound forward.

At 21:23, the camera caught the door open. "This may be her," the officer said.

Sean stared at the screen. The officer clicked the mouse and there she was. His Abby. A smile crossed her lips and he could see the dimples even in the grainy image at this awkward angle. She said something to one of the officers. Though she gave a faint smile when she collected her book bag at the end of the conveyer, he saw the upturned mouth and slightly furrowed brow.

"I don't see anyone with her," Sean said.

"Can we look at other recordings that trace her path?" Pacini asked. "And how about cameras in the library?"

"Yeah, we can hit up the other cameras that would have caught her on the way to the library. But the building doesn't have the coverage you'd expect. The justices don't want images of what goes on here leaked, so many of the non-public areas don't have cameras."

"The library?" Pacini repeated.

The chief's eyes dropped to the floor.

"Nothing in the library?"

"I'm sorry, there's not."

Sean didn't know what to make of that.

Pacini pointed at the screen. "We've got someone else coming in the door."

On the monitor, the court's bronze and glass door opened. The officer working the computer said, "That's just one of the law clerks."

From Sean's own days as a Supreme Court law clerk he knew that the officers were required to memorize the faces of all thirty-six of the justices' clerks. Sean stared at the screen and a familiar face looked back at him: Malik Montgomery.

The monitor went dark. The rest of the recording had been erased.

CHAPTER 14

Sean sprinted out of the police office and down the long hallway to the elevator. He stabbed the button several times. Abby hadn't been at the library since yesterday, but he was desperate to close the distance between himself and the last place he'd known his daughter to be.

The elevator opened and he slapped the button to the third floor. The stool where the elevator operator normally sat, a throwback Sean never understood why the court continued, had a folded newspaper sitting on it.

He got off the elevator and turned left into the librarian stations. He took another left into the massive Reading Room. The carved oak walls and balconies were lit by only a few reading lamps, and shadows cast about the room. The library smelled of old books and wood polish. Sean walked the center aisle, looking at the long stretches of wood with lanterns and globes perched on them. The tables were bare, except for two with tablets and some books and papers spread across them. Sean walked over to one and saw a blank legal pad and two *U.S. Reports* opened, but nothing else. Abandoned research.

At the next table, he pulled the chain on a brass lantern. In the shallow light he saw a Tax casebook, not a source someone working on a Supreme Court case would normally consult. Something a law student would read. Under the book was a spiral notepad. He picked it up and flipped through the pages: Abby's meticulous handwriting. Then he saw her book bag, its contents scattered across the red carpet. Dread gouged into him.

Pacini and Police Chief Martinez came into the library, and he called them over.

"Abby's things," Sean said, his voice echoing.

Pacini looked at Sean, then darted his eyes about the Reading Room. More officers came into the library. "Get the lights on," Pacini shouted.

The chandeliers from the high gilded ceiling came on, and Sean paced the shelves along the north wall. Pacini and Martinez directed officers to the back of the Reading Room. Pacini pointed to the narrow stairs that led up to the stacks. Sean continued clicking on the lamps affixed to the tall bookshelves. He told himself to stay calm, but he started running from aisle to aisle.

"Abby!" He tore through the federal reporters, the state reports, the congressional record sections. *"Abby!"*

He heard a voice from above. One of the officers on the balcony near the stacks. Pacini raced up the small iron staircase. Sean couldn't hear them, but the speed at which Pacini ran to the officer sent a tremor through Sean's body. He watched as an officer staggered out toward Pacini. He was a young guy and he bent over, vomiting near the staircase.

Sean ran to the stairs, but he felt hands on his arms. Two officers, one holding each bicep, were saying something, but he couldn't process the words. Pacini also was yelling something he couldn't make out. Their grip tightened as he started up the stairs. But he managed to break away.

"No, Sean, no!" Pacini yelled as Sean pushed through to the dark crevice between two massive bookshelves.

Abby's body was twisted, shoved into the bottom shelf. Blood was smeared on her face, her hair matted. She was pale white.

And that's the last thing Sean would remember from that day. That terrible day.

CHAPTER 15

"Are they still out there?" Emily asked. She was bundled under the covers, looking toward the bedroom window. Long rays of sun hit the bed through an opening in the curtains, and she shielded her eyes with a hand.

Sean looped his tie. It was supposed to be a return to the morning routine, but nothing felt the same. Had it really been only two weeks? He glanced out the window.

"They're still there, but it looks like the village manager shooed away the van." A FOX 5 News van had blocked their single-lane street for the past week. Sean finished knotting the tie and sat on the bed. Emily's eyes were hollowed out and the lines on her face more pronounced than he'd ever seen them. He put his hand on her arm, but she rolled over, her back to him.

Everyone had assumed that *she* would be the strong one, the one holding their family together. And why not? That's what Sean would have predicted. She was the center of the family. She kept the trains moving while Sean spent his days, evenings, and most weekends on the fifth floor of the Justice Department building. And more than that, she had mettle that he did not, emotionally and physically. When they were in law school and Emily got pregnant, he panicked while she took charge and made sure her pregnancy didn't interfere with either of them graduating. When Ryan was rushed to the ER with an asthma attack, she was the one who sprang to action while Sean floundered. If Emily had a migraine, she'd still go about her day—she had natural births for all three children, no epidurals for Christ's sake—while Sean would be curled up in a ball if hit with a minor cold. She was Superwoman.

But the death of Abby was the ultimate devastation to Emily, and Sean didn't resent her for not living up to expectations. In an odd way, Sean loved her more for it. For now, and for a change, it would fall on him. Sean would have to be the strong one. Emily had found her Kryptonite: the knowledge that she would never again see or speak to their beloved daughter.

He stood and gazed out the window again. "Oh shit," he said. Emily rolled back over. "What?"

"Cecilia's chewing out one of the reporters." Sean pulled his suit jacket over his arm and shuttled downstairs. He opened the door right as the bell rang, and Cecilia barged in.

Before Sean shut the door, Cecilia turned toward the small group huddled on the sidewalk outside his picket fence. "Just try to get a fucking quote from me ever again, Steve. You're dead to me— and I'll make sure you're dead to every single one of the Supreme Court Bar. See how you'll do reporting the appellate beat when no one will talk to you." She slammed the door.

"What was that about?" Sean asked.

"I just asked him what the fuck he's doing. He's the goddamned Supreme Court correspondent for the network, yet he's out there like some grimy TMZ paparazzi."

"I don't like it, but he's got a boss and a job to do like the rest of us," Sean said.

"Bullshit," she said. Debating with Cecilia never had an upside, so he dropped it. Her eyes fluttered about the living room at all the flowers. "It looks like a funeral home in here." She paused, at a rare loss for words, seeming to realize the insensitivity of the remark.

"We've got enough flowers and casseroles for a lifetime," Sean said. "Sorry for calling on short notice. Emily's still not feeling well, and I didn't want Ryan to have to take the bus to school. Not yet, anyway."

"I'm happy to help. Are you sure they're ready to get back to school? And I'm sure the law firm will survive without you for a while."

"Ryan's therapist said it'll be best for both boys to get back to their routine. And what am I going to do? Sit around all day? I'd rather be busy." Sean had already read two books on how to cope with losing a child. Both said that men often throw themselves into their work out of a misguided idea that they need to appear strong. And to avoid dealing with the grief. The books advised against going back to work too soon. But the books were wrong.

Cecilia frowned. "How are the boys?"

Sean lowered his voice since his sons were in the kitchen nearby eating breakfast. "Jack's doing pretty well. I think he doesn't fully understand. Ryan is trickier. He's putting on a strong front, but he's hurting."

"Can I say hello?"

In the kitchen, the boys were at the granite counter with the Cheerios, bagels, and orange juice. Like *Before*.

"Hi boys."

"Cici!" Jack said. "Are you giving me a ride to school?"

"Nope," Cecilia said. "Your dad's taking you. I've got to take this creature." Cecilia tousled Ryan's hair. He normally would have laughed and feigned struggle, but today he just tolerated it.

"Hey Dad," Ryan said.

"Yes, buddy."

"Malik Montgomery's got a good lawyer." Ryan looked toward the small television on the kitchen counter. "The news said his lawyer refused to comment about his arrest, and you said a good lawyer would never comment or appear on the *Today* show."

"No, I said, you know you have a *bad* lawyer if he *wants* to comment or go on those shows. But you're not supposed to be watching this stuff." Sean clicked off the set and tilted his head toward Jack, a signal to Ryan that the two of them were a team protecting the little guy. It was manipulative, Sean knew, but it also worked. Ryan was right, though. Malik Montgomery had hired a good lawyer—one of the best criminal lawyers in the country, actually, an old Washington hand named Blake Hellstrom.

"Cici," Jack said, "when are those news people outside gonna leave?"

Cecilia furrowed her brow. "I'm not sure. Maybe we should go get the water hose and encourage them to go."

"Yeah!" Jack climbed off the kitchen stool until Sean grabbed him by the arm and hoisted him back up.

"Cecilia was just kidding," Sean said. He eyed Cecilia, whose cocked eyebrow said, *No I wasn't.*

The boys chomped down the last of their breakfast and left the kitchen to gather their backpacks. Sean looked at Cecilia. "When *do* you think they'll go away, Cel? It's not good for the boys." At OSG Sean wasn't permitted to comment on the government's cases, so he had little experience with the press. Cel, though, knew the game well. With her gift for quotable one-liners and her lack of filter, she was a reporter's dream and quite popular with the press corps.

"I honestly don't know when they'll give up," Cecilia said.

"You deal with the press all the time, you've got no idea?"

Cecilia considered the question. "I suppose they'll stay until they hear from you. Have you thought about a press release? You've gotta feed the beast."

Sean exhaled. "You really think that will do it? If I talk, they'll go away?"

"Why would they stay? How many guys want to stay the night after they've convinced the girl to have sex?"

A terrible metaphor. Cecilia was famous for them. He glanced out the square windowpanes on the front door. Without thinking any further, he marched outside. Cecilia was calling after him, but it was too late. He found himself standing on his porch, waving the half-dozen reporters to enter through his front gate. They approached cautiously at first, but once they realized it was an invitation to an impromptu press conference, they began to jockey for position, holding up their mikes, camera operators jostling for the best view.

The reporters started shouting questions over one another. Sean held up a hand. It took a moment, but they went quiet. He then cleared his throat. "I'm speaking to you today for one reason and one reason only: the hope that doing so will get you off my front sidewalk and give my family some privacy. I have two young sons— boys who are grieving the loss of their big sister—and I really hope and expect that you will give them the opportunity to return to their routine; to leave for school without a media spectacle outside their front door."

A reporter with a thin waist and blonde bobbed hair tucked behind her ears didn't waste time. "Mr. Serrat, Jane McKnight from News Channel Eight. How do you feel now that Malik Montgomery has been released on bail?"

"To be honest," Sean said, "I've been focused on my family, and I think it's best that I not comment on the proceedings." That was a lie. Sean thought about Malik a lot. About driving to Malik's row house. About charging the man as he answered the door. About jumping on top of him. Pounding his head against the ground. The way Malik did to Abby. How quickly the old instincts returned. The punch-first-think-later impulses of a fourteen-year-old coursed through his forty-four-year-old body.

The blonde reporter pressed on: "But as a father, aren't you angry that the man who raped and killed—who *allegedly* raped and killed—your daughter is on the streets?"

Sean felt his thumb digging into his palm, the rough scar on his soft, uncalloused hand. "I'm not going to second-guess the prosecutors or judge. It's not productive. I think the best course right now is to let them do their jobs."

Another reporter pushed in front of the blonde. He had puffy bags under his eyes and wore faded jeans and a tight blazer. "Reverend Al Coleman says that bail was granted because the evidence against Mr. Montgomery is flimsy. He said there's no DNA, no witnesses, no physical evidence, and that Malik Montgomery was arrested only because he is black and your daughter was—I quote—'a pretty white girl.' Do you care to comment on that?"

Sean's stomach clenched. He stared at the reporter for what

seemed like a long time, deciding not to engage with the man. But then he began to speak.

"For starters, I think that people who didn't know my daughter should really ask themselves if they are helping or hurting the investigation with comments like that. And if they did know my daughter, they would never suggest she was just a pretty face." He swallowed hard. "Let me tell you what the world lost when my Abby was stolen." At this everything seemed to go quiet, not just the reporters, but the birds, the sounds on the street. As if Sean's mind was filtering out the world.

"Everything came easy to Abby," he said finally. "She was first to walk and talk in daycare, graduated high school and college early and with honors, she was already at the top of her class in law school. We used to marvel at her. But her success isn't what made us so proud. It was her heart, her lovely, kind heart." He looked out at nothing. "When she was ten years old she would stop on the soccer field to help a kid who fell down, even if it meant losing the game. In high school she worked with special-needs kids, but didn't want to include that work on her college applications because she thought it cheapened the relationships she'd built with the children. She went to law school not to get rich or land on Wall Street, but to help the underprivileged. She made mistakes, and she wasn't perfect. But anyone who'd ever met Abby would tell you she was special. So, to call her just some 'pretty white girl' is"—Sean searched for the word—"well, it's disgusting."

The reporter pushed forward unfazed. "But do you think Malik Montgomery's race played a role in his arrest, Mr. Serrat?"

Sean glared at the man. "The color of Mr. Montgomery's skin meant nothing to me when he dated my daughter, and it means nothing to me now." It was getting harder to speak. "Abby went to law school because she still believed in justice—in the rule of law— and she didn't let pessimism sway her trust in the system. And, for her, I refuse to partake in the cynical speculation by people who seem more intent on their own agendas than getting justice for my murdered daughter." His voice broke, but then he recovered. He stared directly into the camera and added, "They didn't arrest

Malik Montgomery because he's black. They simply followed the evidence. Now please, give my family some privacy." Sean felt a hand on his arm.

Cecilia led him inside, slamming the door behind them. She hugged him tight. Then she eased back and examined his face.

"What's the look for?" Sean said. "Was it that bad?"

"No," Cecilia said. "I think you've accidently just become a media star."

CHAPTER 16

Sean sat behind the glass-topped desk in his new office at Harrington & Caine. The space was all packed boxes and bare walls. His lunch, a limp sandwich he'd bought in the firm's cafeteria, was still in its plastic container at the corner of the desk. He studied the visitor who sat across from him.

"Thank you for seeing me, Mr. Serrat. I know this must seem, well, unusual. A surprise."

Sean was surprised—mainly that *this* was the famous defense lawyer Blake Hellstrom, the go-to hired gun for politicians caught with their hand in the cookie jar (or up an intern's blouse) and for multinational corporations centered in the DOJ's crosshairs. This was the lawyer representing Malik Montgomery: portly, with a bad comb-over. His suit, navy with pinstripes, was presumably expensive, but Hellstrom was the kind of guy who could make a $6,000 Brioni look cheap.

"To tell the truth," Hellstrom continued, "in my forty years in practice, I've never showed up unannounced to speak with the victim's family."

Sean tilted his head. "I'd assumed the 'victims' in your usual cases are taxpayers or shareholders."

Hellstrom stroked his chin. "That's true these days, I suppose.

But I was a public defender early in my career and handled many homicide cases."

Sean gazed over Hellstrom's shoulder out the window. The sunny morning had turned dull gray. The tip of the Washington Monument peeked over a neighboring building. Sean's eyes shifted back to his visitor. "So why the break in routine, Mr. Hellstrom? What do you want?" Sean had never been one for pleasantries, but like so many things, they seemed even more pointless in the *After*.

Hellstrom slouched back in the chair, paunch sagging over his belt. "In most of my cases," Hellstrom said, drawing out the words, "I do the best I can for my clients. I turn over every stone, file a mountain of motions, and I eat, drink, and sleep their cases until trial. But I vowed to myself two things long ago, lessons learned early in my career." Hellstrom looked Sean in the eyes. "First, if anyone's going to jail, it's going to be my client, not me. So no matter how badly I want to win, I always play by the rules. Second, if my client goes to jail, I don't take it personally. My clients are not my friends, not my family—they're my *clients*."

Sean began to understand why they called him "the jury master." His manner. Hellstrom had a homespun sincerity—he was a truth teller—and you *wanted* him to continue talking, telling you his story, dispensing his wisdom.

"This morning, one of the associates at my office sent me an e-mail that had a video clip of an interview you gave the press. I normally don't open these types of things." Hellstrom pulled out a handkerchief and blew his nose loudly.

"You may be too young, but do you remember the days before we got deluged with all this YouTube and Internet crap? Anyway, this associate, a young guy fresh out of law school includes a note that says I really should watch it, so I did. And I was struck by your words about—no, *your faith* in—the system."

Sean narrowed his eyes. "I'm not some naïve kid, Mr. Hellstrom, so please don't—"

"Of course not. But maybe I've been doing this too long, or it's the type of cases I handle, but I see things a little differently. I don't know what your experience was at the solicitor general's office, but in my practice there are some cases—usually the big ones—where the government can't see straight. Good people do strange things. Look at the Roger Clemens trial or the Ted Stevens and John Edwards cases."

"So what's your point, Mr. Hellstrom?"

"Please, call me Blake."

Sean waited for a response.

"My point," Hellstrom said finally, "and the reason I came here today, is that I'm convinced Malik Montgomery is innocent."

Sean scoffed and stood. "I think we're done here."

Hellstrom held up his hands in retreat. "Please, Mr. Serrat . . ."

"If your client is innocent, I'm sure he'll be in great hands with you as his lawyer. I just don't see what you hope to achieve by—"

"I'm not sure myself why I'm here," Hellstrom said. "It's the damndest thing. I just kept thinking of that video of you and something compelled me to walk over. Please, if you'll just hear me out."

Sean gave an exasperated sigh and sat back down.

"You're not the decision maker, and the government's gonna do what it's gonna do with this case. But this is your daughter. And, unlike all the defendants I've ever represented, I've never felt the terror I'm feeling with Malik Montgomery. Nothing we say here goes beyond this room and I won't be telling anyone you spoke with me. I just ask you to consider something." Hellstrom raised two fingers. "They have only two pieces of evidence as far as I can tell: One, Malik was at the Supreme Court the night your daughter was murdered. And two, her phone was found at his home."

"No, that's not all," Sean countered. "He lied. He lied about being at the scene of the crime. I know, I was there. Malik looked me in the eye and he lied."

Hellstrom gave a sympathetic gaze. "More than a hundred people were in the court that evening for a reception. Malik should've told the FBI he went in to speak with your daughter, but by that point he was scared and knew the direction things were headed. Malik may be affluent, but he's still had to grow up in this city as a black man. He has good reason to fear the police."

Sean rolled his eyes. "I'm not going to get into a debate about race and the justice system. I think there's a much simpler reason why your client lied: he murdered Abby and deleted incriminating evidence from her phone, which was found hidden in his house."

"Let's think about that one, Mr. Serrat. This kid's a Rhodes Scholar. A Georgetown Law graduate. And a Supreme Court law clerk. If he murdered your daughter, why the hell would he keep her phone? And why hide it at his home when he would know witnesses at the restaurant would place him as the last person seen with her? And if he was such a computer expert that he could wipe the phone clean, why would he be dumb enough to leave the device on so it could be tracked to his house?"

Sean shook his head. "They arrested him for a reason. And there is no one else who—"

"Do you know whether they even looked for anyone else? They arrested him the morning after you found your daughter and after questioning the kid all night. Just twelve hours later. Did you know your daughter was in a relationship that she was keeping secret? That someone had been harassing her? And that she was doing some type of confidential research project concerning nominees for the Supreme Court?"

Sean had heard some of this from Malik that night, but it was the first he'd heard of any research project. "All this according to who?" Sean asked. "Your client?"

At that Hellstrom made no reply.

Sean continued, "They looked for other suspects—and I'm sure that they're still looking."

Now Hellstrom gave Sean a disappointed look.

"After an arrest, Mr. Serrat, the police tend not to look for other suspects. Old codgers like me use that kind of thing to show that even the police have reasonable doubt. If there's no doubt he's the one, there's no reason to look elsewhere."

"Then tell me, why? What use would it serve to arrest the wrong man? Why not go after the *real* killer?"

Hellstrom held Sean's stare. "Now, Mr. Serrat, you're starting to ask the right questions."

CHAPTER 17

Sean took a seat in the back of a lecture room in McDonough Hall at Georgetown Law. He looked down at the rows and rows of twenty-somethings transfixed by Jonathan Tweed. Tweed's secretary had said that Tweed was giving a guest lecture to a colleague's Constitutional Law course. In the nosebleed section of the hall, Tweed appeared much shorter than six foot two. But his boyish good looks were apparent even from this distance, if not from the gazes of the young law students attending the class.

"Professor Barnhizer asked me to talk today about freedom of the press," Tweed said. Sean shook his head. Not a good day to hear about freedom of the press given the group that had been stationed outside his house.

Tweed considered the crowd. "But who would rather talk about something else—let's say, perhaps . . . *sex*."

That elicited a low rumble from the students.

Tweed held a microphone and worked the room like a televangelist about to pass the collection plate. "No, I wouldn't want to disappoint Professor Barnhizer. How about we compromise? Let's talk about both freedom of the press *and* sex."

The students clapped at this and someone whistled.

"Has anyone heard of an eighteenth-century journalist named James Callender?"

The room went quiet. All these years and things still hadn't changed since Sean sat in a Harvard lecture hall: the terror of the professor calling on you and—*gasp!*—you possibly not knowing the answer. The days when you knew it all or, at least, you needed everyone to think you did. The first time he saw Emily was in a classroom just like this one. Their first day of law school. Torts I. He remembered her sitting in the center row, center seat, leaning forward ready to take notes, while he staked out a spot in the back. He recalled her hair, pulled back into a ponytail. Her green eyes and full lips. She was the first to raise her hand and speak. He remembered thinking she was out of his league, better than him. And he was right. But he couldn't take his eyes off of her. After class he'd asked her to join his study group. "Who else is in the group?" she'd asked. Sean had smiled. "Just me . . ." Professor Tweed's voice broke the spell.

"If you think today's paparazzi is bad, well, they had nothing on the muckraker James Callender." Tweed took a sip from a bottle of water. "He actually broke one of our country's first sex scandals. Anyone know the politician involved?"

The room filled with crowded chants of "Washington," "Jefferson," "Madison."

"Getting close," Tweed said. "Think the Federalist Papers." He paced around, then stopped, and pointed to a student in the third row. "That's right, Alexander Hamilton. Our first Treasury secretary."

Tweed strutted back to the lectern. "In 1797, our friend James Callender wrote an exposé accusing Alexander Hamilton of financial improprieties while at Treasury. Apparently, Hamilton had been making payments to a shady character named James Reynolds and was accused of speculating on government funds. His honor challenged, Hamilton wrote a ninety-five-page response to Callender. His explanation?" Tweed gave a mischievous grin. "Hamilton said, 'I'm not engaged in public corruption, I paid the money to Mr. Reynolds because, well, because I was being blackmailed for having an affair with Reynolds's wife.'"

Tweed scanned the crowd. "Not usually the best defense in the court of public opinion: 'I am not a thief, just an adulterer.'" Another smile. "But that was just the beginning for James Callender. From there, Thomas Jefferson hired Callender to secretly write scathing stories about John Adams, Jefferson's opponent in the race for the presidency. Those stories landed Callender in jail in Richmond, Virginia, under the Alien and Sedition Acts—laws that made it a crime to criticize our public officials. Think about that, you could go to jail simply for criticizing the president. How do you think Fox News or MSNBC would fare?" Tweed touched his chin. "It doesn't sound so bad when you put it that way."

More laughter.

"So then Jefferson is elected president, and he decides to pardon Callender and others who were convicted under the Sedition Acts. Now, here's where the story takes a strange turn. Callender gets out of jail and then asks the newly elected president for a job in the government, but Jefferson refuses. Callender doesn't like that and decides on a little revenge. He writes a story based on a rumor he'd heard while serving his time in that Richmond jail. He reports that Jefferson had a child with one of his slaves. A story no one believes, virtually ruining Callender. But it's a story most historians *now* believe is true beyond a reasonable doubt."

Tweed let that sink in. "This vile man, this muckraker, used his words to shine a light on our public figures, and he went to jail for doing it. He died in disgrace for the Jefferson story. Why do I start this lecture about freedom of the press with Callender? Beyond illustrating that sex scandals in our fair city are nothing new, Callender shows that our founders and the framers of the Constitution struggled with the same tough issues we're going to discuss today."

Tweed lectured for another forty minutes before dismissing the class. Sean waited as the students packed their laptops and the circle of after-class suck-ups surrounding Tweed dispersed. He then stepped slowly down to the front of the class.

"Impressive," Sean said. "Not one student sleeping or surfing the Internet."

Tweed looked up from stuffing papers into his satchel. "Sean,

I didn't see you here. How are you? I hope you didn't sit through that entire lecture. I would have stepped out if I—"

"No, I enjoyed it. The students really loved it. I would have liked it even more if I didn't have several modern-day James Callenders outside my house this morning."

Tweed raised his eyebrows and gave a sympathetic nod. "You here early for the vigil tonight? It's going to be a massive turnout."

"No, I'm going to head home and get Emily and the boys—I don't want them to have to come alone."

Tweed's expression turned curious. "So you just came by to say hi or . . ."

"Malik Montgomery's lawyer came to see me today," Sean said.

"Blake Hellstrom? What did he want? He didn't have the balls to ask you to go to the prosecutors for leniency, did he?"

"It was a weird meeting." Sean told Tweed about Hellstrom's proclamation of his client's innocence.

"Did he ask you for anything? I heard he lost a child himself. Tell me he didn't try to use that to—"

"He didn't mention losing a child, and he didn't ask for anything. He just wanted to talk. A private talk."

Tweed turned and erased the white board. "He's a brilliant defense lawyer, Sean, don't trust him."

"I didn't feel like he was playing me. He seemed—" Sean thought about it "—distraught."

Tweed made no reply as he snapped on the caps to the white board markers, but his expression was skeptical.

"You know Malik Montgomery pretty well, right?" Sean asked.

"Yeah, I mean, he was one of my students."

"But he was your research assistant, and you helped him get his clerkship?"

Tweed nodded.

"Do you have any doubts that he did this?"

Tweed looked conflicted. "I don't know the facts, so I can't—"

"But you know this kid, Jon. Is it something he's capable of? Murder?"

Tweed fussed with the straps on his satchel. He started to speak, but hesitated.

"What is it?"

"I understand that there was an incident when he was in college."

"An incident? What kind of incident?"

"I'm not sure. Something popped up in his background check for his clerkship with Justice Sheldon. She called me to ask about him. She didn't give me any details, but said there'd been an altercation with a girlfriend and the police were called. There was no arrest and Sheldon said it seemed harmless, but she wanted to know what he was like." Tweed looked down at the floor. "I keep thinking about that because I told her he was a model student and got along with everyone and that I thought he'd make a great clerk. If I would have known . . ."

Sean considered relieving Tweed of any guilt. After all, how much could he possibly know about his hundreds of students? But he couldn't bring himself to say the words. "Was Abby working on some special project for you? Something confidential?" He'd been thinking about this since the meeting with Hellstrom. Abby loved to talk with Sean about the law: about her law school papers, her law review note, her work for Jon. He couldn't believe she'd have kept something from him, but your children will do nothing if not have their secrets.

Tweed's forehead wrinkled. "I'm not supposed to—"

"Jon, come on."

His friend's shoulders drooped. "I'm helping the administration vet potential candidates for Chief Justice Malburg's seat. I've got students helping me. It's obviously sensitive. We made the students sign confidentiality agreements. Violation is grounds for expulsion."

"Abby was one of them?"

Tweed nodded.

"Did you tell the FBI? I mean, in case it's relevant to the investigation?"

"They never asked. They actually haven't interviewed me yet. I think they believe they've got their man."

"Am I on your list?" Sean asked. "Your students are digging into *my* background?"

"Don't be ridiculous. I wouldn't have students look into your past." Tweed waited a beat. "I personally handled your vetting. You're pretty boring, by the way."

Sean shook his head. "Can I see Abby's research files?"

"I don't think . . ." Tweed trailed off again. "Come to my office and I'll give you the file."

CHAPTER 18

"You ready to go?" Sean said. Emily stood in the entryway of their home. She wore a black dress with a single strand of pearls around her neck. She had on more makeup than usual, but it didn't completely camouflage the dark circles under her eyes, and she looked too thin. Sean couldn't recall the last time he saw her eat.

"I'm not sure I'm up for this." Emily bent over and strapped one of her shoes.

"People need to say their good-byes to Abby," Sean said. "They already delayed the vigil by a week for us, and Jonathan said we don't have to stay for the whole thing."

The drive to Georgetown was silent. A May storm had blown in and rain sprinkled the windshield. The wipers beat back and forth, entrancing them all. He thought about the previous two weeks. It was hard enough navigating the well-meaning, stupid efforts to console. The intrusive calls, e-mails, and texts. Visits to the house. The Serrats were the type of family that would tightly bandage their gaping chest wound, not keep it exposed to the elements. He'd also had to figure out the formalities of death. The cold paperwork. The details about cremation. Picking an urn. He felt a moment of empathy for his father, who'd made the arrangements after Sean's mother's death. When his father died, the military had taken care of everything.

He glanced at his sons in the rearview mirror. Ryan sat quietly, his iPod buds in his ears as always. Jack pressed his nose to the window. Sean reached for Emily's hand, but she kept it just out of grasp.

Why were they doing this? Abby's classmates and friends needed some closure, but his family hadn't even said their own good-byes. A pillow-shaped biodegradable urn for a water burial still sat unceremoniously in the back of the SUV. His daughter's remains tucked in a Bloomingdale's sack. Sean sat at a red light on Sixteenth Street. When the light hit green, he spun into a U-turn.

"Fuck this," he said.

"What are you doing?" Emily said, her brow sprouting lines.

An hour later they inched along in traffic on the Chesapeake Bay Bridge. The strobe of police lights glowed ahead—an accident that had left them stuck on the four-mile bridge over the Chesapeake Bay.

"Traffic should start moving soon," Sean said.

Emily gave an icy shake of the head and gazed wearily out the rain-spattered window.

Sean said, "Look, you didn't want to go to the vigil and neither did I, so I thought we could say good-bye to Abby at one of her favorite places."

Emily continued her stare into the gloom. Sean could read her thoughts: Rehoboth Beach in Delaware wasn't exactly a hot spot in May, they didn't have beach clothes, they didn't have their toothbrushes, and they weren't ready for some getaway. The days of spontaneous outings to the Delaware shore were over. It was one of Abby's favorite places as a kid, but that was just going to make them feel worse.

"Is the water going to be too cold to swim, Daddy?" Jack asked from the backseat.

Emily gave Sean a hard look.

"I don't think we'll be going in the water," Sean said, "but we can go to the boardwalk."

"Can we go on that ride that takes us into the sky?"

"If it's open," Emily clipped.

"I hope it's open," Jack said.

And it was. By nine o'clock the four of them were on the board-walk riding The Sea Dragon, a giant pendulum that swung back and forth into the cloudy night sky. Emily and Ryan on one side, Sean and Jack on the other. When they swung up, Jack laughed and thrust his arms in the air. When the pendulum swung back down, Sean gazed up at Emily and Ryan, both with blank stares, Emily hugging herself from the chill in the air.

After the Monster, Sean took Jack into the Haunted Mansion, which had a sign that read AWARD-WINNING RIDE, undoubtedly an award issued in the 1970s given the state of the thing. After some fairground games, the family walked on the beach toward the hotel. All of them carried their shoes, and the boys, Sean included, had rolled up their trousers. Emily clutched at her cardigan. Sean had envisioned them releasing Abby's ashes that night, perhaps remi-niscing about the great times they had spent on this shoreline since she was a little girl. But instead, they ate cardboard pizza from a vendor and went to their room at the Boardwalk Plaza Hotel.

Emily had barely said a word to Sean since he'd turned the SUV around and abandoned the vigil. Late that night, with the sound of the boys snoring in the double bed next to theirs, he and Emily lay in the darkness.

"I'm sorry," he said. "For some reason, I thought it would help."

"It's fine," Emily said.

"We need to talk. We can't go through this alone."

Silence.

"Did I do something? Did I *not* do something?" Sean said. "I can't get through this without you, Em. Please, talk to me."

She did speak to him. Just when he thought he couldn't feel any more of the peculiar hollowness in his chest or the weight in his arms—when he thought he couldn't feel any more alone—she ut-tered six words: "Why didn't you take her call?"

CHAPTER 19

Sean didn't sleep that night. Every hour or so he'd turn to the red glow of the hotel alarm clock. At six a.m., he slipped out of bed and pushed aside the curtain of the sliding glass door of the tiny suite. He opened the door a crack. The salt in the air filled his lungs. The rain clouds had disappeared, and there was a burst of orange from the horizon. He stepped quietly into his pants and padded barefoot to the door.

A voice whispered in the darkness: "Are you going to watch the sunrise like you and Abby used to do?" It was Ryan.

"I was thinking about it," Sean said. He waited, then said, "Wanna come?"

"That was you and Abby's thing. I couldn't . . ."

Sean felt that lump in his throat again. "She'd want you to." He added, "*I* want you to."

Ryan climbed over his little brother, who was snoring next to him. Sean and Ryan then walked shirtless and shoeless down the stairwell of the hotel and journeyed the sandy path to the beach. Abby was seven years old when they began their covert missions to the beachfront—their "sunrise escapes," as she called them. They continued the tradition into Abby's adulthood. Every summer, from elementary school through high school through college. And just last summer at Nauset Beach in Cape Cod.

"It's weird without her here, isn't it, Dad?" Ryan said. He stared out at the ocean, the sun reflecting off the water.

"Yeah, it is. I think it was a mistake dragging us here. I don't know what got into me."

"I'm glad we came. She's not here, but it kinda feels like she is here, do you know what I mean? The smell of the ocean or the room at the hotel, I can't explain it."

Sean took in a deep breath through his nose and nodded.

"What'd you guys used to do when you'd sneak out?" Ryan asked.

Sean thought about this and his mind flashed to Abby as a little girl, goading him into the cold water where she'd jump on his back. He would bodysurf, her arms wrapped tightly around his neck, gliding through Rehoboth's unsettlingly strong shore breaks, making sure she landed softly. Making sure she didn't get caught in the undertow. Protecting her. His mind wandered to last summer, their final sunrise escape.

"No, really, I've studied all of the past justices—I know them all," Abby said. The sound of crashing waves filled the air.

"All of them?" Sean said skeptically. "There's been more than a hundred Supreme Court justices, I don't think you—"

"Try me. Give me a clue, and I'll guess the justice."

Sean smiled at his daughter. The summer after her first year of law school. Like every person who'd ever studied the law, she was consumed by it. And a bit insufferable, too, with the law jokes and constant legal references. He was surprised since he thought that Abby might be immune, having grown up with the law and Supreme Court around her.

His daughter stuck out her lower lip. It worked as well in her twenties as it did when she was five.

"Okay, okay. How many hints?"

In her best game show contestant voice, Abby said, "I can name that Supreme Court justice in three hints."

"All right. First hint, the justice was a great writer."

"Uh, could you be more general?" She smiled, her teeth gleaming against her tanned face. "John Roberts, Elena Kagan," she added.

"Nope, way before their time."

Abby bunched her lips.

Sean said, "Okay, okay, hint number two: The justice was a bestselling author."

"Sotomayor. No wait, she was after Roberts, so it must be before her time too. Come on, these are too general, give me a real hint."

"Last hint. The justice's picture is in the anteroom right outside the Supreme Court's conference room. Remember when I took you there? The conference room where the justices decide their cases in secret, right next to the chief justice's chambers."

"Of course I remember. You let me sit at the table where they decided Brown v. Board of Education. *I remember John Marshall's portrait above the fireplace, but you're talking about the small room at the entrance, not the conference room itself?" She scrunched her face, trying to conjure the image. "Ugh, don't tell me you're referring to Oliver Wendell Holmes."*

"Not bad! But what's wrong with Holmes? He was one of the greatest writers on the court. Didn't you learn about 'clear and present danger' or 'shout fire in a crowded theater' in Con Law? He came up with those lines. And his dissents were phenomenal. They called him 'The Great Dissenter.'"

"He also was a pig."

Sean threw up his hands, giving her a baffled look.

"In Buck v. Bell *he upheld a mentally disabled woman being forcibly sterilized," Abby said in disgust. "He wrote the poetic line 'three generations of imbeciles are enough.' Lovely. Your hero."*

With her hair blowing in the breeze, and her fiery gaze ready for a vigorous debate, there was no other word for her but exquisite.

"Come on, Abby," Sean said. "You can't judge a man by his one mistake."

"Oh yes you can—if that mistake shows his true character. All the other stuff, it's just cover."

The last comment stung now, just as it did then. Was that what his life had been all these years since Japan, just cover? When he thought about it, he'd really made two oaths that night in Misawa. The first the vow of silence with Kenny and Juan (which he'd broken by going to his father); the second, an oath to God, ironic since back then he hadn't been quite sure that he believed. The Almighty hadn't cured his mom's cancer, after all. But sobbing alone in his room, he'd vowed to never break the law again. To be a better person. To make something of himself. He'd left Japan soon after and his new school gave him the opportunity to reinvent himself. He was on a mission to succeed. By the time his father had retired from the military, Sean had attended five high schools in four years, but gotten straight As. That made for a helluva college essay. Dartmouth offered, he accepted, and once he was in the Ivy League system everything came easy: Harvard Law, a D.C. Circuit clerkship, on to the Supremes, then a coveted spot in the solicitor general's office. It didn't take a psych workup to connect why he had become a lawyer, why he dedicated himself to upholding the law and had become an appellate specialist whose job it was to fix mistakes made in the past by the lower courts.

Ryan's voice reeled him back in. "What'd you guys talk about?"

"What's that?" asked Sean, not understanding.

"You and Abby. What'd you used to talk about when you'd sneak out all those times?"

"She often talked about you, Ryan," Sean said. "And how proud she was of you."

Ryan picked up a shell and studied it. "She did?" There was a skeptical lilt to his voice.

"Oh, she admired you, Ryan. How you're so naturally smart, how you have no fear of public speaking, and how musically talented you are. She struggled with all those things, you know."

"I don't know why she'd admire me. She was the one who was the best at everything. Like you said on the news."

Sean again regretted speaking to the press. "She did admire you. I'm not just saying that."

Ryan's eyes glistened. Sean realized that as hard as he and Emily had tried not to make Ryan feel inferior to his overachieving sister, they'd failed. Parents don't like to admit it, but when a child excels it sends a message to the world: you were good parents. The truth was, Abby was born to achieve and Ryan—sweet, empathetic Ryan—was born to stumble before he'd find himself.

Ryan rubbed his eyes with the back of his hand. "The last time we spoke she was mad at me."

Sean hugged his son. His bare shoulder grew wet from Ryan's tears. Sean was choking back a sob himself. "Brothers and sisters fight. Abby adored you. And she wouldn't want you worried about some silly fight you had."

"But she was really mad at me, Dad," Ryan sobbed.

Sean felt a hand on his back and he turned. Emily. She gripped Jack's hand with her left hand. In her right, a sack that read BIG BROWN BAG. The Bloomingdale's bag. Abby's ashes.

Ten minutes later, with the beautiful red, orange, and purple sky and the sound of waves crashing, they watched as the pillow-shaped urn slowly disappeared into the ocean where it would break down and his little girl's ashes would become a part of this place she loved. Sean wanted to dive in the water and let the riptides take him away. But looking at Emily and the boys, he knew that, for them, he needed to be strong. Cliché as it was, he believed Abby would have wanted it that way.

On the slow walk back to the hotel, Emily reached for his hand. And he knew then that, if for only the moment, Emily was thinking the same thing.

CHAPTER 20

Sean idled the SUV curbside in front of the Starbucks on Rehoboth's main street. He could see Emily through the coffee shop's window ordering their drinks for the drive home. He glanced in the rearview at Ryan and Jack, who were bickering in the backseat.

"Stop breathing on me," Ryan said to his little brother. "You didn't brush your teeth and your breath smells like butt."

"Oh yeah," Jack countered, "well, your breath smells like *dummy*."

Ryan: "That doesn't even make sense, you're such a—"

"Boys, enough," Sean said. They were acting like *Before*. Just an hour ago they were in the midst of saying good-bye to Abby, one of the saddest events of Sean's life, yet here they were back to being brothers. It gave Sean hope. He eyed his phone sitting in the console. He could no longer avoid it. He powered on the device, which buzzed and quivered as e-mails scrolled onto the screen. Then the chirp of an incoming call.

He scanned the caller ID: J. TWEED. Jonathan. He took a deep breath and answered, prepared for the interrogation about why he had skipped his own daughter's vigil. Before he uttered a word, Tweed said, "Sean, thank God you picked up. I've been trying you since last night."

"I'm sorry we didn't make it, Jon. We just weren't up to—"

"It's not about the vigil," Tweed interrupted. "It's about the nomination. Marty Lang has been trying to reach you. They called me hoping I could track you down. The president wants to meet with you—today if possible. They're doing the final vet and you must have made the short list."

"Today? What time? I'm in Rehoboth. The soonest I can make it home will be one o'clock."

Tweed paused a beat. "Rehoboth? What are you—never mind. They want you in the lobby of the Hay-Adams at five o'clock so that should work. Abani Gupta will pick you up and take you to the White House."

Gupta was the lawyer who'd successfully vetted and served as the sherpa for the last two Supreme Court nominees. She was no-nonsense and smart. Sean assumed they wanted to meet him at the hotel since it was right across the street from the White House, and he could easily be shuttled through the gates, hidden behind the tinted glass of a town car.

At any other point in his life, he would have felt butterflies of excitement, the surreal honor of even being on the list. But the death of a child teaches something: your career, your accomplishments, the plaques hanging on your wall, they don't mean shit. If he could get back the late nights he'd spent working his cases and writing briefs, the weekends preparing for oral argument, the conference calls and meetings, he'd trade it all for the chance to walk down the beach just one more time with his Abby. *Before* he'd questioned Emily's decision to give up her career to stay home with the children. And he'd resented her demand that he slow down at work, that he take the job at the law firm. But now he understood. Emily had been right all along.

"I'm not sure, Jon. Let me think about it." He powered down the phone. He watched as Emily stood expressionless in the line at the coffee shop. The boys were still going at it in the back.

"Dad, tell Jack that it's okay to say sitting 'Indian style.' He says it's racist . . ."

"Mom says we should say 'crisscross-apple-sauce,'" Jack defended.

Sean twisted around and was met by Ryan passing him a bottle that had a ribbon around its neck. "This rolled from under Mom's seat."

Sean remembered the bottle from the night he'd found Abby. As he took the glass decanter from Ryan, the note affixed to it came loose and fluttered to the floor in the back. Sean scanned the bottle's label, which had Japanese characters all over it but the brand was written in English. Nikka whiskey. The brand from that night.

"Oh my God, is this you, Dad?" Ryan said. Jack blurted a laugh. They were looking at the back of the note card. All Sean could see was the writing on the front, CONGRATULATIONS ON THE NEW JOB! He reached over and plucked the card out of Ryan's hand. The boys were both giggling.

"And you give me trouble about my hair," Ryan said.

It wasn't a card at all, Sean realized. It was a photograph. Heat engulfed his face, accompanied by a feeling of disorientation. The photo was of fourteen-year-old Sean, drunk and unsteady, hair that hit his shoulders, sleeveless Def Leppard T-shirt. Next to him were two boys, glassy-eyed. One short and cocksure, the other a scrawny Hispanic kid. Written in messy handwriting on the white border of the photo were two words:

THEY KNOW.

CHAPTER 21

He was quiet on the drive home, but his thoughts thrashed through the possibilities. Who had placed the bottle of Nikka whiskey and photo in the SUV? Why? What did it mean? Other than telling his father—who'd seemed more intent on protecting his military career than helping his son—Sean had never spoken about that night. Not to Emily, not to anyone.

His thoughts jumped to the man in the flannel shirt who'd bumped him on the subway. *They know.* The man's face then morphed into his younger self. It was the face from the photo. Not thirteen-year-old Juan, whose brown skin ruled him out, but the other boy. Sean blinked away the image of Kenny wiping the bloody blade on the grass.

But why, after all these years, would Kenny seek him out? Maybe he'd seen the news about Sean's possible nomination to the high court. Or maybe an adversary of the president digging up dirt on the potential nominees found Kenny under some godforsaken rock. In the devastation of the past two weeks, Sean had not thought about Japan. He wasn't worried about himself anymore, and there was something freeing about that.

But the bottle still sent a lightning bolt through his chest. Was it a coincidence that the boy who without remorse killed a storekeeper had entered the scene at the same time Abby was murdered?

He reminded himself that they'd already arrested the killer, Malik Montgomery. They had hard evidence against Malik. But then Blake Hellstrom, Malik's lawyer, came rushing to mind. The doubts ignited inside of Sean, burning through the entire three-hour drive.

At home, Sean retreated to the shower. He closed his eyes, the hot water pouring over him, and lapsed into a crying jag. After the shower, he put on his suit pants, white dress shirt, and a conservative tie for his meeting with the president. He'd considered skipping it, but Emily had said, "Abby loved the Supreme Court. What would your daughter want you to do?"

He went to his home office and sat behind the desk, staring off into space. He was consumed by thoughts of Japan, the bottle, and Kenny reappearing. The isolation was the worst part. He was in this alone. Now was not the time to unload his past on Emily. She was barely keeping it together as it was. And, anyway, where would he even begin after all these years?

There was a knock on the open door, and Ryan popped his head in.

"Preparing for your meeting at the White House?" Ryan asked. He had a thick folder in his hand and placed it on Sean's desk. "You left this in the car."

It was the file Jonathan Tweed had given him: Abby's vetting research. She'd been assigned to dig into the past of the front-runner for the nomination, Senator Mason James.

He'd analyzed Abby's file at the beach and found nothing out of the ordinary. Newspaper articles, speeches, campaign expenditure reports, Facebook and Twitter posts, printouts from high school reunion websites, the senator's voting record, and a stack of Internet research organized in folders and covered with highlighter, all focused singularly on the impressive career of Mason James. Sean assumed there were now several such files throughout Washington focused on himself.

"I probably should prepare, but I figure that I just need to be honest. Thanks for asking, though. Hey, you know the meeting is supposed to be secret, you can't tell—"

"I know, Dad," Ryan said. He let a long moment pass, then said, "Is that Abby's stuff you were looking at last night?"

Sean nodded.

Ryan's eyes settled on the floor and he lingered at the doorway. He then bit on a thumbnail.

Sean asked, "Is there something you wanted to talk about?"

Ryan continued working the nail.

"Ryan?"

When his son lifted his gaze, more tears. Sean wondered if it was possible to run out of tears. If so, the entire Serrat family must be getting near empty.

"About what happened at school—the Facebook messages about the weed," Ryan muttered. "I'm so sorry, I—"

"Buddy, stop." A family crisis just two weeks ago, those events seemed trivial now. On top of his grief, Ryan shouldn't be carrying around guilt about inappropriate Facebook messages and made-up pot sales.

"You don't understand," Ryan said. He continued to cry and seemed to be having a hard time catching his breath, like when he was a little boy. "It's about Abby."

Sean digested that. "Abby? What about Abby?"

"Remember I said she was mad at me?" Another sob. Ryan was sucking his breaths in gulps now. "It's because of the weed."

Sean gave him a confused stare.

"I went to her for help. I was scared."

"Scared? Scared about what? What are you talking about?"

"The man from Chipotle."

The guy in his Facebook messages. The man in red. The dealer. "I thought Chipotle Man was made up, that you were just trying to impress your friends?"

Ryan looked away and wiped his nose with the back of his hand. "I got weed from the guy, Dad." He whimpered. "He gave it to me for free. I was supposed to sell it and give him the money and keep some for myself, but I got scared, so I flushed it."

Confusion was replaced with a surge of anger, but it didn't have the energy it once did. Sean drew a deep breath to slow the pounding in his chest. "What's it have to do with Abby?"

"The dealer. He said he was gonna hurt me if I didn't get him the money. I went to Abby for help."

The words bounced around in Sean's head. Abby knew about this? And she hadn't come to him? He remembered her call. Her last ever to Sean. That goddamned missed call.

Ryan was crying again. "Abby went to see the guy. She paid him what I owed, but he said it wasn't enough. He said we'd better come up with five thousand bucks or he'd go to the press—he knew who you were. He ripped her necklace from her neck, said she could get it back when he got the five grand. Abby thought she was being followed, and she was scared and gonna go to you for help."

"When? When did she say she was going to talk with me about this?"

"The day she was killed."

CHAPTER 22

"I'm so sorry, Dad. I'm so, so sorry." Ryan's nose was running and his face red.

"You should be," Sean said. Ryan seemed like he might hyperventilate, but Sean had no urge to comfort him. He was consumed by wrath for the man who had threatened his children. The man who had taken something that Abby had worn every day since Sean gave it to her for her college graduation: an antique necklace worn by Sean's mother. Abby wasn't wearing the necklace when they found her body. Agents thought that the killer may have taken it that night. But apparently they were wrong.

"This guy, when is he usually at Chipotle?" Sean's head was throbbing.

When Ryan didn't respond immediately Sean walked around the desk and put his hands on Ryan's shoulders as if to shake him. "Stop crying and answer me. Where can I find this guy? The Chipotle in Bethesda? When's he there?"

"He hangs out there after school. He usually wears a red shirt and ball cap so kids know he's the guy who sells."

Sean checked his watch, 3:15 p.m. He had to be at the Hay-Adams hotel at five. He shook his head in disgust and stormed out of the office.

• • •

The Chipotle on Old Georgetown Road was filled with the after-school crowd. Booths with squirrelly teenagers in designer clothes, laughing and screwing around. The line to order was fifteen kids deep. How did he get here? He remembered getting into the SUV, but the rest of the journey was a blur. Everything was coming at him at once. The drain of saying good-bye to Abby that morning. The trauma of the last two weeks. He needed to stop. And think. Was he really going to confront this guy? What would that accomplish? He should go to the police. Talk to the agents assigned to Abby's case. All that made sense, yet he still found himself standing in the back of the queue.

He was in a daze, half looking for the man in red, half thinking about the many times he and Ryan had shuffled through this very line. Ryan loved Chipotle. The boy would choose a chicken burrito with guac over five courses at The Inn at Little Washington.

Then Sean saw him. A man in his twenties, skinny—what Ryan would call a "tweaker"—walked into the restaurant. He had a ferret face with a patch of whiskers on a pointy chin. He wore a red Washington Nationals shirt and backward-facing red ball cap. Chipotle Man.

CHAPTER 23

Sean worked his way through the line. He glanced again at Chipotle Man, who was now sitting at a booth with two meaty guys, both in T-shirts with their hair dyed white-blond. It was hard to keep watch when the team behind the counter started calling to him. Chicken or beef? Black or pinto beans? White or brown rice? Sean answered without thought, returning his eyes to the drug dealer. A teenage girl approached Chipotle Man's booth. She and the man in red talked, then he gestured to the door. The girl, who had flat brown hair and looked about seventeen, hurried out of the restaurant. Chipotle Man gave a grin to the two blond guys, then followed after her.

Was this how kids made a buy? Sean imagined Ryan following this protocol. Or Abby approaching this skeezy little man. Sean paid for the burrito and threw the softball wrapped in foil in the trash can as he rushed out the glass door.

He snapped his head back and forth looking for Chipotle Man, but he wasn't out front. Sean walked down the broken sidewalk toward the back of the building and peered around the corner. The girl was standing with her back pressed against the brick wall, Chipotle Man facing her. He was uncomfortably close, and she was shaking her head and looking at the ground.

Chipotle Man yelled at her. *"Do it, bitch!"* He stepped back and unbuttoned his pants. The girl started to cry.

"Hey!" Sean shouted. It just blurted out before he'd had time to process the situation. He shouldn't be here. Why was he doing this?

The red hat pivoted sharply to Sean. The girl said nothing but her eyes screamed for help.

"Leave her alone," Sean said, walking toward them.

Chipotle Man stepped in Sean's direction and looked him in the eyes. "Who the fuck'r you?"

He was shorter than Sean and skinny, but he kept his hand tucked in his front pocket, concealing something. A weapon? Sean ignored him and shouted to the girl.

"Get out of here." When she didn't move he yelled, *"Go!"*

She shot past him and around the corner, leaving Sean and the man in red alone. The back of the restaurant was nothing but dumpsters and trash strewn on gravel.

Chipotle Man made a show of his hand inside his pocket.

Sean said, "I don't want trouble. I just have a couple questions for you, then I'll be on my way."

Now Chipotle Man looked puzzled. His eyes swept over Sean as if trying to place him.

Sean said, "You had some dealings with my son and my daughter, and I'd like to talk about that. You also have my daughter's necklace, which I'd like back." It was ridiculous that he'd place himself in this situation over a piece of jewelry, family heirloom or not. But this was about more than the necklace.

"That's where I know you from," Chipotle Man said with a scoff. "You're the dude on TV."

"I want to talk with you about what happened with my children. I don't need to involve the police."

"Damn right you won't involve the police. Not a good career move. And you don't want that pussy son of yours ruining his Harvard application."

Sean felt something primal taking over, like that night at Malik's house. Electricity shooting from the back of his neck to his chest through his arms to his balled fists. His eyes stayed on the man's hand, which remained tucked in the pocket.

"When's the last time you spoke with my daughter?"

"I don't have to answer your questions," Chipotle Man said. He was twitchy and kept wrinkling his nose. Sean's experience with meth-heads was limited to episodes of *Breaking Bad*, but the guy fit the part.

"Did you follow her? Did you threaten her?"

Chipotle Man scoffed. "You playing detective, Daddy? Sorry Holmes, but I didn't have nothing to do with what happened to your slut daughter." He pulled his hand from the pocket and picked at his arm.

Sean rushed him, ramming Chipotle Man against the wall. He was outside himself for a moment. Sean shoved his forearm against the man's throat. Chipotle Man's eyes bulged.

"What the fuck, man?" Chipotle Man's voice had raised an octave, the bravado gone.

Sean was shaking, adrenaline overloading his system. Through gritted teeth he said, "Don't you *ever* speak that way about my daughter again. Do you understand me?"

Sean felt a hard blow to the side of his head. The next thing he knew, he was on his side on the gravel. Chipotle Man's two friends, the blond guys, looked down at him. One kicked him in the stomach.

The blonds each grabbed one of his arms and pulled Sean to his feet. He'd had the wind knocked out of him and was gasping for air.

Chipotle Man got close to his face. "I didn't hurt that whore daughter of yours. Go ahead and call the police if you don't believe me. All you'll get is your little boy in juvie and everyone will know your daughter blew me to cover your son's drug debt."

He hit Sean hard in the jaw, and Sean tasted blood. The next blow was to the eye. Then they let go of Sean's arms, and he slumped to the gravel.

He was on the dirty ground. Beaten and bloody. Alone. And nearly late for an appointment with the president of the United States.

CHAPTER 24

Back at home, Sean stared into the bathroom mirror, dabbing his swollen eye with a washcloth. His dress shirt had droplets of blood on the collar, so he tore it off. Now the dilemma. Did he go to the White House meeting or make an excuse? Emily's voice played in his head.

What would your daughter want you to do?

He looked at the white undershirt. No blood had seeped through. In the bedroom, he slid the dimmer up so there was just enough light not to wake up Emily, who had gone to bed when they arrived home from Rehoboth. He found a clean shirt in the closet and slipped out of the room. Sore from the beating, he winced as he eased on the shirt.

He checked his watch. He had thirty minutes to make it the seven miles from Chevy Chase to the Hay-Adams hotel downtown. He called and confirmed that Jack was doing okay at his play-date, and that the neighbor would drop him back home before dinner. On his way out the door, Ryan called to him.

"What is it?" Sean said. "I'm running late."

"I need to talk with you . . . Whoa, what happened to your eye?"

"I don't have time to explain. What do you need?"

He held a folder in his hand. "I think I found something in Abby's file. I think it may help—"

"You've helped enough, Ryan. Now I have to go." Sean slammed the door.

CHAPTER 25

The Oval Office was as it appeared in photos. It was oval, for starters, with wood floors covered by an oval rug embroidered with the presidential seal. The Resolute desk. And the president's personal touches: a bust of Abraham Lincoln, a Norman Rockwell painting. Sean sat upright on a beige couch and glanced at his reflection in a glass-topped coffee table. The swollen eye looked terrible. What would he say if the president asked? Hit a door? Too cliché. Bee sting? Wouldn't explain the gash. Mugged? Too many questions. Maybe the president wouldn't ask. That seemed unlikely, but Abani Gupta, who'd picked him up at the Hay-Adams, hadn't asked. Nor had the president's chief of staff.

The ride from the Hay-Adams to the White House grounds had been surprisingly quick. He'd imagined a holdup with security, but it was just a matter of the town car driver flashing an ID, a dog jumping into and out of the trunk, and Sean showing his license then signing a visitor log.

For past Supreme Court nominees, he'd heard of candidates being led through an underground tunnel from the Treasury building into the White House or clandestine meetings outside of Washington. But there was no cloak and dagger here, further confirming that Sean wasn't a serious contender. The press corps would hear of the meeting, as the White House intended, showing that the president was doing his due diligence before choosing the inevitable nominee, Senator Mason James. He shouldn't have bothered coming.

The door opened and the president strutted into the room. Sean stood. He'd never met the man, who was shorter than expected. His famous hair looked as perfect as it did on the Halloween parody masks, as did his glowing white teeth.

"Ouch," was the first thing the president said. "They told me you looked like you'd been hit by a truck, but I had no idea."

"I decided some exercise might help relieve stress, but the bike trail didn't agree." Sean borrowed his friend Jonathan Tweed's accident for himself. It seemed to work. The president didn't ask questions, just gestured for him to sit.

"I first wanted to give you my condolences about your daughter," the president said. He sat on the other sofa across from Sean. "It's a tragedy, and I'm embarrassed as hell that we had to call you in here at this time."

"Thank you, Mr. President."

"Mr. Serrat, I'm going to give it to you straight, if that's all right with you?"

That expression always struck Sean as odd. Would you normally *not* be straight with someone? Only politicians had to announce when they were being sincere.

"We'd pretty much made our decision on the nomination. And, while you were high on the list, for a variety of reasons, we'd gone in a different direction."

Sean nodded again, not surprised and unsure what to say.

"But my chief of staff showed me your interview about your daughter. Your words about our justice system and the no-B.S. views on the interest groups really stuck with me." The president leaned forward. "Look, you're no stranger to the administration or my predecessor's administration, so we never had any concerns about your views on the law. And certainly no qualms about your ability to do the job. Hell, everyone says you were the smartest lawyer at the solicitor general's office. Your family story is damn compelling, too. Your father was a bona fide hero."

Sean started to understand. Mother dead at a young age. Father, a retired general who died in Lebanon while serving on an anti-terrorism commission. (*Quite a guy.*) Daughter, murdered. A political trifecta that might offset the usual assault on a nominee. His stomach churned.

"Listen," the president went on, "I can't afford a fight over the nomination right now. I need somebody who's going to immediately resonate with the public. And word has it that you're a bit, well, independent. Someone described you as a brilliant introvert, and we need someone who can quickly get out there and win over the public—and the vipers on the Hill."

"Someone who will kiss a few babies," Sean said. "Interpreting the Constitution deserves nothing less." The words came out with more of an edge than intended. But the president smiled.

"I hear you," the president said. "Look, you're here because this video, for my team—and for me—was a game changer. I haven't made any final decisions yet. Our plan is to put your name out there again along with some additional information about your personal story and see the reaction. I just wanted to be up front about why you're here now, so late in the process."

The president stood, and Sean took the cue to stand as well. "So we've gotta decide this thing soon," the president said. "My team will call you either way. But I want you to know that if it's not you this time, it won't be your last shot. We've still got two justices in their seventies."

Sean didn't have the energy or enthusiasm to say much, and the president didn't seem interested in hearing anyone talk but himself. Politicians. Abani Gupta appeared in the doorway ready to whisk Sean out of the Oval Office.

"Again, I'm sorry about your daughter," the president said as Sean neared the door. "And please, get some ice on that eye."

CHAPTER 26

When Sean got home the only remains from dinner were an empty pizza box, crust-filled plates cluttering the kitchen counter, and the smell of Domino's. He loosened his tie and lumbered down to the basement. He was exhausted. Ryan and his little brother sat on the floor facing the flat-screen playing *Mario Kart* on the Wii. Emily was probably in bed.

"Daddy!" Jack said with a gap-toothed smile. He jumped up and hugged Sean's waist. Ryan just stared at the television screen maneuvering his motorcycle-riding gorilla around the track.

"Did you have fun at Dean's house?"

Jack nodded. "Yep. And Ryan got us pizza and hot wings. Mom said it was okay."

Sean said, "Thanks for ordering it and feeding him, Ryan."

Ryan's eyes stayed fixed on the screen and his jaw clenched. Sean had been hard on him, and his son's remorse seemed to have shifted to anger.

Sean went upstairs to his bedroom, glancing at the bundle under the covers. There was a faint smell of vodka in the air again. If Emily didn't come out of this soon, he'd need to call someone. Maybe it was time for her parents to come stay. He could hear the usual commentary on how expensive yet small his house was, the terrible traffic, and the unfriendliness of the store clerks. He might explode if Emily's parents, as they did every visit, mentioned the dangers of living in a major city. That look from her mother: *We warned you . . .* Maybe it wasn't the right time for them to come.

In the bathroom he stared into the mirror, dabbing his eye lightly with his ring finger. His blood-spattered dress shirt remained draped over the bathtub from earlier in the afternoon. He thought about the teenage girl Chipotle Man had pushed against the wall, and imagined Abby dealing with the man. He thought of Chipotle Man ripping the gold chain from Abby's neck. She wouldn't have given it up voluntarily. The necklace and pendant were antiques. They'd been worn not only by Sean's mother (someone Abby had never met but was always fascinated with), but also by Abigail Adams, one of Abby's heroes.

Sean's fists were bound into hard balls. In a fog, part anguish, part anger, part utter irrationality, he made a decision he would later relive in agony over and over. Sean went back to the bedroom, searched Emily's jewelry box for a tiny key, and opened the lockbox he kept hidden in the back of the closet. Inside was a small black box that had the word TAURUS on the front of it. He removed the .357 Magnum. It was cold and heavy. He slid in the small safety key above the handle and unlocked the hammer so the revolver was fireable. He tucked it in his waistband and bolted out of the house.

CHAPTER 27

No one seemed to notice the black SUV idling across the street from the Chipotle. At 8:45 p.m. on a weeknight, traffic was surprisingly light by Bethesda standards, and Sean had a clear view through the restaurant's large front window. There were only a few customers. The place must be closing soon. He'd seen Chipotle Man get up and walk around the restaurant and speak with a group of kids, but for the last fifteen minutes all he could see was the top of the red ball cap peeking over a booth.

He felt the gun at the small of his back. He'd bought it years ago when the neighborhood was experiencing a rash of burglaries, but had never fired it. And he had no intention of firing it tonight. He just wanted to talk to Chipotle Man. To get some answers. He would try to catch him alone, but was prepared for another three-against-one situation. He assumed the mere sight of the weapon would scare off these small-time criminals and prevent another beating. There was, of course, the obvious question: Why not just call the police? He had no answer. Had he lost his shit? He was starting to think so. But for some reason he just didn't care.

The restaurant started to clear out. The two blond guys, the ones who had worked him over earlier that day, left, but Chipotle Man stayed behind. That was good. A few minutes later, Chipotle Man got up from his booth and did a complicated handshake with a black kid. He opened the glass door, lit a cigarette, and began walk-ing down the street.

Sean waited until Chipotle Man morphed into the shadows be-fore pulling the SUV from the curb. It took only a minute before the comical red outfit appeared in his headlights. Sean surveyed the path ahead. On the right, tall brick apartment buildings and dated commercial office space. On the left, the campus of Bethesda–Chevy Chase High School. A high school, a perfect place for a drug dealer to skulk around at night. Sean drove past Chipotle Man and turned into B-CC's campus. He parked in a secluded spot near the front of the main building. Sure enough, the skinny man in red made his way onto school grounds. Another burst of adrenaline flowed through Sean, heightening his senses. The man walked past the steps to the main entrance and veered down a path to the rear of the school.

Sean climbed out of the SUV. The school grounds were sur-prisingly empty. And dark. Any after-school activities were proba-bly long over, and the building looked locked up tight. Sean trailed Chipotle Man down the path. *Turn around and go home,* the voice whispered in his head—but he continued to follow. At the end of the sidewalk, he crouched on his heels and peered around the corner. In the shadows, he could see three figures, one of them wearing a hat. There was a smell he hadn't encountered since col-lege, and the glow from the tip of a joint.

He wasn't sure what to do next, so he decided just to watch. Hopefully, he'd catch Chipotle Man alone. It was a long ten min-utes, and he felt creepy lurking at a high school. He saw an outline of someone on a mountain bike riding into the parking lot, but the biker disappeared into the gloom.

Finally, movement. Two of the figures were heading toward Sean. His eyes darted around. No place to hide. Two teenagers nearly bumped into Sean as they turned the corner.

"Unless you want to get arrested," he said, "I suggest you boys leave now."

Panic in their eyes, they scurried away, apparently buying the fake cop routine.

Sean looked around the corner. There was still the outline of a hat and the flare of another joint. He stepped toward the man. The glow of the joint went out and there was a dark blur. Chipotle Man was taking off.

Sean sprinted after him. Chipotle Man was darting toward a short chain-link fence to the left of the main building. In the dim light, Sean could see a scoreboard and realized that the man was headed to the football field. Chipotle Man raced down the bleacher stairs and jumped another fence and disappeared onto the field. Sean followed, taking the stairs two at a time, aluminum thundering with each step. He vaulted the fence and continued after him. Chipotle Man came into view again. He looked over his shoulder and stumbled, allowing Sean to gain on him.

Sean was close, but the man was just out of reach. He felt the gun slipping out from his waistband. Sean willed himself a burst of strength and he dove, catching Chipotle Man around the legs and bringing him down. As Sean also hit the ground, the gun fell onto the field.

Chipotle Man sat in the grass for a dazed moment. He stared at Sean and then his glance moved to the gun. Both men paused a beat, and then simultaneously scrambled toward the revolver. The next thing Sean saw was the skinny man, panting and out of breath, standing over him, the barrel aimed at Sean's head.

"Are you fucking crazy?" Chipotle Man shouted. He was breathing heavily and he let out a barking cough.

Sean held up his hand, shielding his face. "I just want to know what happened to my daughter."

The man hit Sean in the head with the butt of the gun, sending him flat on the field. The man stood over him.

"I didn't touch your daughter," Chipotle Man shouted. "Get that through your dumb-ass head. And I don't got her cheap-ass necklace no more if that's what this is about."

Emily, Ryan, and Jack's faces shot through Sean's mind as the blood from the gash on his head dripped into his eyes. This had been a mistake. Another terrible mistake. He looked up at Chipotle Man. "What . . . happened . . . to it?" His mouth was dry, voice hoarse.

"Happened to what, motherfucker?"

"The necklace . . ." Sean struggled.

"Some guy bought it back for her."

It didn't make sense. Who would she have gone to for help? He looked up at the man, who seemed to be debating what to do. Sean was feeling faint, but he fought to stay conscious.

"Who was he?"

"How the fuck am I supposed to know?"

"Who . . ."

Chipotle Man's eyes narrowed. The last thing Sean heard before things went dark was "He was some rich dude in a suit, like you."

CHAPTER 28

When Sean came to, he was laid out in the grass on the football field. His arm was outstretched and a hand cinched around his wrist. He felt another swell of nausea. He looked up and saw Chipotle Man, the veins in the man's thin neck bulging, as he struggled to drag Sean across the field. He had one hand around Sean's wrist, the other holding a phone to his ear.

"I don't think I've got a choice," Chipotle Man said into the phone.

In the distance behind the man Sean could see lights winking through gaps in the trees. If Chipotle Man wanted to kill him, he assumed he would have done it already. Maybe he just needed to give the guy a way out.

"I'm not gonna tell anyone," Sean said. His throat was still dry, his voice raspy. "I just want to know about my daughter."

Chipotle Man stopped and let go of Sean's wrist. His arm flopped to the ground. Into the phone Chipotle Man said, "Hold on a minute." He crouched down near Sean's face. His clothes smelled of cigarettes and weed. Breath foul. "Shut your fucking mouth or I will put a bullet in you." He stood and brandished the gun—Sean's gun.

Chipotle Man then went ramrod straight, his eyes bugged, and he collapsed. Sean shoved the man's limp body off of him and strained to sit up. He wiped the blood away from his eyes with his own shirt and tried to focus on the silhouette standing before him.

He was pale, his face disfigured from fear. And he was holding a steel rod—the kind used in construction—in his right hand.

Ryan.

CHAPTER 29

Sean stumbled across the field, his arm around Ryan's shoulder, like some wounded quarterback who'd had his bell rung. His pulse was hammering at his temples, but he wasn't dizzy anymore and was gaining his footing.

"Wait," he said.

Ryan stopped and looked at his father. His eyes darted around the field.

"I need to go back," Sean said. "The gun."

Ryan was shaking his head, but Sean held up a finger for him to wait. He made his way back to Chipotle Man. In the center of the field, the skinny man lay unconscious on his side. Sean leaned down and started to move in to take a pulse, but he could see Chipotle Man's chest heaving up and down. The man's hat was nearby on the ground and Chipotle Man's hair seemed matted with blood. Sean winced with pain as he bent over and scooped up the gun.

A siren's wail penetrated the quiet. It was not a continual blare, but a quick on and off. Red lights swirled from the front of the school. Sean hobbled quickly to Ryan, and they reached a tall chain-link fence that bordered the field. They ducked through a hole someone had cut into the fence and trekked into a small patch of woods. As they headed into the trees, Ryan stopped and said, "My bike."

"We'll have to leave it." That decision was confirmed when flashlight beams touched the brush. Sean clutched Ryan's hand and ran, the branches stinging his face and arms.

He was losing his breath, but he kept running until Ryan's hand slipped free. Sean turned back. Ryan was on the ground hugging his knees. Sean crouched down. He'd seen this before.

"Are you okay?"

Ryan was breathing heavily and didn't respond.

"Look at me," Sean whispered.

Ryan's eyes lifted.

Sean said, "It's gonna be okay."

"But I hurt him."

"He was going to hurt me," Sean said. "You saved me, Ryan."

Ryan wiped his eyes with the back of his hand. "But what if he's dead?"

"He's not dead," Sean said. "He was moving when I went back. It was no worse than when he clocked me on the head. He'll have a major headache, but he'll be okay."

The tension in Ryan's face seemed to fade a little.

"Are you okay to move? We really need to go," Sean said, as he scanned the shadows. He rose and offered Ryan his hand.

Ryan grabbed it and hoisted himself up, and they continued their escape through the trees.

CHAPTER 30

From the brush, they cut through the Capital Crescent Trail, the only light a sliver of moon through the cover of trees.

"How'd you find me at the school?" Sean asked as they walked side by side, the sound of gravel under their feet. He was struck by his son's bravery, but he also was concerned. Emily was right, Ryan was a gentle, sensitive boy. And he'd already been through so much with Abby. Whatever anger Sean had felt toward Ryan earlier in the day had vanished.

Ryan said, "You were so mad when you left the house, and I was worried, so I rode my bike to Chipotle. I saw you parked and watching him, so I followed when you left."

Sean nodded. His son had been right to worry.

"I think someone else was following you too, Dad."

Sean gave his son a quizzical look.

"At the school. I was going to come talk to you, but I saw this guy on a motorcycle. He parked and followed you."

"Was he a blond guy built like a refrigerator?" Sean asked, thinking of Chipotle Man's muscle.

"I don't think so. I only got a quick look at him, but I don't think he was blond. He took off his helmet and the main thing I remember is that he had a mark on his face, a mole, I think."

Sean shook his head. "I didn't see him."

"You said you had to go back for a gun. You had a gun, Dad?"

"I'll explain later. I'm just glad you came, buddy. If it wasn't for you, I might not be standing here. Thank you."

Ryan seemed to stand a little taller at that.

"Where's the metal bar you hit him with?" Sean asked.

"I threw it as far as I could when we were running through the trees."

They found an opening on the trail and peered out at the school. The police were gone. The cops must not have seen Chipotle Man on the football field, or the man had regained consciousness and slipped away. Sean led Ryan to the SUV and they both climbed in. Ryan started crying. Sean wasn't sure if it was the sight of him bloody and beaten in the overhead lamp or the weight of what had just happened bearing down on his son. He reached over and hugged Ryan, holding him tight as he let it all out.

"You brave boy. You sweet, brave boy."

CHAPTER 31

The tree-lined streets of Chevy Chase were quiet but for a dog barking in the distance. At the front gate, a few newspapers were piled
up, but thankfully, no reporters were staked out. Under the yellow
porch light, Sean hugged Ryan again and he braced himself as he
pushed open the door. If Emily was awake, he'd have some explain-
ing to do. And Sean had no idea what to say. But the house was
still.

"Why don't you hit the sack," Sean whispered, as they both
slipped off their shoes. Ryan gave his father another hug. He tip-
toed up the stairs while Sean went into the kitchen. Sean didn't turn
on the light. He opened the refrigerator, pulled out a bottle of
water, and took a long gulp. The voice came from the dining room.

"Where have you guys been?" The light clicked on. Emily's
gaze softened when she got a look at him. "Oh my God, what happened?"

Sean walked to his wife and gave her a long embrace. Over
her shoulder in the dining room he saw piles of photographs spread
across the table. Emily put her hands on Sean's arms and examined his face.

"I got mugged," he said finally. "I was in the gym's parking lot
and two guys came out of nowhere. They clocked me good and took
my money. They threw my keys into the trees by the lot. I didn't

want to worry you, so I had Ryan ride his bike over and bring me a spare key." They were not a couple who lied to one another, and already Sean regretted it. He should tell her everything. But he was deterred by the weary, demolished look of her. Was the old Emily even still in there?

"Are you okay? Did you call the police?" Emily tucked strands of hair behind her ears.

"I'm fine, and I'm not calling the police."

"Why?"

"We don't need more attention, and, besides, they knocked me to the ground before I got a good look at them, so it would be pointless." The first rule of holes, Sean always told his children, is that when you're in one, stop digging. But here he was with not just a shovel, but an excavator.

"I think we should call," Emily said.

"No," Sean said. It was firm and final, and to his surprise, Emily didn't fight it. "You're going through some pictures?" he asked, a clumsy change of subject.

Emily followed his eyes to the table and said, "Abby's baby pictures, from before we had a digital camera. I'm having them and all our pictures digitized so they're preserved."

Sean gave a fleeting smile. "That's a great idea, Em." He walked to the table and looked over the photos. Birthday shots, first day of school, family vacations. He picked up a recent one.

"Remember this?" he said. It was from last Halloween. They were the Avengers. Ryan as Captain America, Jack as the Hulk, and Abby as Black Widow.

Emily nodded. "You told her the costume was too revealing."

"It was," Sean said. "I told her she was so beautiful that she didn't need any more attention."

"And what did she say?" Emily asked.

"What do you think?"

A smile briefly graced Emily's lips, but then the vacant stare reappeared. "Let's clean you up." She took his hand and led him to the bathroom, where she pulled out a plastic container filled with Band-Aids and ointments. Her Mother's Kit. She gestured for him to sit on the toilet seat as she ran a washcloth under warm water at the sink.

Sean winced as Emily softly dabbed at the crusted blood on his face. She ran the cloth under the water and a brown and red swirl disappeared down the drain. She cleaned the blood from his hair. More brown and red in the sink. They both stared absently at the blood. Before long Emily was crying. And so was he.

CHAPTER 32

After Emily returned to bed, Sean went to his home office and stared at the computer screen. He was too wired to sleep, so he scanned the fifty-seven e-mails he'd received from work. In one, a partner asked Sean to help pitch an appeal to a pharmaceutical company tomorrow. Sean typed out a reply that he would attend. What was he going to do otherwise—sit around the house and imagine conspiracies that didn't exist? Make some more terrible decisions? He eyed the bottle of Nikka whiskey that stood on his desk on top of the photo of Sean, Kenny, and Juan.

He'd been a fool. In not wanting to accept that Abby was gone, not wanting to allow the grief to take hold, he'd lost his way. Temporary insanity. They had the man who'd killed Abby, Malik Montgomery, and everything else was just a distraction. Noise. If Kenny was truly back from Japan, it was probably because he'd seen Sean in the newspapers and thought he could get something out of it. It had nothing to do with Abby. As for Chipotle Man, he was a small-time drug dealer. Neither Kenny nor Chipotle Man would be able to find the Supreme Court building on a map, much less get inside and hurt Abby.

His foolishness tonight had nearly gotten him seriously hurt. Worse, he'd put Ryan at risk. He flashed to his son standing on the football field, clasping the rebar, face sallow. Sean grabbed the bottle of whiskey by the neck and placed it in the wastebasket. He stared at the photo then crinkled it into a ball. A voice snapped him out of it.

"I thought I heard someone still up," Ryan said. He leaned on the doorframe.

"Hey, what's up? Can't sleep?" Sean asked.

"I forgot to show you what I found," Ryan said. He held up a folder. "It was in Abby's stuff." Ryan walked over to the desk and opened a manila folder from Abby's vetting research file. He placed his index finger on some writing in faint pencil on the inside of the folder: SCOTUSgirl@gmail.com.

"An e-mail account," Sean said. "Did you try to log on?"

Ryan gave his father a sideways look.

"Oh yeah," Sean said. They'd reset all the passwords and locked Ryan out of the computers after the Facebook fiasco. He gestured for Ryan to come around to his side of the desk as he started punching keys on the computer.

"What's 'SCOTUSgirl' mean?" Ryan asked.

"SCOTUS is an acronym for the Supreme Court of the United States."

"That sounds like an address Abby might use," Ryan said.

A Gmail page appeared. Sean said, "What do you think for a password?"

"There's some words written on the other side of the folder," Ryan said. He flipped over the file and directed Sean to two words scribbled on the outside, CHADWICK and WAVERLY. Sean typed them in one at a time and neither worked.

He typed LUCY, for the family's dog. Abby adored the Labrador, and took it hard when the old dog died shortly after Abby left for college. Ryan nodded.

A lockout again.

"How about 'Povie,'" Ryan said. "I know she used that as a password before." For her entire life, Abby loved words—big words, obscure words, complicated words. And she had a penchant for making up words. When she was little she called stuffed animals "la-la," her favorite hamburger place "gookie," her baby brother "gi-gi." It was part of their family lore. And her made-up word for the family dog was "Povie."

Sean typed in P-O-V-I-E and clicked the mouse. He was in.

"There's no e-mails," Ryan said. He stood behind his father, hunching over Sean's shoulder.

Sean grabbed the mouse and clicked on the Inbox. Ryan was right. No e-mails. He clicked on the Sent Mail folder. Nothing.

"Someone must've gone through here and deleted everything," Sean said.

"Or maybe she never used the account," Ryan said. "Why would she? She's had her own e-mail account through Georgetown."

Sean didn't answer and continued to move about the page. He opened the Drafts folder, and there was one e-mail written in draft form. He clicked on the little mail icon and lost his breath when he read the message:

Meet me at library Sunday, 10pm.

The night Abby was murdered.

CHAPTER 33

The next morning, Ryan and Jack ate their breakfast at the counter like always. Sean thought that the best way to keep his imagination from running wild was to return to work. The boys should return to school because things couldn't be normal for them until things were, well, normal. But the Gmail message snatched hold of his thoughts and wouldn't let go. And he fought it, but Japan and Chipotle Man were back in his head. He glanced out the window and happened to catch Frank Pacini taking out his dog, a large, perpetually nervous Afghan hound. Pacini and his wife had sent flowers and a lasagna to the house, but Sean otherwise hadn't heard from him since the night in the library.

"Ryan, can you wait with Jack until Dean's mom is here to take him to school? I need to talk to the neighbor for a minute. I'll give you a ride when I get back."

"Sure," Ryan said.

Sean kissed Jack on the top of the head and hurried out the door. He found Pacini standing on the patch of grass that bordered the street. He wore a gray suit and was waiting awkwardly for the dog to finish its business.

"Frank," Sean said as he walked over.

"Sean, how are you?" Pacini said. "Ouch, what happened to your eye?"

"Long story involving me, a bike, and a patch of gravel." Funny how when you repeat a lie a few times you start to believe it yourself.

"Are you holding up okay? Ginger said she's called Emily a few times, but hasn't been able to reach her."

Emily lay in a stupor of depression meds swallowed down with Grey Goose, so Sean saved the obligatory *we're doing the best as could be expected* and cut to it. "Do you think you have the right guy? Did Malik kill Abby?"

Pacini looked at his dog and his forehead wrinkled. "That's something you really should discuss with Patti."

Patti Fallon was the lead prosecutor assigned to the Malik Montgomery case. Because Abby was killed on federal property, the Justice Department asserted jurisdiction.

"I've had a couple of calls with her. She seems like one of those prosecutors who's a true believer."

Pacini shook his head. "She's good, Sean. One of the best prosecutors at Justice."

"I'm sure she is, but I just wanted your take—your honest take on the case."

"You should talk to Patti," Pacini said. When Sean gave him a hard glare, Pacini added, "We're both scheduled as witnesses to fend off Montgomery's motion to suppress, so we shouldn't be talking about the case. We could be forced to disclose anything we talk about on the witness stand."

Pacini was right. Plus he was career FBI—he wasn't going to budge.

"I spoke to Blake Hellstrom," Sean said.

At this Pacini's eyes widened.

Sean said, "Hellstrom swears his client is innocent."

Pacini scoffed. "That's his job. Tell me you're not having doubts about the prosecution because of something Hellstrom said?"

Sean shrugged.

"They've got the right man, Sean. Given all the heat they're taking on the race stuff, they wouldn't have moved on Malik Montgomery if they weren't confident he's guilty. And trust me," he looked Sean in the eyes now, "there's more evidence than you know about."

"Like?"

"Like, ask Patti."

Sean sighed. "I found an e-mail," he said finally. "An account I think Abby opened. In a draft e-mail file there was a note asking someone to meet at the Supreme Court library the night she was murdered. She was with Malik that night at dinner, so she had no reason to send it to him." For obvious reasons, this was all he would tell Pacini. What else would he say? *My son and I beat up a drug dealer who bothered Abby. And, by the way, my co-conspirator from a childhood murder left me a bottle of whiskey.* The e-mail, though, was something to grab onto. Something real.

But Pacini wouldn't bite. "You should tell Patti about it."

"You know that using draft e-mails is how people who don't want an electronic trail often communicate? The sender writes a draft and then the other person logs on to the e-mail account and reads the draft and deletes it so there's no transmission over the Internet." Sean heard the desperation in his own voice. "The Supreme Court discussed the technique in *U.S. v. Ahmed,* the case about the government's surveillance program. Malik said she was seeing someone, so maybe . . ."

Pacini just looked at him. It was a pitying look. Sean thought about how this all must sound. The grieving father clinging to complicated scenarios and supposedly unanswered questions in order to avoid letting go of his murdered daughter.

Pacini was probably right.

CHAPTER 34

"Sean, I appreciate the information, I do," Patti Fallon said, her voice coming from the SUV's overhead speakers. Sean was driving Ryan to school, and he merged onto the chaotic traffic circle on Connecticut Avenue. "But my priority right now is winning the suppression hearing. If Blake Hellstrom gets the evidence thrown out, nothing else will matter. It'll all be over."

Sean glanced at Ryan, who fiddled with his iPod Touch. His earbuds were in, and it was hard to tell if he was listening to the call.

"I hear you, Patti, but what Hellstrom says makes sense. Malik is too smart to have left the phone and video evidence behind. It's too convenient. And this e-mail I found suggests that Abby was meeting someone else that night."

There was a long silence. Then: "I promise you, Sean," Fallon's voice had the hint of an edge to it now, "we understand those issues. Hellstrom has made the same points to me and my team. I've got my best people working this case, career prosecutors. The best agents investigating. We're considering *all* the evidence, not just the defense's points."

"Is there evidence I don't know about? Something you haven't told me?"

"Let's talk about it when you come in for the meeting on the hearing. I'll give you an update on everything. Right now, I need my people to focus on the suppression hearing. They're working around the clock, and now we're going to have to determine if we need to give Hellstrom the e-mail you found."

"I'm not trying to make things difficult for you, Patti."

"Of course not. And I understand that this isn't easy for you. I just hope you understand that there are agents investigating the facts, that we know how to win cases."

"I understand all of that. And I'm not trying to be a meddler. But *you* need to understand that this is my daughter. And I'm not interested in winning. I'm only interested in the truth."

Sean disconnected the line. He didn't appreciate being handled, treated like he was a nuisance. At the same time, he probably shouldn't have been so curt with Fallon. She was a pro and just making her case.

"The prosecutor didn't seem too interested in the e-mail, huh, Dad?" Ryan said. He was listening after all.

"I think she's just tired. There's a big hearing coming up. And she probably has to tell Malik's defense lawyer about the draft e-mail, and I suspect she doesn't want to."

"Why's she have to tell the defense lawyer?"

"There's a rule about it. It's not like on TV where the prosecution can sandbag the defense. The government has to give the other side anything exculpatory—anything that might help the defendant."

Ryan gazed out the SUV's window. "Is that why you didn't tell her about what happened with the man from Chipotle? Because she'd have to tell the defense?"

"No. I'm still just trying to figure out what to do. I shouldn't have brought the gun . . ."

"What's Mom think?"

"I'm working on that, too—how to tell her."

Ryan furrowed his brow, but didn't inquire further. "You know what I don't get?"

"What's that?"

"I don't get why Abby's files had no notes. You ever see her school notebooks? She'd jam them full with notes. She tried to teach me note-taking, and I couldn't keep up—she would write down everything. And she typed like crazy on her computer. But those files you have, they don't have any notes. That can't be all her work."

His son was right. Since elementary school Abby had been a fervent note-taker. She'd once told Sean that to learn something she needed to write it down, in longhand. The notebook they'd found in the library that night, her notes from Tax class, were jammed full with single-spaced notes. Sean thought of his friend Jonathan Tweed's reluctance to give him Abby's files.

"Did you check her laptop?" Ryan asked.

"It's missing," Sean said. "Whoever broke into her apartment probably has it." Sean spared his son an alternative theory: Abby had the computer with her that night in the library and the killer took it.

"Even if she used the computer, she'd still have some handwritten notes," Ryan said.

Sean pulled behind the procession of yellow school buses slowly making their way up the hill to the front of the middle school.

"Hey, Ryan."

"Yeah?"

Sean gave his son a crooked smile. "Wanna miss school and help me with something today?"

CHAPTER 35

Sean gazed up at the massive portico of the Supreme Court as the morning sun reflected off the white marble steps. Even under his Ray-Bans, which he wore to conceal his bruised eye, it was blinding. He was one of the few lawyers at OSG who liked to enter the building through the 1,300-pound bronze doors—until the court closed the front entrance for security reasons. It made him feel patriotic, American, to trudge up the forty-four steps, through the iconic doors, and into the marble palace where the country solved its problems, not through rioting in the streets, but through the opinions of nine justices declaring the law of the land. Now, the building was just a crime scene. A place of horribles.

Sean followed Ryan's gaze to a homeless man who sat on the sidewalk jingling coins in a cup. Ryan. Predictable, wonderful Ryan. On cue, Ryan dug into the pocket of his jeans for whatever balled-up bills or stray coins he had. His son walked past the small crowd of protesters who seemed to have taken up permanent residence on the sidewalk in front of the building and dropped the money into the homeless man's cup. Ryan said something to the man, prompting a toothless grin.

When he returned, Ryan let out a loud sneeze. It was May in the District, which meant an oppressive pollen count. Sean had called Jonathan Tweed's office. Tweed's secretary, always friendly with Sean, told him that Tweed had just left to take a group of students on a field trip to the Supreme Court. The school was just down the street from the court, so Sean gambled that he might catch them on their way.

Sure enough, Sean saw a parade of law students led by Tweed marching down First Street. As Tweed reached the sidewalk in front of the court, he noticed Sean and waved. He said something to his students and pointed for them to assemble on the court's plaza.

"Another surprise visit," Tweed said. "Nice to see you. I'd heard through the grapevine that your face looked like you'd been in a bar fight, but you don't look so bad. Though reportedly the president was disappointed you wouldn't be suitable for a television appearance."

"Not that it matters," Sean said. "He pretty much told me that I'm not ready for prime time."

"I don't know, I heard you made an impression. And not just for your messed-up face. You might want to keep your phone nearby. I get the sense they're deciding on the nominee soon."

Sean drew his mobile from his pocket and displayed it to Tweed. "I turn this on only when I need to make a call. I deleted all of my messages last night and already the voice mail is full—all reporters."

"I'd keep it turned on," Tweed said. He then shifted his gaze to Ryan. "Shouldn't you be in school, mister?"

Ryan smiled.

Tweed looked back at his students, who were all whispers and stares. "Justice Carr is doing me a favor and agreed to meet with them. He's walking over to the Supreme Court Historical Society with us and then to lunch."

"He sure seems generous with his time, particularly at the end of the term." The Supreme Court issued all of its decisions from the term no later than the end of June, so May was usually a busy period at the high court.

"The man shouldn't play poker. I come out of our regular game with more free court visits for my students than I know what to do with. I'm surprised he has time to write his opinions. I suppose that's what law clerks are for. You two want to tag along?"

"I'm not sure I'm up for that today," Sean said.

"Aw, come on, it will be educational." Tweed turned to Ryan. "It might even justify you playing hooky."

Ryan grinned, but his attention was now fixed on a motorcade of Segway-riding tourists moving down the street.

"So, I assume you didn't track me down just to say hello?" Tweed said.

"I just had a couple questions. About Abby."

Tweed nodded.

"Did she mention any problems she was having? Come to you for help?" Sean thought of Chipotle Man's remark about the man who'd bought Abby's necklace. *He was some rich dude in a suit, like you.*

Tweed crumpled his brow. "Problems? No. Is there something I should know about?"

"She apparently was getting hassled by a drug dealer. It's a long story, but I wondered if she came to you for help?"

"If she'd come to me, you'd know about it. I wouldn't keep that from you. And I'm sure Abby knew that coming to me with something serious, for better or worse, was as good as telling you herself."

Sean scrutinized his friend's face, deciding to believe him. And Tweed was right, Abby would assume that anything she said to Tweed would get back to Sean.

Tweed pointed to his students, who were now huddled around Justice Carr, who'd come outside to meet the group. The broad-shouldered Carr, in slacks and button-down shirt, held court near one of the fountains, the students staring admiringly at him. Sean thought of what it must have been like two decades before, post-game at Notre Dame Stadium, Carr surrounded by coeds, signing autographs for fans.

"I've got to get up there before they embarrass me," Tweed said. "So, want to come along?"

Sean caught Ryan's eye. Sean nudged his head away from the building, silently asking if Ryan wanted to ditch the meeting with

Justice Carr. He knew the answer. For an eighth-grader, nothing could ruin a surprise day off from school more than a history lesson. Even one from a Supreme Court justice. Ryan's eyes widened and he gave the slightest nod. Abby had always been fascinated by the court and awestruck by the justices. But not Ryan. When Sean had arranged for Ryan's sixth-grade class to attend an argument and meet with a justice afterward, Ryan fell asleep at the long table in the Nan Rehnquist dining room as the justice was speaking to the kids.

"I think we're gonna skip out, but I appreciate the offer."

"You sure?"

"Yeah, you remember the last time Ryan met a justice," Sean said.

Ryan blushed.

"Of course, the famous cat nap." Tweed slapped Ryan on the back. "Don't worry, I've done much worse. Ask your father. On second thought, ask him when you're eighteen." Tweed flashed another smile.

"Yeah, I'll hold off until you're old enough to get into R-rated movies," Sean said. He was only half kidding. Tweed had left OSG under an ugly cloud after getting caught on a conference room table with one of the Bristow Fellows, the interns at the office.

Tweed continued, "Well, call me if you need anything and I'll—"

"Just one more thing," Sean said.

"Yeah?"

"The files you gave me. Abby's vetting files. They didn't have any of her notes. Do you have them?"

Tweed's eyes swept the area. "The students followed strict guidelines," he said quietly. "All research was done only at the school, all notes in paper, not electronic form, and they turned everything in to me. Nothing left our research area next to my office. And I locked up all research and notes. Only I have access to the files, and I gave you what I had."

"So her notes wouldn't have been on her laptop?"

"They shouldn't have been. I didn't want anyone leaving

something on an unsecure computer or accidentally printing something or e-mailing the wrong file. I'm old-school about vetting. Only paper files, code names for the nominees, everything locked in my safe. The only file is the one I gave you."

Sean said, "It's impossible Abby didn't take any notes, Jon."

"Unless my secretary screwed up when she made you a copy, or some superspy broke into my safe, that's all there is."

Sean arched a brow.

Tweed blew out a sigh. "I'll check when I get back to the office."

They said their good-byes, and Sean and Ryan were making their way toward the street when a voice called out to them.

Sean turned and saw Justice Carr heading their way. He had a confident gait for a man with a noticeable limp, and Sean was reminded of seeing Carr during the Senate confirmation process. The media had loved Carr. Beyond his good looks, he was one of those rare brain-and-brawn guys. There was endless footage of him making the courtesy rounds with the senators; scenes of the young, vibrant Carr walking the halls of the Hart Senate Building, his limp ever the reminder of his glory days with the Fighting Irish. The YouTube clip of the tackle that ended his football career had more than a million hits. The only criticism he'd faced during the entire confirmation process was a senator's quip that Carr's limp seemed to grow more prominent as the date of the confirmation hearing drew closer.

Sean knew what was next: more awkward condolences. They always seemed to bring Ryan down rather than help. "Why don't you wait here, buddy. I'll be just a minute."

Sean approached the justice on the plaza and they shook hands.

"I just wanted to say how sorry I am about your daughter."

"That's very kind, and I appreciate it."

"She was an amazing young woman."

Sean lapsed into silence. Next to the well-meaning but misguided comments ("she's in a better place," "at least you have other children," "time heals all wounds," and other such nonsense), what bothered him the most was the deification of Abby, particularly from people who didn't have the foggiest idea who she really was.

On the very day they'd discovered Abby's body, Sean had met Justice Carr for the first time at the Georgetown event. Sean had mentioned that Abby had met Carr, but the justice had no recollection of her. Yet now, Carr thought she was "amazing." Why do people feel the need to say these things?

"I trust you'll let me know if there's anything I can do?" Carr continued.

Sean just nodded and walked away.

CHAPTER 36

Abby's apartment was only a few blocks from the bustle of the Capitol, Senate buildings, and Supreme Court, but on a weekday morning it was as tranquil as the burbs. The denizens of the Hill rose early and left behind only the sound of the old trees rattling in the morning breeze. Sean and Ryan plodded down the stairwell to Abby's basement apartment.

The crime scene tape was gone from the door. Sean pushed it open and a pile of mail fanned across the hardwood. Neither he nor Emily had notified Abby's credit card companies, utilities, Internet, or phone providers of her death. Her lease was paid up until summer, so there was no rush to empty the apartment. Agents had already searched the place, yet here he was. The desperation was not lost on him.

"Okay, I'll check out her room and you search in here," he said to Ryan. "If you find any of her notebooks, please come get me before you touch anything."

Ryan nodded and Sean walked the narrow hall to Abby's room. Inside, there were stuffed animals from when she was a girl and photos of her family taped on a mirror above the dresser. There was one shot of Ryan playing his guitar and another of Jack making one of his famous funny faces. One of Emily bundled up in a hat and scarf, cheeks rosy, on the grounds of the Homestead resort, and another of Sean on Nauset Beach. A chill traveled through him at the sight of their last sunrise escape.

Sean shook it off. He would not let emotions get the better of him. He was there to find Abby's notes. It was a loose thread that needed to be fixed, and he wanted to feel like he was doing something. He searched her small desk, the dresser, and closet. He looked in the wicker baskets under the bed, inside the laundry basket, and even scrunched the stuffed animals to see if there was anything hidden inside. He found nothing.

Before leaving the room, he eyed a political poster pinned to her wall, VOTE "NO" ON PROP 9. Despite growing up in D.C., seeing the foibles of elected officials—and having Sean as her father—Abby had never turned cynical about politics or politicians. He was reminded of the last time she'd called him on his own cynicism.

"You always say people deserve a second chance, so why not him?"

Sean rolled his eyes. A politician caught having an affair with an intern did not deserve a second chance.

"What if his wife was a horrible person?" Abby argued. "What if he'd found his soul mate?"

"You believe in soul mates?"

Abby looked at Sean and then over to Emily, who was on the couch reading a book. "Of course I do." She turned back to her argument: "You just wouldn't give him a second chance because he's a politician. Why do you hate them so much?"

"I don't hate them that much."

"No? Name anyone you hate more than politicians."

Sean thought about this one. "Child molesters," he said. Then, with a tiny smile, "And radio disc jockeys."

Ryan was at the bookshelf, removing one book at a time, fanning the pages and peering in the empty space on the shelf. Sean helped him finish the search. They found nothing. Defeated, Ryan sank into the small sofa. Sean sat at the round bistro table just off the galley kitchen. He began absently flipping through the mail he'd stacked on the table.

"I'm hungry, Dad. Are you?"

Sean continued examining the junk mail and envelopes. "I'm a little hungry. Something sound good to you?"

"Burritos," Ryan said.

Sean thought about it. "I'm not sure there's any Mexican places near here."

"I know a place . . ."

Ryan flashed a grin, like *Before*. It took a second, but Sean caught on. "You won't catch me in another Chipotle the rest of my life."

Sean liked the feel of the smile on his face as he continued to scan Abby's mail. He came upon the telephone bill; the landline Abby opposed as unnecessary and archaic, but that Sean insisted upon. He opened the envelope and read the first page. Nothing caught his eye. Some calls to her grandparents, some to New York, and a smattering of out-of-state numbers he didn't recognize. But on the second page, an unusual entry: COLLECT CALL FROM SUSSEX II CORRECTIONAL INSTITUTION, WAVERLY, VA. There were two similar entries on the third and fourth pages of the bill. Who would Abby know at a prison? He didn't think she was doing any prison clinic work with her law school.

"Hey, do you know if Abby knew anyone in prison?" Sean asked.

"Prison? I don't think so. Why?" Ryan walked over to the table and took a seat.

"Abby was accepting collect calls from someone at this prison," Sean said, handing one of the telephone-bill pages to his son.

Ryan looked it over. "She never said anything to me. Look the place up on the Internet."

Sean pulled out his mobile. "My phone's nearly dead. We'll have to wait."

"Maybe not," Ryan said. He placed his iPod Touch on the table.

"I thought that was just for music?"

"It doesn't have a phone, but you can get Internet if there's a Wi-Fi signal."

Sean thought about this. "So that's how you sent the Facebook . . ." Sean stopped. "Is that why I saw you standing in the neighbor's yard that night? You were stealing a Wi-Fi signal because we'd locked you out of the computer." Sean couldn't help but break a smile.

Ryan's face flushed.

"Well, get to it, do the search," Sean said.

Ryan tapped on the device and frowned. "Wi-Fi's not working down here, either."

"We haven't shut off the service, but maybe the cops unhooked it," Sean said. "How about we go somewhere for lunch that has Wi-Fi. I actually think I know somewhere you'd like."

"Is it—"

"No," Sean interrupted. "It's not Chipotle. And I don't care if Chipotle has Wi-Fi." He smiled again.

"Dad," Ryan said, staring at the telephone bill.

"Yeah?"

"Look at the name of the town." Ryan put a finger on the center of the bill.

Sean read the words above his son's finger. WAVERLY, VIRGINIA. It sounded familiar but he couldn't place it.

"Abby's notes on the folder," Ryan said. "She wrote 'Waverly.' Maybe she was going there. And maybe the other word Abby wrote on the folder, 'Chadwick,' is who she was going to visit."

CHAPTER 37

Sean and Ryan edged forward in the lunch line at Ben's Chili Bowl. The place was less than three miles from Abby's apartment, and they'd been coming to Ben's for chili dogs and half-smokes since Ryan was a little boy—before gentrification made the place fashionable.

After ordering, they waited for their food at a table in the back of the restaurant. They faced a large mural depicting famous African Americans in history, many of whom had spent muggy summer nights during the civil rights era filling the booths and tables at Ben's. Ryan gazed at the wall and said, "Remember when you used to quiz me on the names of everyone on the mural?"

Sean nodded as he fumbled with Ryan's iPod Touch. He turned into such an old man every time he tried to operate any type of touch screen. The images inevitably moved uncontrollably around the screen, or disappeared, or zoomed in or out too far.

"Need some help?" Ryan said with a smirk.

"Only if you're buying lunch," Sean replied. He caught the Wi-Fi signal and searched the Internet for the Virginia Department of Corrections. On the tiny screen he read that Sussex II was a Security Level Four facility. It housed inmates with life sentences, but who were not disruptive or predatory.

"You can search inmates by name," Ryan said, pointing to a miniature search icon.

Abby had written two words on her file folder, "Waverly" and "Chadwick." The prison was located in the town of Waverly, Virginia, so Sean tapped in "Chadwick." A grid-like list appeared. Sean handed the iPod Touch to Ryan to adjust the image so it fit the screen:

DOC Number	Offender Name	Gender	Race	Release Date	Location
2150867	Chadwick, Michael D.	Male	Black	08/14/2055	Green Rock Correctional Center
21356793	Chadwick, Tyrone G.	Male	Black	05/07/2032	Bland Correctional Center
21002384	Chadwick, Duane E.	Male	White	10/01/2043	Deerfield Correctional Center
21042463	Chadwick, Malcolm E.	Male	Black	06/22/2067	Haynesville Correctional Center
22147018	Chadwick, John K.	Male	White	12/27/9999	Sussex II State Prison

Five names. But the only inmate in the Sussex facility was John K. Chadwick. Ryan quickly pulled up several newspaper stories mentioning the man's name, which reported that John Keith Chadwick was serving a life sentence. He'd been convicted in the nineties of murdering a college classmate, his girlfriend. She'd been raped and suffered a fatal blow to the head. Like Abby.

CHAPTER 38

By late afternoon they were on I-95 South en route to Sussex prison. Traffic was heavy, and Sean trailed a large semi that was muscling its way to an exit. Sean had called the prison to try to speak with John Chadwick, but was told that prisoners could only make, not accept, calls. They could, however, receive personal visits. In what had been a number of impulsive moves by Sean of late, here they were. Driving to a prison out in the middle of nowhere.

"Turn. Right. On. Route. Six. Twenty-five," the navigation system directed. It had been more than three hours on the road, but Sean and Ryan had used the time to talk. About rock bands. About how Jack didn't fully understand that Abby was gone. About how Mom was doing. Sean realized it had been a long time since he and Ryan had really talked. Somehow Sean had become one of *those* parents. The "Washingtonians" he rolled his eyes at: competitive, achievement-obsessed, more interested in talking *at* Ryan about how to get into Harvard than hearing about his son's thoughts and dreams. He'd always considered himself an involved parent, and in superficial ways he was. He showed up at the parent-teacher conferences and soccer games and plays. He helped with homework. But one eye was always on the clock or his phone. He didn't have time for the little things. The board games Emily played with the kids on Sunday nights, Taco Tuesday, or her Thursday reading hour.

They rolled onto Musslewhite Drive in Waverly, Virginia, following the signs to the prison's visitor lot. The facility was a foreboding campus of tall fences and concrete structures on hundreds of acres in the vast open land of rural Virginia.

Ryan gazed up at the guard tower. "Do you think we'll be able to get in?" He seemed fascinated with the idea of going inside a prison.

"I was told that if we got here before five o'clock, we'd have a shot." Sean had called an associate at his law firm and asked her to set up a visit with Chadwick. To his surprise, the associate managed to arrange a same-day visit. The efficiency of the private sector. He picked up the phone and a twenty-five-year-old with an Ivy League degree made calls, faxed in the necessary forms, and he was in. It would have taken weeks to arrange such a visit when he was in the government.

"Do you think we'll see any scary prisoners?" Ryan asked. He had a gleam in his eyes.

"You're going to have to hang out in the waiting area, I'm afraid." Sean didn't know what he was walking into and didn't want to risk Ryan dealing with a convicted murderer. God knows what the guy might say or do when approached by strangers. Ryan frowned, but he didn't debate the point.

Sussex II, as it turned out, ran an efficient operation and Sean was through the checkpoints, scanners, and searches in less than ten minutes. A burly man in a tight-fitting corrections uniform escorted Sean to a visitor's room. In all his years at the Justice Department and as a lawyer, Sean had never been inside a prison. He expected to be separated from John Keith Chadwick by a sheet of glass with each of them talking into telephones, but Sean was ushered into a tidy conference room painted institutional beige. The man sitting at the table in the room likewise was not what Sean had expected. No prison muscles. No face tattoos. No scarred veteran of the penal system. Just a doughy man with blond hair and a baby face, despite being in his forties. He wore a blue short-sleeved collared shirt and plastic-framed glasses. Under the glasses, kind eyes.

The correctional officer gestured for Sean to sit down across from the prisoner and said he'd be right outside if Sean needed anything. The click of the door's lock was unsettling, and Sean was surprised to be left alone with the man. But he relaxed when he saw that the prisoner was cuffed and had chains dangling from his wrists that were attached to anchors on the table.

"You're Abby's father?" John Chadwick asked.

"That's right."

"I recognized you from the newspapers. I'm really sorry for your loss. She was a great girl." Chadwick had a hint of a Southern accent. Not country bumpkin, more Southern gentleman.

"Can I ask how you knew her?"

Chadwick wrinkled his brow. "My case. I thought that's why you're here. To take over my case." He shifted in his chair.

"I'm sorry, that's not why I'm here." He didn't say more. Most lawyers liked to talk, to hear their own voices. Sean had learned that you get more information if you wait and listen.

Chadwick sat back and considered him. After a long silence, he said, "Then why are you here?"

"You had several calls with my daughter and I was, well, surprised. She'd never told me about you."

Chadwick sighed, a drawn out audible exhale. "You don't know anything? She didn't mention me?"

Sean shrugged.

"Abby was going to try to reopen my conviction—get it thrown out. Get me out of here. Prove I'm innocent."

Sean narrowed his eyes.

Chadwick said, "Look, I know how that sounds, believe me. Everybody in here is innocent. But I really am. And the DNA is going to prove it."

"There's DNA evidence?"

Chadwick leaned forward and rubbed his chin with the back of a chained hand. "I was a senior in college and I had a bad drinking problem. My girlfriend, Natalie, was murdered."

Sean looked into Chadwick's eyes, but said nothing.

"The night she was murdered," Chadwick continued, "we'd

had a fight. She didn't like that I was going to a party. She'd been trying to get me to stop drinking. As usual, I didn't listen and went out. I woke up the next morning in my dorm room. I had no idea how I got there. And I had a bruised hand. The next thing I know, the police are knocking on my door. Natalie was found dead, beaten to death, and she'd been sexually assaulted. And I've been locked up ever since. But I didn't kill her, Mr. Serrat. I loved her."

"You didn't mention the part about being found guilty at trial after your parents hired an expensive defense lawyer," Sean challenged.

Chadwick locked eyes with Sean. "So you do know about my case," he said. "You're right, I was convicted. But that was before DNA testing was routine and as sophisticated as it is now. Natalie scratched whoever attacked her. She had skin under her fingernails. Six months ago I learned that they still have the evidence samples. The blood type was A positive, the same as mine. But DNA can prove it wasn't me. Abby was going to help."

Sean examined the man. If he was lying, it was Oscar worthy. But Sean found it hard to believe that Abby wouldn't have mentioned this. And she wasn't even licensed to practice law, so unless the representation was through a law school clinic, something was off here.

"Do you know how Abby found out about your case? Did you contact her?"

Chadwick lifted his gaze to the ceiling, thinking. "I'm not sure how she found out. I didn't contact her. She just showed up one day and asked to speak with me. I don't get many visitors. It was a chance to talk to a woman who wasn't my mother, so I said why not?" Chadwick cocked his chin at the door. "And then this delightful young woman came in. I felt terrible when I heard what happened, and not just because she was helping me. She seemed like a nice person, a good person."

Sean nodded. On that much the two men could agree. "What did you and Abby talk about when she visited? Maybe there's something I can do." It was a cruelly hollow offer, but he needed information.

"She just wanted to know anything and everything she could about my life back then. What happened the night Natalie was killed, what happened with my trial, who my friends were then, pretty much everything I could remember."

"How many times did she visit you?"

"Twice in person, but we mostly talked on the phone, though she stopped accepting my last few calls."

"Do you remember if she took notes when she interviewed you?"

"Oh yeah, she sat right where you are, scribbling away."

"Was there anything in particular she focused on? Something she kept coming back to about your background or your case?"

Chadwick moved his eyes to the ceiling again. "She seemed most interested in who could have actually killed Natalie. That's the problem my lawyer at trial had. I mean, if it wasn't me, then who? Abby was obviously focused on the DNA, but she said we needed to give them another reason to reopen the case."

"And do you have any ideas about who might have killed Natalie?"

Chadwick shook his head. "I don't. Trust me, I've had years to think about it. So me and Abby just went through everyone I knew. Everyone Natalie knew."

"Can you give me those names?" The officers had allowed Sean to bring in a white notepad and pencil, issued to him at the security check point. He would have to return the unused portion of the pad and the pencil before he could leave the prison.

Chadwick perked up. "Absolutely." He looked Sean in the eyes. "I've spent my entire adult life behind bars. I was guilty of being a spoiled kid, guilty of drinking way too much, and guilty of being, pardon my language, an asshole. But I didn't kill Natalie."

Sean didn't respond to the assertion of innocence—a proclamation he was sure had been declared an infinite number of times behind the walls of Sussex. He hunched over the table, ready to write. "Let's just go through the names."

Chadwick began listing all of his friends from college. His frat brothers, his classmates, Natalie's friends. Sean wrote down each name.

"Anyone else?"

Chadwick thought some more. His eyes flashed. "One more. I can't believe I forgot to mention him. We weren't super close or anything, but my roommate. Mason James. You may have heard of him. He's done really well for himself and even tried to help me out. He's a senator now."

CHAPTER 39

They drove with the windows open, the air humming through the SUV like a wind tunnel. Since he was a baby, the sound had always soothed Ryan. And the push of air helped keep Sean alert. It was nearly nine o'clock and they'd decided to plow through rather than stop for fast food on I-95. They'd spent the first part of the drive talking about Chadwick. It appeared that Abby had been deceiving the man as part of her effort to vet Senator James. Or maybe she really intended to help Chadwick with his quest to reopen his case. Sean had considered keeping the information to himself, but he and Ryan were in this together. And talking about it, hearing it out loud, helped Sean organize his thoughts.

Could Abby have stumbled across something that got her killed? Could he seriously think that Senator James was capable of murdering Natalie Carlisle? Or Abby? There were similarities. Both were young, beautiful women. Both suffered traumatic head injuries. The evidence was inconclusive on whether Abby had been raped, but tests showed that she'd had intercourse shortly before she was killed. But Chadwick didn't seem to suspect Senator James. To the contrary, when Sean pressed him, Chadwick had said, "Trust me, Mason James is the last person in the world who'd rape and kill Natalie." He didn't explain why.

Lurking in the back of Sean's mind: Was the pain of Abby's

murder making him search for something that just wasn't there? The books he'd read about coping with the loss of a child all said that grief does strange things to people. There was proof in Emily's crippling despair. And in his own hunt for Chipotle Man.

Sean gazed at Ryan, who also was lost in thought. His son's brown hair tousled in the wind. The boy seemed older. Ryan tinkered with his iPod and Linkin Park started wailing through the SUV's speakers.

"What are you thinking about?" Sean asked.

Ryan paused for a moment. Gaze still fixed out the window, he said, "Is it true what they say about grandpa?"

Sean turned to Ryan. It wasn't a question he'd expected. "Who are 'they'? Who said something about your grandfather?"

"On the news, they said that your dad—"

"I told you not to watch that crap, Ryan. I expressly said you're not to—" Sean caught himself. Old habits. "I'm sorry. What did they say about my father?"

"They said he was a hero. That he got killed trying to save some people during an attack at a hotel in Lebanon."

Sean nodded. "That's true."

"He was a soldier?"

"No, not when he died. He'd been a general in the Air Force. After he retired, he was on an anti-terrorism commission, which is why he was in Beirut."

"Why didn't you ever tell us?"

That was a fair question, one Sean hadn't really come to terms with himself. "They never gave me any details about his death, so there wasn't much to tell. But I'm honestly not sure why, Ryan. My father and I had a complicated relationship. When my mother died when I was ten, he kind of checked out of my life. By the time he'd left the country for his new job things were pretty bad between us." That was an understatement. Another victim of Japan had been their relationship. His father, a one-star general, had been the base's commanding officer. When he wasn't at work, he was at the O-Club, slowly building a reputation as a booze and pussy hound. Sean, in turn, had acted out, drinking and partying and fighting, often being brought home after curfew by the base police. But nothing really seemed to catch his dad's attention. They rarely fought, or even spoke, for that matter. What he remembered most from his teen years was the silence. Heavy silence. And the one time he had come to his father for help—over a killing, no less—his dad had let him down again. The General was a politician. In the military, but a politician nonetheless. So when Sean told him about the store-keeper, his dad chose to hide the problem. Bury it. Within the week, the General had made up some story about a sick relative and shipped Sean off to his aunt in Cleveland, then was stationed back stateside three months later himself. Sean always wondered if leaving the post early in Japan had ended his dad's chance for more stars on that uniform he loved so much.

By Sean's senior year in high school his dad had retired. He'd also managed to get sober. The day Sean was leaving for college his father tried to make amends. Tried to bring up the storekeeper and what had happened. Wanted to talk before he left the country for the new job. But it was too late. The last thing Sean had said to him was, "Go work out your twelve steps somewhere else. We're through."

Ryan continued, "They interviewed one of your old friends on the news. He said that when your dad died, you didn't take time off school. That you used it as motivation to succeed. He said that's why you may become a Supreme Court justice."

Sean shook his head at the armchair psychology. Why the hell was the media focusing on his father now? Then he remembered that during his White House meeting, the president had mentioned his dad. *Our plan is to put your name out there again along with some additional information about your personal story and see the reaction.*

"It wasn't my father's death that motivated me," Sean said absently.

"No? Then what was it?"

"Mom. You. Jack. Abby."

For years his oath had been his motivator. He'd channeled all of his guilt and shame into unbridled ambition. But when Emily came along the focus changed. He wanted to be a better person not for the vow of a distraught teenager, but for *her*. She believed in him, pushed him to be better. She became the family he'd always wanted. And by the time they'd had their third child, he'd long ago siloed away his past. Emily and the kids were all that mattered. It was why he couldn't bring himself to tell her about Japan. He liked the version of himself reflected in her eyes.

"Is Mom gonna be okay?"

"Yes. She's just having a rough time."

"Don't you think we should tell her about everything? And about what happened at the school last night?"

Sean kept his eyes on the road. "I'm not sure."

"Why? You think she can't handle it?"

"I didn't say that. I just think she's really struggling right now, and I don't want to pile on. You know what I mean?"

Ryan turned to his father. "You both always say that keeping things to yourself doesn't help anyone. That we need to trust you guys enough to tell you things."

"I know. But this is different. I've never seen Mom this way. I just don't know if she's ready."

"I think she's stronger than that, Dad."

Sean chewed on his lip. "You're a smart kid, Ryan. A really smart kid."

CHAPTER 40

Sean's street was dotted with lamp light as he rolled toward their colonial. The sidewalks were lined with recycling bins and brown sacks filled with plastics, bottles, and cans.

"Shit," Sean said as the SUV neared their home. Ryan, who'd dozed off, sat up and rubbed his eyes with balled fists. Another news van was parked in front of the house, this one blocking the drive-way. Sean pulled alongside the van and gestured for the driver to move aside. The unshaven guy in his thirties, eating a bag of chips, finally noticed him, gave a lazy nod, and started the van's engine. Before the vehicle moved, however, another man, this one in a blazer and holding a microphone, appeared next to the SUV's opened driver-side window.

"Mr. Serrat, I'm Eric Wall with WUSA 9 News."

Sean held up a hand and shook his head, but that didn't stop the reporter. "Do you care to comment on the upcoming evidentiary hearing? Do you think the FBI committed an illegal search? Should the evidence against Malik Montgomery be thrown out?"

Sean turned to Ryan. "Just look forward and don't acknowl-edge him." Sean waved for the van's driver to pick up the pace.

"The NAACP says Malik Montgomery is being railroaded," the reporter said. "Do you have any doubts about Mr. Montgomery's guilt?"

Sean glanced over the reporter's shoulder to the front of the house. He saw a form in the window. He looked the reporter in the eyes. It must have been a hard look because the guy stopped talking midsentence. Sean's window hissed up and the reporter nodded to the driver of the van, who finally rolled from curb, giving Sean access to the driveway. Sean pulled up the drive. He and Ryan climbed out of the SUV and started quickly toward the door when something troubling caught Sean's eye. In the front yard, near the steps. Ryan's bike.

CHAPTER 41

"I've been trying to reach you," Emily said. She stood in the shallow light of the kitchen. Her eyes were bloodshot, hair a mess. "You can't keep doing these disappearing acts. Why didn't Ryan go to school? Where were you? And why didn't you pick up your phone?"

Sean answered none of it, but turned instead to Ryan. "Why don't you go get cleaned up and I'll make you some dinner. I want to talk with Mom."

Ryan nodded and disappeared out of the kitchen.

"Em, I'll explain everything. But first, how did Ryan's bike get here?" They'd left the bike at the high school last night.

Emily stared at him. "That's what I've been trying to call you about. They found a dead body at the high school today. You were right over there last night. Maybe the same guys who mugged you . . ."

Sean's pulse started to thud. He tried to keep his composure, but he felt wobbly. His face was on fire. "Who?" he asked. "Who was killed?"

Emily had a concerned look on her face, and she reached for her iPhone on the counter. She tapped on the device and then held the screen up for Sean to see.

It was a blow to the gut. No, a brass-knuckled sucker punch that left Sean struggling for air.

Chipotle Man.

His real name was William Brice, "Billy," the story said. He was twenty-seven and had a past conviction for selling drugs. An unnamed source with the Montgomery County police said they believed his murder was drug related, but the investigation was ongoing.

His knees nearly buckling, Sean steadied himself on the counter.

"What? What is it?" Emily said.

Sean remained quiet. He forced in several more slow, deep breaths. "What's Ryan's bike have to do with this?"

"The police found the bike at the school. Ryan's name and number are engraved on the frame. They're looking for witnesses and wanted to know if he was at the school last night and maybe saw something."

His wife met his stare. She looked gaunt. Her cheeks sunken.

"What did you tell them?" Sean asked.

"You're scaring me, Sean. What's going on?"

"What did you tell them?" he asked, his tone more desperate.

"I said Ryan wasn't at the school last night. I said he was with you."

CHAPTER 42

Sean sat across from his wife at the dining room table. The photographs of Abby were still scattered across its dusty surface. He told her about Chipotle Man. About Ryan hitting the man to protect Sean. And he told her about the visit from Malik Montgomery's lawyer. About Abby's secret e-mail account and vetting research on Senator James. And about the visit to Sussex prison and the connection to the senator. It should have been a full confession, including telling her about his boyhood friend's possible reappearance. But he stopped himself. There was already too much to take in, he justified. He had tried many times over the years to tell her about Japan. There was the time in law school, when she'd caught him researching whether Japan had a statute of limitations for murder. When she asked about the scar on his hand. Or about why he'd had such a bad relationship with his father. He'd always had an excuse not to speak up. And here he was again. But he just couldn't risk causing her more pain. Risk seeing that look in her face—a look that said *I don't know who you are.*

Sean rubbed a hand over his face. "You told the officer I was mugged last night?"

"Yes, at the gym. It's near the school, so he really wants to speak with you."

"Did you mention Ryan? Or his bike?"

"I just said I thought Ryan rode over and brought you a key, but that I didn't know how his bike got to the school."

Sean's mind played things out. "What if the cop who came today tracks down the kids who saw me last night at the school? Or what if they find out about my fight with Billy Brice? And what if they talk to Ryan's school or the principal or someone connects Brice to Ryan's Facebook messages about the man in red?" They were rhetorical, clipped questions. The sound of desperation.

Emily reached for his hands. "You need to stop," she said. Her tone was resolved. She took in a deep breath as if to steel herself.

"We need to do three things," she said after a long silence. There was no doubt here. He didn't know if the lack of hesitation was to convince Sean or herself. But there was something reassuring about the decisiveness. He saw a glimmer of Emily from *Before*.

"First," she said, "you're going to call Cecilia tomorrow morning and get some advice. You tell her that you fought with Billy Brice. You don't mention Ryan. Not even to Cecilia. From this moment forward, Ryan was home."

"But you told the cop—"

"I was mistaken. Ryan was here, in his room, and I'd thought he was with you. I'm obviously not thinking straight . . ." She gestured to her disheveled hair and threadbare robe.

"Second," Emily continued, "we need to talk with Ryan." At this she revealed a tiny break in the façade. She seemed to be fighting back a sob. "We need to prepare him for the police approaching him with questions. But I don't think we should tell him this guy Brice is dead."

"But what if he finds out at school? What if—"

"He can't take this right now, Sean." More firm: "We can't tell him."

Sean agreed with her that a death on a teenager's conscience was too much to bear. He knew that more than anyone. And something about Emily wanting so desperately to keep the secret to protect Ryan reaffirmed his own decision to keep Japan from her. But he wasn't sure how they could prevent Ryan from finding out.

"What if he sees the news or hears about it? It will be better coming from us," Sean said.

"He doesn't read the newspaper," Emily said. "And there are murders all the time in D.C. I don't think the kids notice anything outside their own little worlds."

"But this one was here, in Bethesda. And it happened at a school." Sean thought about Chipotle Man's face, how it went blank and he collapsed when Ryan hit him. But when Sean had gone back for the gun, he was breathing. He was alive. Sean had a sinking feeling that the man might still be alive if Sean had called for help.

It was then he realized a way for it to work. Sean had gone back to get the gun while Ryan waited near the woods. He looked at Emily who was massaging her temples. "For tonight I'm okay if we don't tell him," Sean said. "But this isn't the end of the discussion, Em. For now, if he finds out on his own, we say that when I went back to get the gun, Brice attacked me again and I hit him. I delivered the fatal blow."

Emily held his gaze for a moment, then nodded. She called for their son, who thundered down the stairs. She told him to listen carefully. She told him about the officer returning the bike. And she told him that it would get his father in trouble if anyone found out about the fight with Chipotle Man. If anyone asked to talk to Ryan about what happened that night, he wasn't there and didn't know anything about any of it. If they pressed him, he was not to say a single word and direct them to his parents.

"If you weren't at the school, there's no reason the police will need to speak with you," Emily said. "And there's no reason for you to say anything. But if you tell anyone—I mean, *anyone* about what happened—it could have serious consequences for Dad."

"But why can't we just tell the truth, that I was just helping Dad? The guy's okay and he hit Dad first."

Emily's lips tightened and she and Sean shared a glance, silently acknowledging that the course they had chosen was contrary to everything they had ever taught their children about morality, about life. Emily put a hand on Ryan's shoulders and fixed her eyes on his.

"Dad and I just need some time to think about this. Dad made a mistake bringing the gun, and the police won't understand. So for now, we need to keep this to ourselves. Can we count on you?"

"Yes," Ryan said, unenthusiastically.

"I mean it, can we *trust* you?"

"Yes," he said, this time with conviction. "What about my bike? What do we say?"

"It was stolen. We don't know when. Keep it simple."

Ryan managed a nod.

"Tomorrow you're going to school like any other day. We need to show the world we're getting back to our routine. That means no more secret outings with your father." Her gaze flicked to Sean, then back to Ryan. "And not one mention of Chipotle Man. As far as you're concerned, he never existed. He's an urban legend you'd heard about in the halls at school, the man in red."

Sean: "And what do you do if the police approach you and want to talk?"

"I say I want to call my parents who are lawyers."

"Exactly. I'm sorry to put this burden on you, son."

Ryan nodded, seeming no worse for the wear. Sean imagined that for Ryan, there was something exciting about it all, something satisfying about him having to clean up after Sean for a change.

Emily kissed her son on the forehead. She offered to make him dinner, but he said he wasn't hungry and he went up to bed.

Sean gave his wife an admiring once-over. He could swear that her face had more color and her eyes more light than just an hour ago. After another long silence, he said, "You said there were three things we need to do." Her eyes met his. "What's the third thing?"

Emily walked to the living room and peered out the window. "As soon as the reporters are gone, we're going to go find the metal pole that Ryan used on Billy Brice."

CHAPTER 43

Sean and Emily pushed through the branches and brush in the woods that bordered Bethesda–Chevy Chase High School. The moon broke through gaps in the canopy of trees like white laser beams. Emily guided their way with the flashlight app on her iPhone, clicking it off periodically when she heard a car on the street nearby or rustling in the trees. The ground was soft, a mix of twigs and leaves. It was hardly a perfect grid search, but they tried to methodically work their way across the area.

They stepped carefully, their eyes sweeping across the terrain searching for the rod of steel that Ryan used to protect his father.

"What if we don't—"

"*Shhh.*" Emily held a finger to her lips. "Did you hear that?" she whispered. She wore her black workout pants and jacket. Sean likewise wore all black—Adidas running pants and matching shirt. If anyone came upon them, they were two joggers looking for their lost dog.

Sean stood motionless, listening. At three in the morning all was still but for the whoosh of the wind. But then, the crack of a branch.

"A deer?" he whispered.

"There," Emily said, pointing. Sean caught a shadow darting between the trees. Maybe a neighbor investigating? A cop? Or, God forbid, had a reporter followed them? But they had been careful to make a show of turning out all the lights at bedtime and had waited for the news van to leave before slipping out of the house and jogging to the school.

Another snap. Someone was running toward them. Sean gripped Emily's hand and they ran. Drooping branches lashed their faces and arms as they darted through the brush. They could hear someone trampling behind, pushing through, stems snapping. They ran until they reached the street. They raced through a small business complex and crouched behind a white work van parked in the lot. They were breathing raggedly, but both managed to keep quiet. Emily cupped a hand over her mouth as a dark mass emerged. They watched as the figure, face shrouded by shadows from a distant streetlight, walked deliberatively toward them. A man. He had something in his right hand. He held it close, almost touching his thigh as he walked.

The ring of a phone slashed through the quiet. Em made the slightest gasp and clutched Sean's arm. The man put his phone to his ear and said something Sean couldn't hear. The guy turned back toward the school and disappeared into the darkness.

CHAPTER 44

On January 20, 2009, Chief Justice John G. Roberts, Jr. swore in Barack Obama as the forty-fourth president of the United States. As Obama placed his hand on the Lincoln Bible and echoed the oath of office recited by the chief, something unusual happened: the chief justice accidently left out a word, a mistake repeated by Obama. To avoid the crazies saying that Obama wasn't *really* the president, everyone decided that the chief should administer the oath a second time. So, the next day, the chief ventured over to the White House and they did it all again. A do-over.

Why Sean awoke that morning thinking of the Roberts-Obama oath debacle was beyond him, but he assumed it was because events had inspired a do-over of his own oath—to protect his son. As a teen, he had sworn to uphold the law, to be a better person, to *not* be like his own father. But here he was covering up a homicide all in the name of protecting Ryan. He was momentarily back in his living room thirty years ago, his father pacing nervously, chain smoking. *You will tell no one. Ever. This is about more than just you, Sean.* History was repeating itself.

He and Emily had stayed awake talking until sunrise. It was as much a strategy session as a debate over how they should proceed. After the scare of being chased, they'd discussed sending the boys to stay with her parents, but Emily insisted that they would not flee their home. To protect Ryan they needed to show the world that things were returning to schedule. If someone was determined to hurt the kids, she said, there was nothing they could do about it anyway. Sean was troubled by the fatalism, Emily's sense that the safety of their children was outside of their control, but he decided not to fight it. School was probably the safest place for the boys anyway. And nothing suggested they were in any danger. For all they knew, the guy who chased them last night was a police officer patrolling the area or an overzealous member of the neighborhood watch, spooked by a recent murder in their community.

Most of their deliberations that night focused on whether Sean should turn himself in and plead self-defense in the murder of Billy Brice. He said he should do it; she'd have none of it. She wouldn't put the boys through worrying about whether their father would be taken away from them too. This was about more than just Sean, she said. In the twilight before he'd fallen asleep, he'd realized that right and wrong were not so clear anymore. Equally unclear, his indictment of his father for keeping quiet about the storekeeper.

He reached across the bed for Emily, but she was gone, her pillow bunched, her side of the bed no longer warm. He went downstairs—his joints cracking, muscles still aching from his encounters with Brice and his goons—and found Emily standing at their opened front door waiting for Jack to finish tying his shoes. Jack already had abandoned any proper bow and was stuffing the white laces into the sides of his Chuck Taylors.

"Daddy!" Jack called out when he noticed Sean watching them.

"Morning, big guy. Mommy taking you to the bus stop?"

Emily nodded. Routine, she had said last night. They had to return to their routine.

"There's coffee made," she said. "I've got to face all the sad looks sooner or later, so I thought I'd take bus duty today. I also called Jack's teacher. She said I could volunteer in his class this afternoon to see how he's adjusting to being back."

Sean nodded. Em was starting to resemble his wife again.

"You got Ryan out the door?" asked Sean.

"Bright-eyed as always," she said.

"And he seemed okay?"

Emily nodded. "We need to trust him."

"I do," Sean said, "I really do."

"Have a great day, Daddy," Jack said as they left the house.

By the time Sean had showered, shaved, and dressed, Emily was waiting for him in the kitchen. She led him to the dining room. The table was no longer covered with family photos. Instead, there were four small stacks of Internet printouts.

"I couldn't sleep so I did some research on Senator James. I think I found something."

Sean gave her a puzzled look.

Em gestured to the stacks of research. "James grew up in Leavenworth, Kansas. His dad was a guard at the federal prison there." Emily handed him a sheaf of papers. On top was a story from the *Kansas City Star*. The headline read LHS STUDENT MISSING.

"While he was there a girl from the school went missing. Her name was Melissa Foster. They never found her."

"Lots of girls go missing every year," Sean said.

"But he knew her, Sean." Emily shuffled through the stack and fished out another printout, this one a page from a high school yearbook. It was a dedication page to the missing girl with a montage of photographs of Melissa Foster. In one, she sat on the hood of a car next to a handsome teenager. A young Mason James.

"When he was in high school his family moved to Lee County, Virginia. Apparently his dad took a position at a prison there. That year another girl went missing."

"Did anyone ever suggest he was involved in the crimes? He's in public office. Someone surely would have—"

"No," Emily said. "But they probably weren't doing searches of his name with terms like *missing girl* or *murdered*. And think about it, Sean. A missing girl in Kansas, a missing girl in Virginia, then John Chadwick's girlfriend in college. What if when Abby contacted Chadwick at the prison, James or his people found out and were afraid she'd uncover something? James's father worked in corrections, so maybe they had someone keeping an eye on Chadwick's visitors. What if Abby connected the murders to James?"

Sean looked at his wife. She was all caffeine and jitters. She picked up another sheet of paper. "I also found newspaper stories about his career. When he was a prosecutor, James's claim to fame was that he'd never lost a case. There was one trial, though, where everyone thought he was going to lose, but before it went to verdict, the lawyer for the defendant was arrested for drug possession, resulting in a mistrial. Also, James won his first run for attorney general after his opponent was caught having an affair with a staffer. In his Senate run, his opponent withdrew for undisclosed personal reasons. His adversaries always seem to have convenient little mishaps."

Sean processed it all. Newspaper stories about missing girls and speculation about James sabotaging his adversaries wouldn't pass the laugh test with a prosecutor or the press. But it was no more speculative than the conspiracy theories racing through Sean's mind all week. Had they both succumbed to grief-stricken insanity?

Em must have seen the skepticism in his face, and she retreated to the kitchen. Sean stayed at the table reading through Emily's research.

"You're going to want to see this," Emily called out to him.

Sean came into the kitchen where Emily was now standing in front of the sink washing the boys' breakfast dishes. Sean eyed the bumper sticker under the magnet on the refrigerator, which seemed to be mocking him: STAND UP FOR WHAT'S RIGHT, EVEN IF YOU'RE STANDING ALONE.

Emily pointed a sudsy dish brush at the small television on the counter. The *Today* show anchor, a black woman with high cheek bones, reported, "The president has scheduled a press conference today to announce his nominee for the U.S. Supreme Court to replace Chief Justice Malburg, a thirty-year veteran of the high court who announced her retirement last month. NBC has learned that the nominee will be a member of Congress. Senator Mason James. It will be the first time since Justice Hugo Black was appointed in the nineteen-thirties that a sitting senator would join the country's highest court."

"I guess I didn't make the cut," Sean said. "Do you think it was the eye?" Sean gestured to his eye, still swollen from the encounter with Billy Brice. Em turned back to the dishes, unamused.

More from the television: "Before joining the Senate, James gained prominence as a prosecutor and went on to become the attorney general of Virginia, where he was known for his aggressive enforcement of the state's laws, yet still managed to garner support from leaders in both political parties. This will be the president's second chance to fill a vacancy on the court. The Senate recently confirmed Thaddeus Carr as the latest justice to join the high court." The screen flipped to an image of Justice Carr on the National Mall, throwing a football to one of his law clerks. "Carr, a former federal judge and college football star, was confirmed quickly by the Senate. The administration is hoping for a similarly smooth confirmation this time around, though some are already criticizing the choice of Senator James . . ."

"What are we going to do?" Emily asked.

"What can we do? It's not like we have proof he's done anything wrong."

"We have Abby's investigation of him. We have John Chadwick."

"I don't think having a college roommate convicted of murder disqualifies one from serving on the high court. And even Chadwick doesn't think that James killed Natalie Carlisle. Quite the opposite."

"You've never been one to believe in coincidences."

"Life has challenged a lot of my beliefs," Sean replied, letting it hang there.

Emily turned back to the sink again. The clinks and clanks of the dishes grew louder.

"I worry that we're just trying to make sense of something that's never gonna make sense," Sean said.

Emily spun around, weariness still etched into her face. "So we just drop it? Pretend that this all doesn't have something to do with Abby?" Emily pursed her lips. "Would she want us to drop it?

Would she, Sean? There's something more to all this, I know it. And I think you know it too."

Sean faced his wife. A long moment of silence passed between them. Then he kissed her. Hard and with longing. And she kissed him back until they were on the floor.

If they were going to chase crazy conspiracies, they'd be doing it together.

CHAPTER 45

"So what the fuck was so secret that we couldn't do this over the phone?" Cecilia said as she and Sean walked the gravel path that bordered the National Mall. She wore a silk blouse and flowing slacks and large-framed sunglasses, never mind that the sun was buried behind thick black clouds overhead. "And what's with meeting on the Mall? Only two kinds of people meet on the Mall: agents in bad spy movies and annoying tourists."

Sean couldn't help but smile. Cecilia was the only person who still treated him the same since Abby's death, and he loved her for it. Sean's eyes roved the promenade. He saw no spies, but they were in fact surrounded by tourists. A Japanese couple taking photos of the Capitol and a heavyset couple studying a map as their three kids ran ahead.

"I've done something really stupid." He stared off into the distance at the Washington Monument. Organ music from the carousel outside the Smithsonian floated over on the wind.

Cecilia looked at him skeptically. "Oh, I can't wait to hear this. The sordid life of Sean Serrat. Did you get a speeding ticket? No wait, someone found out that you don't recycle and hate people who own Priuses."

"I killed someone," Sean said.

Cecilia guffawed. When Sean held her gaze, she removed her sunglasses, her stare boring into him.

"I'm telling you this as my lawyer right now, Cel, so the privilege applies."

"You're freaking me out, Sean. Quit screwing around."

Sean told her everything. Well, almost everything. He'd omitted Ryan from the details.

"This drug dealer, Billy Brice, he died from just a single whack on the head?" she asked.

"I didn't think I hit him that hard. It was just a small steel rod, like the ones used in construction. And when I left he was breathing. I thought he'd just got knocked out."

"I think the prosecutors will believe self-defense. Did they find the gun on him?" Cecilia asked.

"No, I took it with me. That's the problem—it was my gun."

"You own a gun? And you brought it with you? What were you thinking?"

"I *wasn't* thinking. But I thought he knew something about Abby and his friends had worked me over pretty good earlier that day." Sean gestured to his eye. "I just brought the gun to protect myself, but things got out of hand."

"Ya think?" Cecilia scoffed again. "Have you told anyone?"

"Just Emily."

Cecilia let out an exasperated sigh, and Sean could read her thoughts: *That's all Emily needed.*

"Did anyone see you near the school?"

"Two teenagers. They were buying pot from Brice, I think. It was dark, and I don't think they got a good look at me."

"Anyone else?"

"I can't be sure, but I had a feeling I was being followed."

"Followed?" She squinted at him, as if this was all just a bit much.

This was tricky. Only Ryan, not Sean, had seen the man following him, the man with a mole on his face. Emily had been firm that they keep Ryan out of this. "There was a guy on a motorcycle I saw a couple times, but I didn't get a good look at him. I would normally chalk it up to paranoia, but when Emily and I went back to search for the rebar someone chased us."

Cecilia frowned, but stayed quiet, lost in thought, as they veered off the path and onto Twelfth Street. The Old Post Office Pavilion clock tower ahead read eleven a.m. There was a low rumble of thunder in the sky. "I'm not a criminal lawyer, you know that," she said.

"I know, but I won't go to anyone else."

"I suppose it won't matter. If no one got a good look at you, hopefully that should be the end of it."

Sean grimaced. "Actually, the police came by the house and talked to Emily."

Cecilia snorted. "You might have started the discussion with that little gem. So someone did see you? What did the cops want?"

"The police found Ryan's bike at the school," Sean said. "His bike was stolen some time back. When the police processed the area around the campus, they found it. They came by to see if Ryan had been there and seen anything."

"How'd they know it was Ryan's bike?" Cecilia asked, her tone skeptical.

"His name's engraved on the frame."

"So, you're telling me that Ryan's bike just happened to be at the school. Happened to be there that night?"

Their eyes met.

"And you're going to tell the police you were at Bethesda Sport and Health that night working out at the gym?"

"I'm not sure. That's what Em told them. She also misspoke and said Ryan was with me."

Cecilia shook her head. She was getting annoyed with the Ryan-wasn't-there game. "When I go to the gym," she said finally, "they check me in at the front door with a scanner." Cecilia pulled keys from her handbag and showed him a key fob with a bar code on it. "Does your gym do that?"

Sean nodded.

"So won't there be a record of you not going inside?"

Sean looked at the ground.

"We're not going to say you were at the gym," Cecilia said.

"No? Where was I?" Raindrops started falling, but Cecilia didn't move.

"You were with me, at my house for a visit. Both you and Ryan were there."

Sean looked at his old friend and shook his head. "You can't, I can't ask you to—"

"When Helen died," Cecilia interrupted, "my parents didn't understand why I was catatonic with grief. They were in denial, thought she and I were just roommates. Helen's family didn't invite me to the funeral, and I had no say in her medical decisions." Cecilia swallowed. "I wouldn't have gotten through it if it wasn't for you and Emily. You were there for me. And you were at my house the night Billy Brice was killed. We ate pasta. End of story."

CHAPTER 46

Sean sat behind his desk at Harrington & Caine reading judicial opinions and briefs a partner in the tax group had sent him. *Routine,* Em had insisted. As if it wasn't hard enough to concentrate on work, he'd been asked to help on an appeal involving an excruciatingly boring corporate tax issue. The office phone rang and he examined the caller ID: "202" and no other number. The same camouflage as when he worked at the Justice Department. He hesitated, then picked up.

"Mr. Serrat?" the voice said. He recognized the Indian accent. Abani Gupta, the lead member of the team vetting Supreme Court justices for the White House.

"Hello, Abani, how are you?" Sean put both elbows on his desk and leaned forward, phone pressed to his right ear.

"I'm well, thank you," Gupta said, brushing aside the pleasantries. "Look, I know you probably heard the news already that the president decided to nominate Mason James, but he asked me to reach out to you personally."

"Thanks for the courtesy, but it was unnecessary."

"Off the record, this was incredibly close. But Senator James had been in the works for months, and the president decided that the country needed to know the nominee sooner rather than later."

Sean hated that tired D.C. phrase, *sooner rather than later.* "I understand," he said. "You really don't need to explain."

"No, but the president wanted me to convey it. And he wanted me to tell you, and I'm quoting him here, 'I meant what I said about next time.'"

Sean made no reply.

"You should know," Gupta added, "I haven't been asked to convey that or any similar message to anyone else the president met with about the high court nomination."

Sean's other line rang. "Again, I appreciate the call. Best of luck with—"

"There's one more thing, Mr. Serrat," Gupta said quickly, sensing he was about to hang up.

"Yes?"

"This is a little awkward, but the president wanted me to ask you for a favor."

What could the president want from him? He couldn't possibly expect Sean to publicly endorse Senator James? That wouldn't happen.

"What is it?"

"We hoped you could assist in the preparation of Senator James for his confirmation hearing. You're the leading expert on modern constitutional law, and we'd hoped you could give the senator a primer on con law. Help prep him for the hearing."

"Forgive me, but I find it hard to believe that the president is dealing with the staffing of the murder boards."

There was a sharp silence. Most lawyers, whatever their politics, would not reject an invitation from the White House to participate in the murder boards, the practice sessions held to get a nominee ready for the Judiciary Committee hearing. It was an honor and sought-after credential in Washington. Sean assumed the invitation served two purposes here: it would help prepare Senator James and further position Sean as a future nominee.

Gupta finally replied, "Actually, this came directly from the president. He personally approved every member of the murder . . . of the prep team. He wanted the leading experts in every area and, I'm not trying to flatter, no one came close to your expertise on con law."

Sean's stomach twisted at the idea of assisting Senator James. Then again, a member of the team would be privy to inside information and possibly the FBI's file on the senator. As Sean kicked it around, a plump figure appeared in his doorway. Mable, his assistant. She looked flustered, conflicted about intruding.

He cupped the receiver. "Everything okay?"

"I'm so sorry," she whispered, "but your son's school called on the other line. They need you to come pick up Ryan."

He took that in, held up a finger, then said into the phone, "I've got to go, Abani, but okay, I'll do it."

Gupta said, "That's great news. I'll be e-mailing you some encrypted files and—" Sean hung up.

"Is the school still on the other line?"

"No, I'm sorry. They said Ryan is okay, but there was a fight. They need you to come pick him up. They tried calling your wife, but couldn't reach her."

Emily was volunteering in Jack's class today, so she must have turned off her phone. Sean sank back into his chair and studied Mable.

"All this drama isn't quite what you signed up for when I started at the firm, is it?"

"It's really my pleasure, Sean."

"Between the press calls and my family situation, I really admire how you've handled things. I also appreciate you unpacking and arranging my office so nicely." Sean looked about the room. Gone were the boxes and bare walls. The framed artist rendition of him arguing in the Supreme Court was hung alongside his many awards. Books were neatly stacked on the wooden shelves. And prominently displayed on a work table in the back of the office, the vase where he kept his fifty-two feather quill pens—one for each of his arguments at the high court—souvenirs that the court gives advocates arguing a case.

"It's been no problem, though the reporters are something else. One even called me at home."

"I'm really sorry about that."

"My husband grumbled, but then he saw you on the news talking about your daughter. We have a girl in college. And my Henry, who's not a very emotional guy, he says to me, 'Mable, you help that man with whatever he needs.'"

"Thank Henry for me. My wife and I would love to take you both out to dinner once things return to—" he stopped himself. "Once things slow down." Sean got up and walked to the coat hook near his door and removed his suit jacket from a hanger and slipped it on.

As he walked out of the office Mable said, "One more thing, Sean."

"Yes?"

"Did the detective catch up with you this morning?"

Sean gave her a confused look.

"You must have missed my e-mail? A detective stopped by this morning when you were out."

"No, did he say what it was about?"

"He was with the Montgomery County police and needed to talk with you about something. He said he was with the homicide section."

CHAPTER 47

Sean approached the entrance to Ryan's middle school. He thought about the last call from the school over Ryan's Facebook messages. He marveled at how his perspective had changed. His parental problems from *Before* now seemed almost silly.

He entered the building and headed to the main office. The woman at the front desk gave Sean a sympathetic gaze. She said that the principal would be right with him. And he was.

"This is starting to become an unpleasant routine," Sean said, shaking the principal's hand.

The principal blew out a long sigh. "Ryan and two boys had a scuffle," he said. "Ryan was clearly just defending himself, but county policy requires us to suspend everyone involved—it doesn't matter who started the fight."

"I understand," Sean said. "Do you know what—"

"We're making an exception this time and not suspending any of the boys," the principal interrupted. "I had a chance to speak to some of the kids who saw what happened. It seems that the two other boys involved said unkind things about your daughter. Much of it racist. Ryan apparently tried to walk away, but they blocked his path and there was some shoving. Some of the things these boys said, well, between you and me, they had it coming . . ."

Sean felt the hairs on the back of his neck rise. What kind of kids would taunt a boy about his murdered sister?

"I also spoke with the parents of the other boys. All agree, if it is acceptable to you, that we keep this in-house. The parents of the other boys were reluctant at first, since Ryan apparently got the better of both kids. But once they heard the circumstances, the parents were appalled. They assured me that there would be consequences at home for their sons. Given county policy, it's the best I thought I could do." He looked to Sean for concurrence.

"Is Ryan okay?"

"His eye doesn't look much better than yours," the principal said. "But he's okay, and the other kids fared worse. Ryan took them both down."

"I think you handled this just right, Jeff. As you know, this has been a hard time for my family, so your support means a lot to us. I can't condone what he did, but . . ."

"Like I said," the principal replied, "I would have loved to suspend only the other boys. Go see your son, Mr. Serrat." The principal gestured toward a small conference room.

Sean opened the door and Ryan stood quickly. His eye was swollen. "I'm sorry, Dad," his voice broke. "I tried to walk away. But they called Abby a whore and said that she wouldn't have gotten killed if she didn't have Jungle Fever. They called her 'Abby Kardashian' and they—"

"*Shhh,*" Sean said. He put a hand on Ryan's chin and examined his eye.

"You're okay?"

A nod.

"Then that's all that matters."

CHAPTER 48

Emily and Jack greeted them at the door. Emily inspected Ryan's eye and retrieved some frozen peas. Jack was all questions. What happened to your eye? Did you get in a fight? Did you win? Does it hurt? How much? More than a bee sting? More than the flu shot? Are you in trouble? Whose eye is worse, yours or Dad's?

Ryan finally managed to escape to his room for a bit. Emily said they all needed to get out of the house, to do something normal. So they decided to tempt fate and go out to dinner. Not to any of their usual haunts in Bethesda where they might run into people they knew. They chose downtown, a place called Central Michel Richard.

Sean parked the SUV, and they walked on F Street past Honest Abe's Tourist Shop, tackily located on the same block as Ford's Theatre where John Wilkes Booth shot Lincoln. The rain was coming down again, and the brisk wind felt good on Sean's face. He took pleasure in the anonymity among the crowds of tourists with their wrinkled maps and rain ponchos, the Serrats hidden under their umbrellas.

As they fast-walked to the restaurant, Jack said, "Hey, Daddy, want to hear a joke?"

"I'd love to hear a joke."

"Knock knock."

"No, no, no, I've heard all your knock-knock jokes. No interrupting cows or boo-whos, give me something new," Sean said.

Jack thought about this as they walked. Then: "Okay, my friend told me a new one. Why'd the man get fired from the orange juice factory?"

Sean was surprised—it actually was a new joke. "Please tell me, why did the man get fired from the orange juice factory?"

"He couldn't concentrate," Jack said.

Sean barked a laugh.

Jack said, "I don't get it."

The bistro was all earth tones, light wood, and glass. Comfort food in style. The place was filled with the downtown after-work crowd—groups of three or four men and women with overly polite manners, client dinners, probably—and couples in their early thirties.

None of the Serrats, particularly Emily, was ready for a dinner out that meant a table for four, not five. But Emily was trying mightily for the boys. And for the briefest of moments, the scene resembled something from their former life. Jack—in a collared shirt, ironed!—slathered too much butter on a chunk of fresh bread. Ryan let the napkin sit rolled up on the table and not on his lap. And Emily studied the menu. She had the Loup de Mer with mushrooms. Just water, thanks, no wine. Sean and the boys ordered the homemade fried chicken, an unhealthy main course Emily normally would have shut down (Popeye's and KFC were forbidden in the Serrat home), but tonight she said nothing about the high-end version.

Sean devoured his food. He realized it was the first time in recent memory he'd eaten anything substantial. He looked over at Emily, who likewise was on a mission to consume her entire plate.

It was an hour of peace, of normalcy. But the asylum wouldn't last.

As the boys clinked their silverware, finishing their Chocolate Lava Cake dessert, and Sean sipped a cappuccino, he saw Emily's shoulders slump. A quiet gasp. What—

Then he saw them. A group of eight leaving Central's private room. The four men wore suits, shirts open at the collar. Their companions, women in their late twenties, cute and tipsy, stepping carefully in their tall heels. They tottered around the diners as they left the place. Sean found himself standing, staring at the last couple, a black man and his date. Sean and the man locked eyes, neither moving. The man's companions seemed to notice Sean. One of the men doubled back and touched his friend's arm, guiding him out.

A flashbulb lit up the room. A waiter quickly shooed away the man with the camera—a photog who'd caught the stare down between Sean Serrat and Malik Montgomery.

CHAPTER 49

"It's already on CNN's website," Emily said. She gripped the humming laptop with a single hand and carried it to Sean, who was seated at the kitchen counter scrolling through the hundreds of work e-mails on his phone. With the boys upstairs in bed, the house was quiet save the sound of rain whipping against the windows.

Sean glanced at the laptop's screen and read the headline: SHOWDOWN BETWEEN ACCUSED KILLER AND VICTIM'S FATHER. He had to hand it to the photog. The guy not only trailed them to the restaurant unnoticed, but the shot was perfect. Sean's tense jaw, cold stare; Malik's glare back. The photograph was deceiving because that was not how Sean remembered the scene. To him, Malik had just looked surprised, maybe embarrassed and regretful, but no menace in his face. And Sean, too, did not recall feeling the icy hatred depicted in the photo. He and Emily in fact shared doubts about Malik's guilt. They were just taken aback seeing him there, living his life. Sean could imagine Blake Hellstrom sitting his client down and giving an exasperated lecture. *You can't be seen out having some grand old time when there's a young girl who will never have another night out. And what were you thinking glowering at her father that way?* Malik would protest: *We were in a private room. I had no idea her family would be there. I didn't glower at him.* And, until trial, Malik would never again be seen in public living the life Abby would not have, much less having fun. Maybe the Serrats should follow suit.

"I told you not to read this stuff," Sean said.

"I don't know how you can just avoid all the news and ignore what they're saying about our family," Emily challenged. "Just bury your head in the sand."

Sean didn't take the bait. This fight had no winner. Emily was right, though. In some weird form of denial or avoidance, he'd shunned all news. He understood that Abby's murder had sparked (another) national discussion about race and justice. And to some extent, having reporters focused on her case could help uncover the truth. But he just couldn't stomach watching the media try to fill a twenty-four-hour news cycle by stretching out the twenty minutes of information they had. He turned back to his phone, but could feel Emily's eyes on him.

"Did the files on the senator arrive yet?" Emily asked.

"I'm still making my way through work e-mails. I'm starting to feel guilty. I get asked several times a day to help with a business pitch or to read someone's brief, and I just ignore them."

"Anyone who asks you to do anything right now is an ass," Emily said. "They can wait. And if they can't, to hell with them." With that, she marched out of the kitchen, leaving the laptop on the counter.

Sean squinted at his phone's screen. Most of the e-mails from work had nothing to do with Sean. He'd learned quickly that for a firm with more than one thousand lawyers in nine offices, Harrington & Caine had lax e-mail policies. Daily he received firmwide e-mails from colleagues seeking contacts with different companies, or information about particular judges, or selling opera tickets, or even lost-and-founds. If Sean ever lost a paperback in the firm's bathroom, he decided, he'd take the ten-buck loss rather than subject colleagues to the mental image of him reading while on the toilet.

He scrolled down until he saw two e-mails from Abani Gupta, which he presumed included the Senate questionnaire and other vetting materials on Senator James. The first e-mail included password-protected files, the second contained the password for the files. Half-assed security, all things considered. Gupta asked Sean to attend a meeting with Senator James the next morning. Short notice, she apologized, but they were on a tight schedule. It would be a quick meet-and-greet with the senator to set a schedule for Sean to help him prepare for his confirmation hearing. Sean replied that he would attend. The files were too large to open on his phone, so he spun the laptop around to log on to his e-mail account. The CNN website was still on the screen. He noticed that the site had loaded more photos of Sean and Malik's showdown at dinner, including new shots of the Serrats leaving the restaurant. If only he'd pulled open the umbrella sooner to shield them from the aggressive photographer. The editor at the website had carefully cropped out Ryan and Jack from the photos, as if that made up for the indecent spectacle of it all.

Sean's eye focused on one of the shots. They were just outside the restaurant, Sean looking away as Emily stalked forward, head up, her expression trancelike. A male figure was in the background. Sean leaned in closer to the screen. He blinked several times to make sure he was seeing clearly. But there he was, faded into the backdrop of the shot. Same scraggly hair, same flannel shirt.

His thoughts were interrupted by Emily's scream.

CHAPTER 50

Sean stumbled off the kitchen stool and raced to the family room. If it had been *Before,* he would have expected to find a big spider or the appearance of the killer in a horror movie (the only two things that ever seemed to scare Emily). But life was different now, and fear heaved in his chest. Emily was backing away from the window, the curtains still fluttering from where she'd whooshed them shut.

"Are you okay? What's going on? What is it?"

"Somebody's out there."

Sean instinctively pushed in front of Emily, shielding her from the window.

Ryan was now on the stairs. "Everything okay?"

Sean opened the curtains covering the French doors to a slit and looked outside onto their back patio. He could see the outline of someone, probably just a reporter skulking around, but there was a glare from the family room light. He gestured for Emily to turn it off. When the room went dark, his heart tripped at the sight of the man. His hair was soaked and strings of it fell across his face. He glared into the window, a menacing tilt of the head. The wet flannel shirt stuck to his thin frame.

It was him. A drenched rat emerging from the sewer. What did he want? Why was he outside the restaurant earlier that night? And why was he here at the house? Sean thought of his gun, but it was locked upstairs. And the gun had already caused enough trouble. Sean took in a deep breath and moved toward the door.

"You're not going out there?" Emily said. It was both a question and a command.

"I'll be okay, lock the door behind me. And have the phone ready to call 9-1-1 if needed."

Before Em could protest more, Sean was on his back patio, facing his boyhood friend, Kenny Baldwin. Kenny moved into the shadows and was looking around, nervous, the rain still coming down hard. Kenny's eyes met Sean's. They stared at one another, not saying anything until Sean finally began with a single word: *"Why?"*

"We can't talk here," Kenny said. "He may be watching."

"Who? What are you—"

"Let's take a ride and I'll tell you everything."

Sean gave a *you've got to be fucking kidding me* expression. "I'm not going anywhere with you." He looked back at the house. Two dark masses were in the window.

"You will if you wanna know what happened to your daughter."

CHAPTER 51

"You're doing what? No, Sean. Who is this man?" Emily's face was wrinkled with worry and disbelief.

Ryan paced the family room, a caged animal. Mercifully Jack, who could sleep with a jackhammer outside his window, was still in bed.

"He has information about Abby." Sean made long eye contact with Emily, realizing that Ryan was watching them. "I know him. I'll be fine."

Ryan said, "Is this about what happened with the man from Chipotle? Is this one of his friends? I don't think you should go, Dad." Ryan peered out the window. Rain drops bounced off the flagstone. Kenny sat inside the darkened SUV in the driveway. Sean knew he was there by the flash of a lighter through the tinted glass.

"You need to trust me on this." He looked at Emily. There was a long silence. But he could see retreat in her face.

"Mom, seriously?" Ryan said.

Emily stepped away from the door. "We need to trust your father."

He felt a warmth come over him at the words.

Sean went out into the thrashing rain and climbed into the

SUV. He was met with the smell of smoke and something sickly sweet. Sean looked at Kenny, whose pupils were saucers. Then he saw the glass pipe in his lap. Then the blade Kenny was holding, and Sean knew he'd made a terrible mistake.

CHAPTER 52

"I ain't here to hurt you," Kenny said. "I just need some money to get outta town, and I wanna set some shit straight with you." His grip tightened on the small blade.

Sean couldn't help but think of that night in Japan.

"Drive," Kenny demanded.

Sean considered fighting his way out. But the cabin of the SUV was too small and he wanted to get this man as far away as possible from his family. He started the vehicle and reversed slowly down the driveway. Kenny crouched low in the seat as they reached the street in front of the house. Sean studied the man in the weak light. His teeth, covered in metallic braces when he was a teen, were now decayed. He was puffier in the face, but the rest of him was too thin, all ropey muscles and bone. He had crude tattoos and sores on his forearms.

Sean pulled from the drive and proceeded down the street, the wipers slashing away the heavy rain. When they were a few blocks from the house, Kenny sat back up. He was twitchy, agitated. His glance kept flicking to the side-view mirror, like he was worried someone had followed them.

Sean said, "Money is no problem. I'll give you whatever you want. Just take it easy."

"Don't tell me to take it easy, motherfucker," Kenny shouted.

His eyes bugged and a vein in his neck kept bulging. Kenny gestured with the blade for Sean to turn right, taking them to Connecticut Avenue.

Sean kept his eyes on the road, playing out his next move. Should he crash the SUV into a lamppost or another car? Should he jump out at a light? Or should he take the risk and hear the man out? Before he could decide, Kenny said, "Pull onto the interstate."

Sean veered onto the Beltway and the SUV picked up speed, streams of rain racing over the moon roof. Ahead was a blur of brake lights.

Kenny turned to Sean and said, "I didn't fuckin' touch her, you got that? And if he says I did"—Kenny pounded the dash with his fist—"he's lying. I just told her what he wanted me to say. He's trying to set me up. I ain't goin' down for this."

Sean's jaw clenched, realizing that Kenny was referring to Abby. In the most calm tone he could manage, he said, "You talked to my daughter?"

Kenny started ranting. "The deal was I'd fuck with you. Let you see me, mess with your head. Tell your daughter about what we did in Misawa. But that was it. I didn't touch her. The dude's lost his mind."

"Who, Kenny? Who are you talking about?" Sean's knuckles were white on the steering wheel as the SUV accelerated.

"Who do you think, man?" Kenny spat out, as if it was the most obvious answer in the world.

Sean thought about who else knew what had happened in Japan. Sean had never told anyone other than his father, and he was dead. That left only Sean, Kenny, and the other boy there that night.

"Juan?" Sean said.

"*Pfft.* You really did just leave and never look back, didn't you?" Kenny pushed the wet hair out of his eyes. "Juan offed himself right after you left Misawa."

Sean took that in. "I didn't know."

"Of course you didn't," Kenny said in disgust. "Your daddy made sure of that."

"What are you talking about?" Sean felt Kenny's stare on him as he pushed down the interstate, the wipers swishing full speed.

"How did you think no one ever found out 'bout us? Your dad wouldn't let the Japs on base to question anybody. They needed his permission. The General shut it down. Saved us both."

Sean thought back to that night, to the time after he'd confessed to his dad. The General had disappeared for a while, but Sean had assumed he'd gone to the O Club, where he spent every night drinking. *You will tell no one. Ever. This is about more than just you, Sean.* It had all seemed so irrational. A plan built more on convenience and fear for his job than Sean's well-being. A decision to keep quiet—keep it buried—not an actual cover-up.

"Then who, Kenny? Who had you do this? Is it Senator James?"

Kenny shook his head and pointed the blade to an exit sign. "Get off here." He directed Sean to the parking lot of a roadside motel. The place was a two-story flophouse with rows of rooms facing a parking lot filled with old cars and U-Hauls. Water poured down from sagging gutters on the flat roof. Across the street, a group of men huddled in the doorway of a caged liquor store. All stared at the luxury SUV as if an alien ship had landed on the block.

Sean pulled under a lonely street lamp, leaving the engine on. His heart was thumping and he was scared, but something made him think that Kenny wasn't going to hurt him. Kenny seemed scared himself.

"Give me your wallet and phone."

Sean arched his back and lifted himself from the seat and pulled out his wallet. He handed it to Kenny.

"If it's money you want, I can give you a lot more than the fifty bucks I have on me. Please just tell me who is behind all this. I promise, I'll keep you out of it."

"I was just supposed to scare you. That was the deal. I didn't know he was gonna . . ." His voice trailed off.

"Who, Kenny? I can't help if I don't know who you're talking about. You came to my house for a reason tonight. Please . . ."

Kenny seemed to be coming down from whatever he had smoked. "I need help getting outta town."

"Whatever you need."

Kenny thought about this. "Come with me." He opened the passenger door quickly and stepped out into the downpour.

"Kenny, wait," Sean said, but the door slammed shut. Sean jumped out of the SUV after him. He caught up with Kenny, who was heading toward one of the ground-floor rooms in the motel. Sean wasn't going into a sketchy motel room with this man. He grabbed Kenny's arm.

Kenny turned back at him. "It wasn't supposed to go down like this. He fooled everybody."

"Who?"

"He set it all up, he—"

Sean heard a pop and felt a sting of liquid and what felt like bits of gravel lashing his face. He wiped at his eyes, then he saw Kenny's body on the wet ground, head exploded.

CHAPTER 53

Raindrops pounded the windshield as Sean raced down the highway. He was breathing raggedly, and his eyes kept flicking to the rearview to see if anyone was following. In the mirror, he saw the streaks of red on his face. He fought back images of Kenny stretched out in the puddles of brown water in the parking lot, his head a shattered watermelon. The gunman must have been nearby. Sean had ducked down, retrieved his wallet and phone, then jumped in the SUV and taken off.

When he arrived home, Emily was waiting for him at the door. She studied him for a moment, then thrust her arms around him.

It was time. She deserved to know the truth.

"Come with me," he said. "I need to show you something."

In the flickering light of their attic, they sat on two boxes, facing one another. She had a bewildered expression on her face as he dug through another box and found his old Def Leppard album. The attic wasn't cold, but Sean had been shivering since witnessing Kenny's murder. He steadied his breathing and pulled out the newspaper clipping about the storekeeper.

And he told her everything.

About a stolen bottle of whiskey from a Japanese liquor store. About three boys and a scuffle with the storekeeper. About a thirty-year-old murder. About the oath. And about how Sean had gone to his father who demanded they keep quiet about the crime. He also told her about his remorse and the shame that prevented him from being honest with her, though he'd wanted to. And how his past had roared back when someone—maybe Senator James— tracked down Kenny Baldwin. He told her about Kenny bumping into him on the subway. About the bottle Kenny put in the SUV. And about tonight, how Kenny said someone had hired him to play mind games with Sean and then something went wrong. He choked up when he reported that Kenny had told Abby about the crime. And he told her that Kenny said Sean knew the man behind it all, but was murdered before he could reveal his identity. He didn't know whether to believe a word of what Kenny had said. But nothing else seemed to explain why he'd reemerged recently, why he'd come to Sean's house tonight, or why he'd been killed.

When Sean finished, Emily was silent. He scrutinized her face in the shadows. Her expression was indescribable. It wasn't betrayal or disbelief as he'd expected. Nor anger. Maybe the expression was just shock—the kind of look someone gets when they fall through the ice into a freezing lake. Except instead of bringing a rope to save her, Sean had brought a hammer. He waited for her to speak, to say something, *anything*. And then she did.

"Did he have a family?" Her voice was quiet, steady. "The storekeeper."

"Yes, his wife worked with him at the store. When I got the life insurance money from my dad's death, I hired a service to see if there were any other relatives. I'm not sure why or what I planned to do, but I thought maybe I could send some money or help them. But the storekeeper's wife had passed away and they found no other relatives."

Emily looked at him. "You've carried this around since you were fourteen?"

This time Sean was the one drowning in the lake. He nodded, not looking her in the eyes. After another heavy silence, he whispered, "Abby's death. It was my fault. I'm being punished." He said it. Finally admitted it to himself. And he now understood. His oath, his deal with God, was an illusory contract. A trick befitting the Devil himself. Give Sean a perfect family and then watch him come apart when it was ripped away. His daughter paid for it all.

Emily stood. She would be leaving, he knew. She would blame him, rightly, for the misery befallen the Serrats. *The Serrats*. It didn't even sound right anymore, without Abby. And with Emily gone, what would remain?

But Emily didn't leave. She leaned forward and wrapped her arms around him. And he cried. A release three decades in the making in the embrace of the woman who'd given him everything.

"What are we going to do?" Sean said, his voice hoarse.

"We're going to make things right," Emily whispered. "But first, we're going to find out what happened to our daughter."

CHAPTER 54

After a restless night, Sean woke to sunshine beaming through the bedroom window, dust floating in the rays. Another headache, this time from grinding his teeth in his sleep. His thoughts immediately went to Kenny, his lifeless body, the blood . . . but he beat them back. Em had said they couldn't let what happened to Kenny cripple them from finding out the truth.

Downstairs, the house was still. A jar of peanut butter sat on the kitchen counter along with Ziploc bags. He looked out the window and the SUV was gone. Already the sun was erasing the evidence of the night's rain. It was one of those D.C. springs where one day it would be dark and pouring rain, the next day sunshine, birds chirping, and everything feeling Disney-movie fresh and new. If only he felt that way. Sean heard the keys in the kitchen door, then Emily came inside. Where would they go from here?

"Sorry I overslept," Sean said. "You got the boys out?"

"Yes. You'd better go get ready if you're going to make it downtown in time."

"My meeting with James isn't until three o'clock."

"I know, but I have somewhere I want us to go first."

He looked at Emily. "Shouldn't we . . . talk?"

She held his gaze. "We will. But we need to get going. There's someone I think we should speak with about Abby."

Sean hastily showered and changed into jeans and a T-shirt—
he would not dress up for Senator James. He and Emily stepped
down their side portico to the narrow driveway. In Chevy Chase,
where many of the houses were built before most people had
cars, the driveways often were makeshift. The Serrats shared their
driveway—a Y-shaped lane wedged between two colonials—with
their neighbor. As Sean walked to the SUV, he saw a man in a
sports jacket and slacks sauntering up the drive.

"Hey," Sean said, chin cocked, "you know the rules. No reporters beyond the sidewalk."

The man reached into his back pocket and pulled out his wallet
as he continued up the drive. Sean glanced toward Emily, who was
next to the SUV. Her face had turned sheet white.

"I'm not a reporter, Mr. Serrat. I'm Detective Whiteside with
the Montgomery County police." The man held open his wallet dis-
playing credentials. "Homicide section."

Sean glanced at the identification and gave the best puzzled
look he could marshal. Kenny Baldwin was murdered in D.C., not
over the border in Maryland, so this could be about only one thing.
Billy Brice.

Emily spoke. "Honey, this is the detective I told you about who
stopped by." It was a tad stilted, but seemed casual enough.

"That's right," Sean said, shaking the detective's hand. "My
wife said you wanted to speak to me about the man who was found
at the high school?"

"Correct. I'm really sorry to intrude, since I know your family
is going through a tough time yourselves, but my boss . . ."

"I understand, detective. I know what the victim's family must
be going through, so I'm happy to help."

"Actually, the victim, his name was William Brice, doesn't seem
to have any family—at least any family who cares about what happened to him."

"I'm sorry to hear that," Sean said.

"It probably seems odd, since you may have read that Brice
was no angel," Whiteside added, "but it's these kinds of cases that
always get me—no family, unpopular victim. I'm the last hope for

justice since no one else really gives a damn." The detective held Sean's gaze for a second longer than comfortable.

Sean said, "I'm happy to help if I can."

The detective studied him for another long moment. "I'm just trying to find anyone who might have seen something. Brice had some marijuana and some harder stuff on him, and we think he was selling behind the high school. If there were some kids buying from him and who saw something, they'd obviously have a lot of reasons not to come forward."

Was the detective suggesting that Ryan was one of those kids? Sean's body stiffened.

"As your wife probably mentioned, we found your son's bike at the school, and we wondered if we could speak with him?"

"I spoke to Ryan," Emily said, now standing next to Sean. "He wasn't at the school that night. He was with his dad, so he didn't see anything."

"How about you, Mr. Serrat, did you see anything?"

"Me?" Sean said. He may have been imagining it, but the detective's tone had an accusatory edge. "No, I wasn't near the school that night. Ryan and I were at a friend of mine's house for dinner."

The detective digested this. "A friend's house?" Skeptical. He shot Emily a look, no doubt remembering that Emily had told him that Ryan and Sean were at the gym that night and that Sean had been mugged. "Do you mind if I ask who the friend is, Mr. Serrat?"

The detective was a beefy man in his fifties, gray hair, seasoned. No dummy. Sean gave the detective Cecilia's name and telephone number. He could feel the detective scrutinizing him.

"Had you ever met William Brice before?" Whiteside asked, his tone again routine, but Sean heard something more. The detective pulled up a photo of Brice on his phone, it looked like a morgue shot. He slid his finger and another image appeared on the small screen. A headshot, a high school yearbook photo by the looks of it.

Sean examined the photos. "I don't know this man. He doesn't look familiar."

"You've never seen him?"

"Not that I recall."

"It's funny, Mr. Serrat, because two of Mr. Brice's friends say that he had a physical altercation with a man who fits your description."

Sean scoffed. Time to play indignant. "They said *I* had an altercation with him? Who are these friends? Are they high on the stuff their buddy was selling?" His credibility challenged, Sean now added with conviction, "I never saw the man before in my life."

"Do you mind if I ask what happened to your eye?"

Sean cocked his head toward the SUV, signaling Emily to get inside. "I had a spill on my bike. Now, if you don't mind, I'm late for an appointment."

Whiteside started to speak, but Sean cut him off, "Have a good day, detective." Sean climbed into the SUV. He inhaled deeply and started the engine. He looked in the rearview mirror, and Whiteside was standing in the path of the vehicle. Sean put it in reverse and the detective stepped aside as they rolled down the drive.

Before the SUV reached the curb, the detective gestured for Sean to roll down the window.

"Let's just go," Emily said.

But Sean slowed to a stop and the window hummed down.

Whiteside said, "I just need to clarify one thing, Mr. Serrat."

"What is it?"

"I don't think you had anything to do with William Brice's murder, just so we're clear."

Sean nodded. Good. This was heading in the right direction. No need to be paranoid.

"You know what the kids called Mr. Brice?"

"Called him?"

"Yeah, sort of his nickname or trademark, so kids knew how to find the dealer without giving any names."

"I have no idea." Sean knew what was coming.

The detective smirked. "They called him 'the man in red.' Ever heard that before? Ever seen that on Facebook or anywhere, Mr. Serrat?"

Sean suppressed a swallow. He tightened his lips and shook his head.

"You're a lawyer, right, Mr. Serrat?"

"Yes."

"So you know the old saying?" The detective now gave him a challenging stare.

"What saying?"

The detective locked eyes with Sean and then peered over Sean's shoulder to Emily. "It's not the crime that will get you—it's the cover-up."

CHAPTER 55

The Starbucks across the street from Georgetown was filled with students, most standing in line with backpacks slung over their shoulders or stooped at tables staring at phones and laptops. It was finals week, and the air was as frenetic as it was back when Sean and Emily were in law school. Then, and now, the entire semester came down to how well you did on a single exam. A test that would determine your class rank, which would control whether you made law review, which would influence how many employers offered you interviews.

Sean and Emily sat at a round table sipping their drinks. If nothing else, the Serrats, like the rest of D.C., were a caffeinated bunch, and this was *Abby's* Starbucks. That's what they used to call it. There was Dad's Starbucks on Eleventh near the Justice Department building, Mom's Starbucks on Connecticut Avenue near the house, and even fourteen-year-old Ryan had his own, the Starbucks on Wisconsin Avenue in Bethesda.

Emily's eyes roved about the coffee shop. The detective had shaken her. On the drive in, Emily had fretted aloud: Had the police talked to Ryan's school and learned about the Facebook posts linking Ryan to Billy Brice? What if a traffic cam or school camera had caught Sean that night? Or, worse, what if someone had seen Ryan? These questions had consumed Sean since he'd learned of Brice's demise. They couldn't be sure that the police had Ryan in their sights, but the detective's cover-up comment could mean little else.

A group of four young women wearing jeans and tight tops came into the shop. Sean followed Emily's gaze. They were ready to take on the world, overconfident yet insecure at the same time, laughing, playing with their phones, and pretending not to notice that the guys were checking them out. Emily blinked back tears. Sean reached for her hand.

After the women ordered, they huddled near the pickup area for their five-shot soy hazelnut vanilla cinnamon white mochas, their Crunch Berry frappuccinos, and other concoctions. Amid the whine of blenders and coffee grinders, Sean saw one of the girls stealing looks at them. She whispered something to her friends and then approached their table.

"Mr. and Mrs. Serrat?" the young woman said. "I thought that was you."

Emily stood and the two hugged. "It's good to see you, Michelle," Emily said. The woman, a Korean American with jet-black hair, gave a fleeting smile.

"Sean, you remember Michelle O'Leary."

Sean nodded and shook her delicate hand.

Emily pulled out a chair. Michelle hesitated, but then waved to her friends, who ambled off, more subdued now. She slid her backpack from her shoulder and sat down.

Emily and Michelle shared an awkward silence, until Michelle blurted, "I miss her so much." She cupped her hands around the cardboard sleeve of her drink and stared at the table.

Sean vaguely recalled meeting her once or twice—O'Leary isn't exactly a common Korean name, so she'd made an impression. He remembered Abby saying that Michelle's family owned a restaurant in Fairfax County, Virginia. She was a hard worker, and Abby had admired her study habits. They'd become fast friends their first year of law school.

"We have some questions," Emily said. She took the girl's hands in hers. "We're trying to understand some things about Abby that may help the investigation."

Michelle nodded, her gaze somewhere far away.

"Was Abby seeing anyone?" Emily had been obsessed with the question ever since Malik Montgomery had made the claim. Plus Billy Brice had said that a rich man in a suit paid him to get Abby's necklace back.

Michelle cleared her throat and swept the room with her eyes. "There was someone," she whispered. "But Abby wouldn't tell me who."

"Michelle, it's okay to tell us, there's nothing we can't handle, there's—"

"Really," Michelle said. "She wouldn't tell me. I noticed she was staying out late, sometimes overnight. I knew it wasn't with Malik because he would call looking for her. I wish I would've known that Malik was so upset about it, I would have covered better for her. I would've—"

"There's nothing you could have done, Michelle," Emily said. "Do you know why Abby didn't tell you who the man is?"

"It seemed weird, but she said it was for my own good. I thought it was someone married maybe. She asked me as a friend to leave it be, so I did."

Sean felt like the wind had been knocked out of him. A married man?

Emily continued, undeterred. "Did she have any problems— things she'd probably share with a friend, but not her mom and dad?"

Michelle's eyes fell to the table. Without looking up she said, "The officer from the Supreme Court asked me the same thing. Looking back on it, that last week, Abby was super stressed out. She said everything was crashing in on her all at once."

"Do you know what she meant? What was crashing in on her?"

"At first I thought it was just about the man she was seeing. She said she was gonna break up with Malik, but she was afraid."

"Afraid of what?"

"Of what he might do. But it was more than Malik." Michelle took a slow drink of her latte. "She said her little brother got into some mess. And she said something about going to a jail out in Virginia. After she went, she said a man approached her and warned her to back off."

"Did she say who that was?" Emily asked.

"She didn't tell me," Michelle answered. "She just called him 'Mole Face,' like he was a rat or something."

Sean and Emily shared a glance. Ryan had seen a man with a mole on his face following Sean the night on the football field. But Kenny Baldwin didn't have a mole. Neither did Senator James.

Michelle continued, "But she seemed most freaked out about some research she'd been doing. She asked me if I knew anyone who could translate some newspapers."

"Translate?" Emily said.

"Yeah, she had Japanese newspapers and she needed them translated."

Sean thought about Kenny Baldwin. *I just told her what he wanted me to say.* Sean remembered his hunt through the attic, Jack saying Abby was up there looking in the JAPAN box. After Kenny approached her, maybe she went snooping and found the newspaper clipping Sean had kept about the storekeeper's death and made a copy. She was a great researcher. Maybe those led to more newspapers. It hit him again that the last thing she would have thought about her dad was that he was a killer.

Emily pressed on. "Did you help her get them translated?"

"I didn't know anyone who spoke Japanese, so no."

"Do you know if she ever got the translation?"

Michelle shook her head. "I would have come to you if I thought it was something serious, but I didn't—"

"Do you have *any* idea who the man she was seeing is?" Sean asked. "Did you ever see him?"

"I honestly don't know," Michelle said. "But I know someone who got a look at him." Apparently Abby had once borrowed Michelle's apartment in Adams Morgan to meet with her mystery man. Michelle shared the place with her older brother, and he'd come home early, interrupting Abby and the guy.

"Do you think we could speak with your brother?" Emily asked.

Michelle nodded and began tapping on her phone. A return chime came quickly. Sean was surprised when Michelle said, "He's on his way."

CHAPTER 56

In the cramped seat of Douglas O'Leary's bicycle rickshaw, Sean held his hand over his eyes, shielding them from the sun as he and Emily bumped and jerked down New Jersey Avenue. Sean had been surprised that Michelle's brother could meet with them so quickly until she explained that he worked nearby: a bike taxi shuttling tourists around the National Mall. In the first of many quirks her brother had, he would speak with them only if they agreed to take a ride. Douglas wore cutoff shorts, white tube socks pulled to his calves, and a straw fedora over unruly ginger hair. He had pale skin with acne on his cheeks and chin. And, unlike his sister, whose eyes brimmed with intelligence, Douglas avoided eye contact. He also had a slight stutter, but that did not slow down his urge to fill all silence with the sound of his voice.

Douglas peddled intensely, twisting around to talk every minute or so. The back of his shirt had a large oval sweat stain. "The groundbreaking for the Capitol was in 1793 and George Washington laid the cornerstone," he said, pointing at the dome. "The District is divided into quadrants and the Capitol is the center of the divide." He curved onto Northwest Drive, then made his way to Madison where he stood on the pedals all the way down the center of the National Mall toward the Washington Monument. He pointed to the Smithsonian building, a red Norman structure that looked like a castle, and told them that the Smithsonian had nineteen museums and nine research centers. He started to explain why the base of the Washington Monument was made from a different color marble than the rest of the monument, but Sean, growing impatient, asked Douglas to pull over near one of the food carts lining the street. Sean pried himself out of the rickshaw and bought three bottled waters from the vendor. He handed one to Douglas. After the man took a long gulp, Sean said, "Douglas, I appreciate the tour, but we have something important to talk with you about, like your sister mentioned."

Douglas exhaled loudly. "I only have a little more of the tour to tell you about."

"I know, but I have an appointment soon and don't have much time. I'd love to finish it on any other day. You're very knowledgeable about the city."

At this Douglas nodded.

Emily spoke next. "Did Michelle tell you what happened to our daughter, Abby?"

Douglas's lips tightened and he looked out in the distance. "Abby was always nice to me."

"You may be able to help us catch who hurt her," Emily said.

Douglas nodded again and then took a long gulp of his water. He crunched the empty bottle and launched it toward a trash can, missing the shot.

Sean said, "Michelle mentioned that one day you came home, and Abby and a man were in your apartment?"

Douglas stared at the tree limbs that swayed above, thinking. "Yes, I remember that day."

"Did you get a look at the man she was with? Could you tell us what he looked like?"

Douglas wiped his nose with the back of his hand. "He wore a suit, I remember."

"That's helpful. Do you remember anything else, how old he was, for instance?"

Douglas tilted his head, his blotchy forehead wrinkling. "Older than her. Maybe your age."

Sean felt a sting in his chest.

"Had you ever seen him before?"

Douglas nodded.

Sean looked at Emily. "You'd seen him before? At the apartment?"

"Not at the apartment."

"Where?"

"I'm not sure. Hey, do you want to finish the tour?"

Sean took in a breath. Patience.

Emily pulled her iPhone from her handbag and tapped on it until an image appeared. Sean looked at the screen. It was a photo of Senator James.

Emily said, "Was this the man?" She turned the screen toward Douglas. He leaned forward for a look.

"Nope. That's not him."

Emily gazed at Sean, hesitated, then pulled up another image on the phone. Sean looked at this one and gave his wife a hard glare. "You can't possibly think that? He's a friend. And her professor, for Christ's sake."

"How many other older men did Abby know?" Emily said. "He left OSG because of an intern, and Cecilia told me he got into trouble when he taught at Yale for getting too cozy with female students." Emily showed Douglas the image of Professor Jonathan Tweed.

Douglas stared at the iPhone. "I don't think so."

"You're sure?"

Douglas nodded.

Their daughter had secrets that she'd kept from them. Kept from her friends. And this mystery man could hold the key to finding the killer. Or he just might be the killer himself.

CHAPTER 57

"Ryan, sweetie, please calm down, I can't understand what you're saying," Emily said, the phone pressed to her ear. They were on the sidewalk in front of the Hart Senate Building, and foot traffic was heavy with Capitol Hill pages rushing about. Sean wanted to snatch the mobile out of Emily's hand, but she shooed him back.

"The detective wasn't supposed to talk with you. He was just trying to get a reaction." Emily raised a finger again. Sean's heart was in a free fall. Ryan must have learned that Billy Brice was dead.

"—he shouldn't have shown you those photos." More listening from Emily. A couple of passersby stared at them, but Sean wasn't sure whether it was because they recognized the Serrats from all the news coverage or because there was something desperate in the way Emily was talking on the mobile phone. Emily finally used her mother's voice. "Ryan, you need to take a deep breath. Calm down. I will be right there, and I can explain everything. It's not what you think. I want you to get a drink of water and try to calm down. Can you do that?" Another beat of silence. "Okay. I love you. I'll be home shortly." Emily ended the call.

Sean began, "He found out . . ."

Emily nodded. "That detective was waiting for him when he got off the school bus. He said the detective showed him photos of Billy Brice; asked Ryan what size shoe he wears."

"What shoe size?" Sean thought about it. "Maybe they found some tracks on the football field or in the woods. What did Ryan tell him?"

"He did what we asked. He told the detective to talk to his parents."

"We should go home now. I can reschedule with James."

"No. I'll go take care of Ryan. I'll stick to the plan and say Brice attacked you when you went back for the gun and you hit him."

"He's not gonna believe—"

"You need to do this," Emily said. "If that man had Kenny or some other creep harass Abby and our family, we need to know. Not just for Abby, but for the safety of our boys. I've got this." Emily looked at him intently. "You need to go to that meeting and look James in the eye and you tell him that if he hurt our Abby, he's not gonna get away with it."

CHAPTER 58

Sean walked down the long hallway in the Hart Senate Office Building until he found SH321. Flags were stationed at either side of the door. He took a deep breath and entered Senator James's office.

A man in his twenties looked over a tall reception desk and asked Sean to take a seat. Perching on a wing chair, Sean glanced at muted C-SPAN on the flat-screen mounted to the wall. How to handle this first meeting with the senator? Should he confront him head on, as Emily wanted? Or should he play it cool and study the situation, learn more? That was more his style, but he was not sure that he could fake cordiality with a man he'd never much cared for, a man unworthy of a seat on the Supreme Court. A man who could be a murderer of women.

Ten minutes passed. Sean had experienced D.C. "make them wait" power plays in the past, but as far as Senator James knew, Sean was there to help. Not a person to play with. A text came in. Emily was nearly home and Ryan had calmed down, which gave Sean a tiny bit of relief. Tiring of waiting, Sean exhaled loudly.

"I apologize for the wait." The receptionist caught the hint. "The senator is at the Capitol and was supposed to have returned by now." The man picked up the phone and murmured something. A man in a dark suit and starched white shirt hurried into the office, hand outstretched.

"Mr. Serrat," he said, handshake too firm. "I'm Brendan Reis, Senator James's chief of staff. The senator sends his apologies. He got caught up on a vote and asked if I could escort you to his office in the Capitol."

Sean followed Reis out of the office and to the basement of Hart where the two men boarded the underground train that connected the Senate office buildings to the Capitol. It reminded Sean of the monorail at Disneyland, except that there were no crowds and the railcars each had the Senate Seal, not Mickey, affixed to the walls.

"The senator has another office?" Sean asked. In his years at the Justice Department, Sean had visited many government agencies, but rarely found himself at any of the congressional facilities or the Capitol. He'd assumed that all the senatorial offices were in Hart or Dirksen or Russell and didn't realize that the Capitol itself housed senators.

"Yes," Reis said. "We're going to his hideaway office. Every senator gets an office in the Capitol building so they don't have to run back and forth. It's small, but really convenient if there are breaks between votes and floor appearances."

They got off the train, and Reis walked Sean through a small archway from the rail platform to the basement of the Capitol. Before them was a dank hallway. Brick walls with caked-on beige paint and a ceiling with exposed pipes. Along the hall were several plain wooden doors, which Sean assumed were storage closets. He was surprised when Reis walked to one of the doors and knocked before turning the knob.

As the door opened, Sean saw Senator James sitting on a couch in a windowless office the size of a small hotel room. Not a suite, a basic room. Another man rose from his seat and stared at Sean. He was tall with lifeless eyes and a slit for a mouth. And he had a mole on his left cheek.

CHAPTER 59

The door shut and Sean felt a bead of sweat slide down his back. His T-shirt was damp. He wasn't sure if it was the cramped quarters or the stony stare from the man with the mole. Though Sean's chest was pounding, he felt vindicated to actually see Mole Face for himself. It meant that he and Em weren't crazy; they hadn't been conjuring conspiracies. The senator was involved in all this.

Senator James gestured for Sean to take a seat across from the sofa. He pointed the remote control at the television and clicked off the set. He glanced at his chief of staff, who had taken a seat at a table near the door, and said, "You can leave us, Brendan."

Reis looked surprised, but left without questioning his boss. The man with the mole, who the senator introduced as his chief of security, moved his muscular frame to the door behind Sean. Sean heard the click of the lock. He forced himself not to turn and look.

Sean spoke first. "Abani Gupta asked that I come by so we can discuss how you want to proceed with the prep sessions." It came out forced. "I thought the most productive route would be for me to give you some suggested reading and excerpts from past confirmation hearings where the committee raised constitutional law questions. We could then schedule a prep session before the formal murder boards."

Senator James narrowed his eyes, still studying Sean. "Or," the senator said, "we can cut the bullshit and talk about your visit to Sussex prison. And perhaps you can explain why you'd have your daughter investigating my background. Did you really think you could steal *my* nomination by digging up dirt on *me?*"

Sean didn't flinch. He'd spent his career training himself to remain calm under tough questioning—oral arguments with nine Supreme Court justices. He sat back in his chair and took in a controlled breath. "I think the real question is how *you* knew anything about what my daughter was doing and where *you* and your friend here were the night she was killed."

Senator James scoffed. "You can't be serious." He glanced up at the man with the mole, who was still standing behind Sean's chair. "I'm sorry about your daughter, I am, Serrat. But you're delusional if you think I was involved. For one, we were at a fund-raiser in St. Louis the night she was murdered. Check it out if you want. And two, why would I kill her?"

"Because she knew something about you that could tank your nomination and probably end your career in the Senate, if not worse. That's why you followed her." Sean twisted around and looked at Mole Face. "That's why you threatened her."

"All she *knew*, Serrat," the senator said, "was that a convicted murderer was a friend of mine in college. That's not worth killing for."

"But it was worth having someone follow her, worth scaring her?" His tone had a sharp, desperate edge.

"You need to take a deep breath, Serrat." The senator was calm, cool almost.

"Fuck you," Sean spat out.

The senator gave an exasperated shake of the head.

"And I don't know where the hell you found Kenny," Sean said, "but whatever it is you think you have on me, I don't give a shit. Tell the world for all I care."

"I have no idea what you're talking about."

"Liar." Sean stood to leave.

The senator nodded at Mole Face, and Sean felt the crushing grip on his shoulders, forcing him back into the chair. Sean started to struggle, but the senator shook his head and the man with the mole released his hold.

Through gritted teeth, James said, "I need you to listen to me here. I had nothing to do with your daughter's death. I had no reason to hurt her. John Chadwick is guilty, and, anyway, your daughter agreed that it didn't make sense to keep talking to him."

"Because she thought she needed to protect me?"

Senator James's eyes narrowed. "No, not to protect *you*."

Sean just looked at the man. The way he said the word *you* suggested Abby was trying to protect someone else.

"I don't know who Kenny is or what the hell kind of crazy nonsense is going through your head, but your daughter had no intention of wasting her time with John Chadwick's rumors. And, really, of all your children, is it your daughter you should be worried about right now, Serrat?" Senator James nodded again to the man with the mole. The man tossed a manila folder over Sean's shoulder and onto the coffee table.

The senator cocked his chin, gesturing for Sean to open the file. Sean waited a few seconds, but his curiosity won out. He leaned forward and slowly opened the folder, which held several photographs. The first was a shot of Ryan under a cone of light from a street lamp. He was on his bicycle at Bethesda–Chevy Chase High School. Sean flipped to the next photo and just stared at it in silence. He knew what crippling despair felt like, but this was something different: crippling defeat.

Senator James leaned forward and tapped his finger on the photograph of a steel bar that appeared to have blood and hair on its end. "Let it go, Serrat. Let it go."

CHAPTER 60

Sean tried to let it go. Senator James was probably guilty of a lot of things, but Sean confirmed that he was out of town at the time of Abby's death. Newspapers reported on his visit to St. Louis, complete with photos of James at several events, his henchman with the mole by his side. Had James hired Kenny? Sean had his doubts. If James knew about Japan, Sean didn't think James would keep that nugget to himself. Kenny couldn't have killed Abby. There was no evidence he'd been anywhere near the Supreme Court the night of Abby's murder. And Kenny didn't fit in with the high court crowd, so he would have been noticed.

But if it wasn't the senator, his henchman, or Kenny who killed Abby, then who? All roads led back to Malik Montgomery. Beyond the Occam's Razor logic of it all, the Supreme Court Police, FBI, and the top prosecutors in the country believed they had their man. Sure, questions existed. Who hired Kenny to mess with Sean? And who killed him? Kenny, a violent drug-addled criminal, could have been delusional, or just trying to play him, and his murder may have nothing to do with Abby. Sean doubted that Kenny was the first person ever shot dead in the parking lot of the Marbury Motel. So, after the confrontation with Senator James, Sean resolved to stop playing detective. To let it go.

Emily disagreed. She was sure the senator was involved in

Abby's death somehow. But the pieces didn't fit and Sean felt they had to try to move forward and let the professionals do their jobs.

Emily still wasn't ready to talk more about Japan, but she at least wasn't spending her days in bed. And they'd just made it over the latest hurdle: Mother's Day. Ryan was a bit trickier. They'd told their son that Sean had delivered the fatal blow to Billy Brice, but Sean didn't think he believed it.

So here Sean was back at work. He'd just finished up an excruciatingly boring meeting with the general counsels of four chemical companies about petitioning the Supreme Court to review a massive jury verdict against them. He'd told them it was a lost cause, and it wasn't the answer they'd wanted to hear. After the meeting, he was pleasantly surprised to have a message from Emily. She wanted to meet for lunch at a place in Dupont Circle. An unusual choice, and a bit of a pain since he'd have to cab or Metro it, but of course he'd come.

On his way out of the building, a woman approached him in the lobby.

"Mr. Serrat?" She held out a slender hand.

"Yes," Sean said. "Can I help you?" Sean's mind searched for how he might know the woman, but he drew a blank.

"I'm Eleanor Chadwick—John's mother." She pushed a strand of gray hair behind her ear.

Sean's face flushed. He'd avoided several calls and ignored e-mails from this woman.

"Yes, hello. I'm running late for a lunch meeting, but would be happy to talk if you could make an appointment with my—"

"Please, Mr. Serrat." She clutched his forearm. Sean looked around. Lunchgoers, in groups of two or three, ambled about the lobby. He hesitated, but then gestured for Ms. Chadwick to join him in a small anteroom off the lobby.

Ms. Chadwick had the weary look of someone who had not slept in weeks. No makeup, dark crescents under the eyes. Her clothes and handbag, elegant and refined from a distance, were frayed.

"We need you, Mr. Serrat."

"I'm sorry, but I reviewed the case and I don't think there's a good faith post-conviction motion here. All I told your son was that I'd take a look."

"Your daughter thought his case had merit, that we could get the DNA tested."

Sean sighed. "My daughter was a law student. She just didn't have the experience yet to make that call." His stomach turned at debasing Abby's abilities.

Ms. Chadwick fixed her gaze on Sean. "You've lost a child," she said. Her voice quivered now. "You know how it feels. Imagine you could get her back, imagine it. You can do this for me. I've lost everything else. My marriage. My home. You could at least get my Johnny back."

Sean swallowed, but he tried to show no emotion. The photo of the bloodied steel rod that probably had Ryan's prints or DNA on it flew through his head along with the echo of Senator James's voice: *Let it go, Serrat.*

Sean steadied himself and said, "I sympathize, I do. But I can't take this on. Has John sought out other counsel? If not, I can make some referrals."

"Johnny hasn't been able to do anything since you visited him."

"If they're restricting his phone access, I'm sure you can—"

"It's not his phone access," she said bitterly. "Johnny was attacked the day after your visit. He's in the prison infirmary."

CHAPTER 61

Sean looked about the restaurant and saw Emily at a cramped two-seater along the wall. Her gaze was empty. Sean walked over and slipped into the chair across from her. After sweeping the area for eavesdroppers or reporters, he filled in Emily on the visit from John Chadwick's mother.

Emily leaned in and whispered, "So we're just going to do nothing? You know he's in the hospital because of Mason James. You have to know that, Sean."

"What am I supposed to do, Em? As long as James has the—" He stopped and twisted around to confirm again that no one was close enough to hear. "As long as he has the evidence on Ryan, we can't risk it."

"What if we got the steel bar and photos back?" Emily said. Her long lashes didn't flutter as she held his gaze.

"How would you propose we do that? Break in to his Senate office?"

Emily gave the slight arch of a brow.

He gave her a *what the fuck* expression: hands held up, eyes wide.

"I'm going to tell you something, but you have to promise not to get mad," Emily said.

He held her gaze, not responding.

"Promise?" she repeated, her green eyes steady.

Sean pursed his lips and gave a clipped nod.

"I think I know where James keeps the file on Ryan. And I think we can get it."

At this, Sean opened his mouth to speak, but closed it. He took a gulp of water, his eyes not drifting from Emily's.

"I've been following him."

Sean nearly choked on the water. "Following who? Tell me you're not referring to Mason James?"

"No, he's too risky. Since his nomination I can't get near him—too many reporters staking him out, and I think he has extra security now. I've been following his henchman. Mole Face." The man's name was Sebastian Finkle, but they still referred to him by the nickname Abby had given him. The guy just didn't look like a Sebastian Finkle. It was a strange name that reminded Sean of a line from a C. S. Lewis novel: *There was a boy called Eustace Clarence Scrubb, and he almost deserved it.*

It had started out innocuously enough, Emily explained. She'd gone to Abby's apartment on the Hill to sort through their daughter's things and afterward strolled to the Capitol. She wandered about the building to see if she could get near the hideaway office where Senator James had shown Sean the file on their son. She couldn't. She'd then found herself outside the Hart building. She didn't have a plan, but was there when the senator and Mole Face walked out of the building. When the two parted ways, she'd trailed Mole Face to the subway station.

"He took the train to Dupont Circle, and I followed him to a condo building. It was the middle of the afternoon so I just hung out in the circle for a little while and, sure enough, he came out. He was wearing a ball cap and sunglasses, like he was trying to hide his face. And he was carrying a large envelope. I followed him as he took the subway to Cleveland Park and he pushed the envelope through the mail slot of a house near the Metro station there."

"So he delivered some mail, I don't see the—"

"You don't understand," Emily said. "I came back to Hart the next day. He followed the same routine. Mole Face left Hart, got to his condo building at around three o'clock, changed from a suit into the ball cap and glasses, and left with an envelope. This time, though, he got on a motorcycle so I couldn't follow."

Sean raised a finger and started to speak until Emily cut him off with a shake of the head.

"Yesterday—three o'clock on the nose—but this time I followed in the SUV. He rode to a home in Arlington. Same drill. Envelope in the mailbox. Three days, three deliveries. Each time he wore glasses and a hat that made it difficult to see his face. And the two times I saw, he wiped down the envelopes before giving them up."

"Did you write down the addresses?" Sean asked.

"Yes," Emily said, a hint of hope in her voice. "I Googled the addresses, but couldn't find anything."

"There could be some valid explanation," Sean said.

"Like what?"

"I don't know," Sean said. "A payoff or something for the senator."

"Politicians usually are on the receiving end of envelopes full of money, not delivering them," Emily said.

"Unless they're not getting a bribe, but giving one—or more likely blackmailing someone," Sean said. He thought of that moment in James's hideaway office when James and Mole Face slapped the folder on the table threatening Sean with evidence against Ryan.

"There's one way to find out," Emily said.

Sean gazed at his wife.

She said, "It's quarter to three and Mole Face's condo is just down the street from here."

That explained why his wife had wanted to meet in Dupont Circle. Whatever Emily had in mind, he owed her this.

CHAPTER 62

The wind pushed a mist of water out from the fountain at Dupont Circle. Several homeless men and women, some holding signs, others with garbage bags stuffed with their belongings, monopolized the benches that ran along the perimeter. Closer to the fountain were children dipping their hands in the water or watching the jugglers, bucket drummers, and other street performers. Tourists from nearby hotels wandered around, taking it all in. The place was as close to bohemian New York as D.C. could manage. Sean and Emily lingered near the chess tables where street prodigies were known to checkmate Ivy League grads.

At just past three, Mole Face fast-walked into the lobby of Dupont Towers, a ten-story modern structure, undoubtedly pricey, nestled next to historic brownstones in the middle of the action. And, just as Emily had described, ten minutes later he came out wearing a ball cap, tight T-shirt hugging chiseled muscles, and aviator shades. A designer-label disguise. An envelope was tucked under his arm. Sean thought again of the folder presented to him that surreal day in James's hideaway office. It would have fit perfectly into the six-by-nine-inch envelope.

They trailed him to the subway entrance, keeping their distance. The Dupont Metro escalator was lined with tourists who gawked at what had to be one of the longest stretches of rotating metal in the country. It must have plunged two hundred feet into the tunnels below. Walkers plodded down the left side of the escalator, standers to the right. Sean kept his eyes on Mole Face's ball cap, which bobbed down the left lane, periodically stopping, probably because of a tourist standing to the left, not catching on to the unwritten rule of the subway.

Mole Face took the red line to Metro Center, the hub of the line. He trotted to the lower level and jumped on an Orange Line train.

"That train heads back toward the Capitol. He's probably going back to his office at Hart," Sean said.

"No," Emily said. "You don't go home, change, then go back to work. He's making another delivery."

And she was right.

Mole Face got off the train at Capitol South. It was indeed a stop near congressional offices, but instead of walking the five blocks toward the dome that dominated the skyline, Mole Face hurried south away from the Capitol.

"What's down there?" Emily asked as they held back, allowing Mole Face to pace just far enough away that they could get lost in the crowd of pedestrians milling about the Hill.

Sean stared ahead. It was an industrial section of Capitol Hill—elevated rail tracks and two smokestacks. "I'm not sure," he said. "I've never been over here."

They stalked Mole Face for three blocks on crumbling brick sidewalks that were lined with dilapidated row houses. Mole Face turned right down a side street, then rambled down the sloped street toward a four-story building. The structure was faded orange with rust stains streaking from metal railings lining a rooftop patio. Mole Face walked to a windswept outdoor parking lot in front of the building.

"Do you know what's in that building?" Sean asked his wife.

Emily shook her head.

They lurked at the top of the hill shielding themselves with some shrubs. Mole Face paced through the parking lot until he stopped in front of a Range Rover. He dug into his pocket and pulled out a scrap of paper. He then fiddled with something in his hand and the Range Rover chirped and its lights flashed. Mole Face opened the vehicle's door. His back was to Sean and Emily so they couldn't see what he was doing, but when he walked away, he no longer had the envelope.

CHAPTER 63

"What the hell is this guy doing?" Sean said. An Amtrak train rumbled past on elevated tracks nearby.

"I'm telling you," Emily said, "I bet you the envelopes have dirt on someone, and Mason James is sending a message."

"How do you think he got into that Range Rover?" Sean said.

"You can buy a universal key fob. You can get one that will open almost any electronic car lock."

Sean gave his wife a sideways look.

She shrugged. "Read about it on the Internet. I was trying to figure out how they got that bottle of whiskey in our car."

A universal key fob could explain how Kenny got inside the vehicle. Another possible connection between Kenny and the senator. He watched as the man disappeared around the corner, turning in the direction of the Capitol.

"Let's get the plate number of the Range Rover," Sean said. They hurried down the hill and through the lot. Sean snapped a photo of the license plate with the camera on his mobile phone. When he turned to continue their tail of Mole Face, the sign on the silver awning hanging over the front of the building caught his eye: DEMOCRATIC NATIONAL HEADQUARTERS.

They caught up with Mole Face again and shadowed him several blocks, keeping their distance and trying to look like tourists wandering the city. That got harder as the man hiked down Third Street and pedestrian traffic became sparse. They watched from afar as Mole Face vanished into a structure near the corner of Third and East Capitol. As they got closer, they were met with a sign that read FOLGER SHAKESPEARE LIBRARY. Emily seemed to read it in Sean's face: *Not another fucking library.*

"I can go in," she said. "You stay here since he won't recognize me."

"No, I'll be fine."

A sign at the entrance of the library bragged that it housed the world's largest collection of Shakespeare materials and rare Renaissance books. As they entered the Reading Room, Sean regretted coming inside. Like the Supreme Court's library, the space was all carved mahogany, long wooden tables, and chandeliers under a gilded ceiling. It was smaller than the high court's library, but it had the same feel. They looked about and didn't see Mole Face, or anyone for that matter. No employees, nobody. Sean assumed that, tucked away in an isolated part of the Hill, the library wasn't on many tourist agendas. He and Emily climbed the steps to a second-floor balcony that overlooked the Reading Room.

They were about to leave when Emily stopped in place, head tilted to the side, listening. From the far corner of the library, below them, whispers. She padded softly toward the sound, Sean at her heels. They stopped just above the hushed voices. The people talking—it sounded like two men—were concealed under the balcony, surrounded by old books. And then they came into view.

Sean and Emily crouched, hoping they wouldn't be spotted. A man, whose back was turned, was poking his finger at Mole Face. The man's whispers grew louder and more heated, and Mole Face seemed to be enjoying it. The man finally let out a disgusted sound and stormed off.

Emily grabbed Sean's hand and pulled him away from the edge of the balcony so their backs were pressed against the wall, just out of view of anyone on the first floor. They watched as the unknown man stalked out of the library. It was then Sean noticed it.

Emily started to head for the stairs to follow the man, but Sean grabbed her arm.

"We need to see who that was," Emily whispered.

Sean shook his head. He didn't need to see the man's face. His limp—an injury sustained on the field at Notre Dame—gave him away.

CHAPTER 64

They held back several minutes, but still managed to catch up to Mole Face and track him back to Dupont Circle. By then, it was late afternoon and Mole Face went to a bar just off the circle. He spoke with a couple of guys at the door. The men were holding hands, hardly an unusual sight in Dupont. From the distance it was unclear if he was friends with them or just making small talk.

"This is where he went every day I followed him," Emily said.

So, Mole Face met with Supreme Court justice Thaddeus Carr. What was *that* about? And who were the recipients of the envelopes Mole Face had delivered? The senator and Mole Face were clearly engaged in dirty tricks. But what could that mean for Ryan? How did it change anything? The senator still had the photos and steel rod.

"I suppose we can try to run the Range Rover's plates. And maybe we can find out who lives at the places where he made the drops," Sean said.

Emily said, "I told you, I already Googled the addresses. I couldn't find—"

"I know someone with much better Internet skills than either of us."

"Who? Jonathan?"

"No, not Jon." Jonathan Tweed was proficient enough that he

could probably figure this stuff out. But Sean wanted to keep him out of this since he was on the vetting team for the senator. Not to mention, Tweed would think that Sean and Em had lost their shit.

"Then who?" Emily asked. She kept her eyes fixed on Mole Face, who disappeared into the bar.

Sean put the phone to his ear.

"Hey, Dad," Ryan answered. "What's up? Do you know where Mom is? She's not home and we're getting hungry and—"

"Mom's with me. We're running late. How about you order a pizza? You can take money from the jar in the kitchen."

"Okay," his son said. He heard Ryan tell Jack about the pizza, which was followed by a "Yes!"

"We hoped you could help us with something," Sean said.

"Sure."

"We need you to do some research for us on the Internet."

There was a long silence on the other end of the phone. "On the computer, by myself?"

"Yes, can you do that?"

"Sure," Ryan replied, with pride in his voice. "What do you need?"

Sean explained. Try to find who owned the Range Rover and who lived at two addresses. He gave Ryan the information.

"No problem," Ryan said. "But Dad . . ."

"Yeah?"

"I need the password. My iPod needs Wi-Fi, and I'm locked out of the computers . . ."

"Sorry, of course. Our password is T-R-U-S-T, trust," he said.

"Aw, come on!" Ryan said, a playful lilt in his voice. Sean felt a warmth fall over him. He hadn't heard Ryan sound like himself since his son's encounter with the detective running the Billy Brice murder investigation.

"Thanks for your help, buddy. You and Jack eat, and we'll be home soon." Sean clicked off.

"So what now?" Sean said to Emily. "We just wait until he comes out of the bar?"

"Actually," Emily said, "I had another idea."

CHAPTER 65

They lingered in the softly lit hallway of the condo building. It hadn't been hard to get in—no doorman, so they just waited for a tenant to exit the lobby doors. The man leaving even held the door for the well-dressed woman with a beautiful smile.

The line of mailboxes at the entrance were labeled. S. FINKLE was in unit 1015. Next thing, Sean found himself outside Mole Face's door. He watched, speechless, as Emily pulled a thin sheath of metal from her purse. She stuck one end in the door's lock, wiggled it around, and the door clicked open. She looked at Sean, seeming surprised herself that the apparatus worked.

"Internet," she explained.

How long had she been planning this? She'd spent the past few days secretly following this man, and, given that she'd acquired burglar tools, she'd obviously planned on breaking in. They were in felony territory. What the hell were they doing?

"This is crazy," he whispered. His eyes darted about the hallway. It was late in the day and people would be coming home from work soon. He then scanned the ceiling, looking for security cameras but saw none.

"The file on Ryan is in there, Sean. We need to do this."

"We don't need to *do* anything. We have a deal with Mason

James—we just need to stay out of his business, and he'll stay out of ours." A deal with the Devil.

"You made that deal, not me," she said. And Sean understood there would be no stopping her. She wanted the file on their son. She'd gone from immobilized over Abby's death to irrationally fixated on protecting Ryan and getting to the truth about Mason James. But who was Sean to judge? He'd acted pretty irrationally himself. And his actions had led to Billy Brice's death. But he couldn't let Emily go into the condo. Their kids needed at least one parent who wasn't at risk for prosecution.

"Fine," Sean said, "but you're not going in—I am. You go out front and keep watch. Call my phone now, and we'll keep an open line. You can warn me if Finkle leaves the bar." The situation had become far too serious to use a ridiculous nickname.

Emily looked hard at Sean but didn't argue. She dug into her handbag for her phone, dialed Sean's number, and confirmed he could hear her on his end. The elevator down the hall dinged.

"Go," Sean said, in a loud whisper. "Keep the line open and you tell me if you see him." Sean slipped into the condo, praying that the person leaving the elevator wasn't Sebastian Finkle.

CHAPTER 66

Sean ducked into a coat closet near the door, his phone pressed hard to his ear. No beeping alarm system, which was a relief, but he heard voices in the hallway.

Emily's voice whispered in his ear. "Coast clear. It wasn't him on the elevator."

Sean let out an audible breath. "Okay, keep an eye on the front and tell me if you see him."

He opened the closet door and scanned the condo. It had large windows that ran from floor to ceiling, the view overlooking Dupont Circle. The place was sparsely furnished, minimalist—straight lines, glass tables, postmodern art on the walls. He began his search, phone at his ear waiting for Emily to warn him to flee. Where would a J. Edgar Hoover wannabe hide his dirt files? He decided to start somewhere private—somewhere most guests wouldn't venture. The bedroom.

He wandered down the hall and into a spacious bedroom, which featured a king-sized bed with a plush backboard built into the wall. It was a clutter-free space, all sleek and no warmth. Inside the walk-in closet were several suits, expensive, neatly aligned. There were boxed shirts and rows of shoes, all appearing freshly shined. All designer stuff. Finkle was quite the clotheshorse.

And then he saw it. At the back of the closet, built into the wall. A safe. It was about two feet square with a digital keypad.

"Unless you also learned how to crack a safe on the Internet," Sean said into the phone, "we have a problem."

When Emily didn't respond, he said, "Em? You there?"

"Get out, Sean!" There was a panic in the whisper. *"He's coming!"*

Sean darted from the bedroom. *Stay calm.* It had taken them several minutes to get from the lobby to the tenth floor. He had plenty of time. He was about to open the front door when he heard the jingle of keys and a rattle from the lock.

He slid into the coat closet again, pulled the door closed leaving a crack, and held his breath. The condo door opened, then shut, and someone shuffled about. Sweat poured from Sean's forehead, dripping into his eyes. He put a hand on his leg to prevent it from jack-hammering.

From the crack in the door he watched as the person paced into the living room. The man's back was turned, but he was dressed in a suit, not Finkle's ball cap and jeans.

Emily's voice pierced the silence: "Sean . . . are you there? . . . Sean?" Her voice reverberated through the stillness, but the man didn't seem to hear it. Sean disconnected the line with a click of his thumb. He risked another peek. The man turned toward the closet and threw his suit jacket across the leather couch. Sean got a clear view of him.

Senator Mason James.

The senator went to a drink cart that was filled with thin bottles and shiny metallic bartender tools. He poured himself two fingers. Sean heard the door open again. Someone else was in the condo, but the visitor was out of his line of sight.

Senator James looked toward the door. "Hey there."

"Hey. You got in okay without anyone seeing you?"

"No problems," the senator said. "Ditched the security guys and came into the building from the back entrance."

Sebastian Finkle walked into Sean's field of vision from the crack in the closet door.

"How'd it go today?" the senator asked.

"Not bad. Got the final package delivered."

"You were careful?"

"Of course. The staff still thinks I'm visiting with my father at the nursing home in the afternoons, so no one has seemed to miss me. Airtight alibi for visiting hours."

That explained Finkle's routine of leaving the office every day at the same time.

James continued. "No violence this time, I trust? We can't have another—"

"Don't worry," Finkle said, "nothing happened."

"And Justice Carr?"

"You were right. He actually showed up. He was *pissed*. Said I could go fuck myself."

Senator James smirked. "He'll come around. They always do. But if not, we don't really need him."

"Yeah, I wondered about that. The others I can understand, but not sure how Carr can help with your nomination."

"It always helps to have support from someone inside the building," the senator said. He took a pull from his drink and studied the glass. "But with Carr, I'm really thinking more of the long game. I wanted to send a message that, when I am confirmed and we're on the bench together, he'll be my bitch."

Finkle let out a dry laugh and clinked glasses with James.

And then something unexpected happened. Senator James and Finkle kissed passionately.

CHAPTER 67

In the smothering air of the closet, Sean's mind raced. Senator Mason James was gay. Married to a woman and gay. The cheating alone could derail his nomination to the Supreme Court. Sean watched as James and Finkle began to undress one another.

Sean realized that a photo of James and Finkle could be valuable. He could make a trade—evidence of the senator's affair for the evidence against Ryan. A secret for a secret. Sean slowly raised his phone and toggled his thumb to the camera app. Was he really going to stoop to this? In the cramped closet it was hard to position the phone to get a visible shot of the men who were now breathing loudly and clawing at one another on the couch. Sean held in a breath and tapped a button on the phone. He hadn't expected the flash or the loud click.

Finkle's head snapped up. His eyes widened, and he pounced over the couch toward the closet. Sean burst out and scrambled for the door.

"Stop!" Finkle yelled as Sean darted out of the condo.

Without looking back, Sean ran with everything he had down the hallway. He thumbed the elevator button rapid-fire. He twisted around and saw Finkle, shirtless, muscles pulsing, bearing down.

Sean sprinted to the emergency stairway and ran full-throttle, skipping steps. He heard the screech of sneakers racing after him

echoing above. He stumbled, nearly nose-diving down the concrete stairwell. If Finkle didn't kill him, the fall damn well might. On
the ground floor, Sean stole a quick look up the stairwell. He and
Finkle locked eyes. Sean pushed through the emergency door
and ran through the lobby and outside. He saw Emily standing
across the street and he caught her eye. He shook his head and
mouthed *Go*. He then raced in the other direction.

CHAPTER 68

Sean had eluded Finkle, assuming the man had even followed him out of the building. He called Emily and they met up at the Friendship Heights Metro station where they caught a cab home.

Ryan was waiting for them at the door. He was pacing about the entryway. "I found them. I found everything you needed." He held a messy stack of papers in his hand.

Sean squeezed him on the shoulder. "Nice work." Sean tried to sound enthusiastic, but he was coming down from the adrenaline rush fueled by his turn as a breaking-and-entering artist and voyeur. His quest to secure hard evidence against the senator had failed. The image he'd snapped was of two blurry masses. On the bright side, James didn't know that. And, photo or not, Sean knew James's secret.

It was good to have some possible leverage against Senator James, but beyond that Sean and Emily weren't sure what this meant about Abby's death. Until then, Emily's working theory had been that James raped and murdered Natalie Carlisle, John Chadwick had taken the fall, and Abby was a threat to James because she could expose the truth. They had no evidence that James or Finkle had killed Abby, but that day in the hideaway office James had confirmed that they'd at least been following Abby and had warned her to back off. And there were those missing girls from

James's past. But his relationship with Sebastian Finkle changed everything.

Sean thought of his meeting with John Chadwick at the prison. The man was certain that the senator had nothing to do with Natalie's death. *Trust me, Mason James is the last person in the world who'd rape and kill Natalie.* Did Chadwick know James was gay? Chadwick wasn't smirking when he'd said it, but looking back, there was a wink to his tone. Was that all this was about—James trying to hide his sexual orientation? Was that why he'd had Finkle follow and then threaten Abby? Was that why he'd been following Sean the night Brice died?

Ryan flattened a sheet of paper on the kitchen counter. Sean couldn't make the kid wait any longer. "So what'd you find?"

Ryan displayed a handwritten list. "These are the owners of the houses for the addresses you gave me." There were two names written in Ryan's messy scrawl. "And here's the owner of the Range Rover. That took longer to find."

Sean read the names. They were familiar, but he couldn't quite place them. Emily looked at them and her brow furrowed.

Then Ryan revealed another sheet of paper from behind his back. His eyes glimmered with pride. "And here's how they're all connected."

He handed Sean a printout from a website. The header read UNITED STATES SENATE COMMITTEE ON THE JUDICIARY—the committee that voted on Supreme Court nominees. Under the header was a list of names, the eighteen members of the committee. Three names were highlighted in yellow marker. Sebastian Finkle had delivered the envelopes to members of the Senate Judiciary Committee.

Ryan smoothed out another sheet of paper on the counter. A news story with the headline THE FOUR HORSEMEN: THE BIPARTISAN OPPOSITION TO THE NOMINATION OF MASON JAMES.

"I ran a search of all their names together and found this story. These three and one other senator announced that they would likely vote against Senator James's nomination to the Supreme Court."

"Great work, buddy," Sean said.

"What's it all mean?" Ryan asked.

That was a good question. It was evident that James was blackmailing the hostile senators on the Judiciary Committee to prevent them from voting against his nomination. And he obviously had something on Justice Carr, whom he appeared to be blackmailing into supporting the nomination.

But all Sean worried about was what it meant for Ryan. What could Sean and Emily do with this information?

The answer came in the form of an e-mail delivered to Sean just before midnight. The e-mail did not show the name of the sender, and it deleted itself from the computer two minutes after Sean had opened it.

Mutual assured destruction.

CHAPTER 69

A week after the break-in at Sebastian Finkle's condo, Sean sat in a conference room in the U.S. Attorney's Office. On the battle-worn table—marred by scratches and stains from years of trial preparation—was a stack of legal pads and a pencil holder filled with sharp no. 2s. The walls, tired and off-white, were bare except for the Justice Department seal, an eagle clutching a quiver of arrows in its claws. Under the bird, a motto written in Latin. Abby could read Latin, but not Sean. He couldn't escape the constant reminders of her that were everywhere.

A black woman, short with thin eyebrows, strode into the room. Behind her, an older man, hound-dog face and thinning hair, and two wide-eyed women in their twenties.

"Sean, so glad you could make it," said Patti Fallon, the lead prosecutor.

After introductions to her team and small talk, Fallon said, "The hearing tomorrow should be pretty short." She was sitting next to Sean, her hands folded on the table. "You probably already know all this, but just so everyone is on the same page, I thought I'd walk you through what will happen."

Sean nodded.

"Malik Montgomery has moved to suppress evidence concerning your visit to his home that night. He's trying to get the court to exclude from the trial that your daughter's phone was hidden in his house. Most important for our purposes, he says that since that search was illegal, everything else that followed should be excluded from evidence."

"Fruit of the poisonous tree?" Sean asked. That was first-year law student territory.

"That's right. So, he's not just trying to exclude Abby's phone, but everything he said to you and Deputy Director Pacini—*and* the surveillance video at the Supreme Court. He argues all of it should be thrown out."

"You can't be serious?" Sean said. "I searched the house, not Frank, and I'm not with the government so what's his basis for exclusion? The Fourth Amendment doesn't apply to searches by private parties. Also, as for Malik's statements, Frank Mirandized him before he talked to us, so those can't possibly be thrown out, can they?"

Fallon gave a satisfied smile. "I'm glad to hear you say all that. Those will be my key arguments. The problem is that it was an unusual situation. Frank was there that night as a friend, but he's still an FBI official. The line between friend and government agent also got a little blurry as the night went on. Blake Hellstrom will argue that Frank's presence alone rendered the whole thing a government search. So the critical question could become consent: whether Malik Montgomery consented to the search. If he consented, it doesn't matter if it was a government or private search."

Sean said, "This shouldn't be a problem. It's hazy, but I remember Malik saying he wanted to help and he let us in. He consented."

Fallon smiled again and scribbled something on a legal pad. She explained that the hearing shouldn't last more than an hour or two. She would call Frank Pacini and Sean as her only witnesses. She wasn't sure who Blake Hellstrom would call as witnesses—the judge didn't require each side to exchange witness lists for hearings on pretrial motions.

"He wouldn't call Malik as a witness, would he?" Sean asked.

"He might."

"Isn't that risky? Aren't criminal lawyers usually loath to put their clients on the stand?"

"Suppression hearings are different, so Hellstrom may take the risk. The law in D.C. is good for him on that. Nothing Malik says at a suppression hearing can be used against him at the trial. Also, Judge Chin will keep me on a short leash on cross. She won't let me get anywhere near the merits of the case or allow me to try to pin him down on the facts."

Sean took a deep breath. "Look, the evidence should stay in, but I need to ask you something."

Fallon lifted her gaze from the legal pad.

"Are you sure Malik Montgomery killed my daughter?" Sean asked. "I mean *really* sure?"

Fallon's eyes flashed. She put down her pen. "I wouldn't be prosecuting him if I didn't believe he did it, Sean. I don't understand the—"

"Have you looked at other suspects?"

"I believe the agents looked at all angles, yes."

"You *believe*."

At this, Fallon exhaled heavily. Her colleague picked imaginary lint from his shirt. A moment passed and Fallon said, "Malik Montgomery was the last person seen with your daughter alive. She broke up with him and witnesses saw them arguing right before she was murdered. Her telephone was found in his home. He lied about being at the court that night. And he had access to erase the court's surveillance recordings."

"But there's no physical evidence," Sean said. "And no witnesses."

Fallon took a sip of her Diet Coke. She considered her words. "It's rare that a prosecution has everything. You know that it's not like television, and, without a confession, most murderers would walk. Here we have a sophisticated perp who won't confess, so we have to go where the evidence leads. And it leads only one place: Malik Montgomery."

"Like I said on our call, it just doesn't make sense how someone so smart would be dumb enough to leave Abby's phone at his house and turned on so it could be traced. Or how he would erase the video *except* for parts incriminating himself."

"My experience has been that even smart people do incredibly stupid things in the stress of covering up their crimes." It was a fair but unsatisfying answer.

"Did you look into my daughter's e-mail account?"

Fallon's lips tightened. "We're looking into it, Sean. But one step at a time. And you're forgetting we have other evidence. Today we need to focus on the motion to suppress . . ."

"What other evidence?"

Fallon let out a breath. "Like that Abby visited the Supreme Court Police office the day she was killed. She reported that a law clerk had threatened her and she wanted to know what could be done about it without ruining his career. We have a police report showing she was there that afternoon."

This knocked Sean back in his seat. That night at the Supreme Court when they searched for Abby the chief of the court's police hadn't mentioned this. He probably didn't know. Some low-level officer probably interviewed Abby and the report wasn't taken seriously until *after* she was killed.

"That's pretty damn important. Why hadn't someone told me this sooner?"

Fallon put her hand on Sean's arm. In a soft voice, she said, "I know this is terrible. I cannot imagine what you're going through. But Sean, Malik Montgomery murdered your daughter. Can we count on your help tomorrow?"

Sean hesitated, then nodded. The group made their stiff goodbyes. As he left, Sean noticed Fallon and her hound-faced colleague meet eyes. They were concerned.

In the hallway, he saw Carl Martinez, the chief of the Supreme Court Police. He was probably there about the hearing as well. Sean felt a surge of anger that the court's police could've possibly prevented Abby's murder.

"Sean," the chief said, walking over. "It's good to see you. How are you holding up?"

Sean gave a *been better* tilt of the head. His jaw tightened as he debated whether to bring up Abby's report to the Supreme Court Police.

The chief said, "It's hard not to lose your faith in everything when you lose a child. When someone takes them from you." There was something about the chief's tone, the look in his eyes. There was a knowing melancholy to it.

"You know?" Sean heard himself ask. He wasn't one to seek comfort in others and had shut down even the thought of attending a parent support group. But at this moment, he wanted to speak with someone who knew. Someone who may have the answers on how to survive the *After*.

The chief studied Sean. "Hit-and-run," he said after a long moment.

"Does it ever get better?" Sean asked.

The chief took in a deep breath and let it out slowly.

Patti Fallon, who must have heard them talking, stepped into the hallway. "We're ready for you, Carlos . . ."

"I'll be just a second," he said.

Fallon hesitated, but ducked back into the room.

The police chief contemplated Sean's question another couple of seconds. "The only thing that helped me was getting the son of a bitch who did it." The chief then looked deep into Sean's eyes and said, "And, you can trust me on one thing: tomorrow we're gonna get the bastard who killed your daughter."

The chief then did something unsettling. Something that explained why he hadn't mentioned Abby coming to the police office to complain about a law clerk. Something that explained how this new piece of highly incriminating evidence against Malik suddenly surfaced. The chief looked Sean in the eyes. And he winked.

CHAPTER 70

Another sleepless night and another crying jag in the shower. It was now close to nine a.m. and Sean gazed out of the cab's window. The E. Barrett Prettyman Federal Courthouse was crowded with television reporters holding microphones and burly men with heavy cameras balanced on their shoulders. The front of the blocky gray building also was lined with protesters. Some held signs while others chanted—*"Free Ma-lik Mont-gom-ery! Free Ma-lik Mont-gom-ery!"*—in the fresh air of the spring morning. A handful of U.S. marshals kept watch.

As Sean and Emily climbed out of the cab, everyone on the plaza seemed to descend on them at once. Sean put his arm around Emily to shield her from the onslaught, but she wriggled her shoulders away. She reached for Sean's hand and led him toward the entrance, moving resolutely through the crowd and camera flashes, ignoring the aggressive questions shouted at them. Halfway to the entrance they were met by Cecilia. She pushed them through the reporters and into the courthouse.

They journeyed through the metal detectors, to the elevators, and through the doors of Courtroom 4. Cecilia took them to their reserved spots in the front row of the gallery. Sean peered over his shoulder. Every seat was filled. He saw familiar faces from both the Supreme Court press corps and the national morning shows.

A court officer walked the center aisle shushing, but the place was abuzz. Sean faced the bench and watched as the court reporter adjusted her equipment and a law clerk nervously shuffled some papers. Patti Fallon sat in front of Sean and Emily at the prosecution table, her hands folded. Calm. Poised.

Sean always admired trial lawyers, the soldiers on the front line. They dealt with real people—people who had something to lose, whether it be their money, their kids, their freedom. In his entire career he'd never participated in a trial. He'd read a lot of trial transcripts, the bloodless record on appeal. But his search was not for the truth. An appellate lawyer's search is for legal errors made along the way. And were there ever errors. Real trial work isn't pretty. But most mistakes and shortcuts aren't enough to reverse a judge or jury's decision. And by the time a case made its way to the Supreme Court, it was in a pretty little package—after years working through the meat grinder of the system, everything usually boiled down to a single legal issue. Sean's job wasn't to stoke the passions of twelve jurors in the heat of trial, but rather to convince nine smart people through a civilized ritual of briefing and thirty minutes of oral argument.

Fallon occupied the space like she owned it. Sean and Emily were there as props for the media. Fallon had called the night before to say she didn't need Sean as a witness. She didn't say why, but perhaps Sean's questions had spooked her.

The gallery grew quiet, and Sean turned to see what had captured the room's attention. Blake Hellstrom walked down the aisle in his scuffed shoes. His left hand clutched a worn barrister's bag, his right a soft guide on his client's back. Malik Montgomery, dressed in a conservative suit and tie, looked younger than Sean remembered him. Hellstrom and Malik strolled through the swinging gate and took their station at the defense table. Malik's father, a handsome man in his sixties in a gray business suit, moved to a seat in the gallery behind his son. Hellstrom approached Patti Fallon and they shook hands. Fallon did not look intimidated, though the lawyers on her team each seemed to swallow hard at the sight of Hellstrom.

A loud chime echoed from the ceiling and everyone stood as the Honorable Mara Chin entered the courtroom. As she took her seat behind the bench, she waved for the lawyers and gallery to follow suit. Emily squeezed Sean's hand, and he pushed himself closer to her on the uncomfortable wooden pew seats in the gallery. Sean had read about Judge Chin in the *Almanac of the Federal Judiciary,* which contained her bio and anonymous comments from lawyers who appeared regularly before her. Chin was in her late fifties, an Obama appointee, liberal-leaning, no bullshit. The consensus: tough but fair.

Judge Chin had dark hair that touched her shoulders and deep smile lines. Her gaze cut to the lawyers and she began.

"Good morning. The court will hear case number 1-2-2-9-9-8, *United States versus Montgomery.* Before the court is defendant's motion to suppress evidence. Counsel, please make your appearances."

Fallon stood. A clear of the throat, then from the diaphragm: "Your Honor, I'm Patricia Fallon and I represent the people."

Blake Hellstrom rose slowly, his chair scraping against the courtroom floor. No straightening of the tie, no preening. He held a slight smile as did the judge, as if they were old friends pretending to act formally. "I'm Blake Hellstrom, Your Honor." Hellstrom looked toward Fallon and added, "I also represent the people—just one at a time."

Laughter filled the gallery. The old lawyer had effortlessly broke the tension in the room. The judge gave an exasperated shake of the head.

"All right, all right," the judge said, giving the room a chance to quiet. "Any opening remarks before we begin, Mr. Hellstrom?"

Hellstrom stroked his chin. "Your Honor, I will keep it short. My client is innocent. The government has no witnesses connecting Mr. Montgomery to this terrible crime. No murder weapon. No DNA or other physical evidence. What they have is a rush to judgment driven by factors that should have no bearing in a court of law. What's—"

"Your Honor," Fallon said, already on her feet. "Mr. Hellstrom is improperly arguing the merits. We're here *today* to hear his motion to suppress evidence—a curious motion given that he's so confident in the supposed *lack* of evidence."

Judge Chin swatted away the bickering with a wave of her hand. "Mr. Hellstrom, save it. The same goes for the government."

Hellstrom flicked an admiring glance at Fallon. "Your Honor, the government has the burden of showing its search did not violate the Fourth Amendment, so I will defer further remarks until we've had the opportunity to hear from *the people*."

The judge looked toward Fallon, who offered a small roll of the eyes, but nodded.

"The government calls Franklin Pacini."

As Pacini took the stand and was sworn in, Sean noticed Hellstrom sneak a glance in Sean's direction. Hellstrom whispered something to Malik Montgomery, who nodded, and both turned back to Pacini. Fallon had warned that Hellstrom may request that Sean be sequestered while Pacini was testifying, a common procedure to avoid one witness from influencing the testimony of another. But Hellstrom, who didn't know if Sean would take the stand, apparently decided against it. Why?

Sean listened as Patti Fallon walked Pacini through that night. From Sean's call, to Abby's apartment, to Malik's place where they found the phone. Emily sniffled and Sean wondered if they both would have been better off sequestered. Fallon skillfully led Pacini down a path to establish two things. First, he was there that night as a friend, not as a government agent, which was important because Fallon argued that the Fourth Amendment did not apply to private searches. Second, that Malik had consented to the search of his home, which again precluded any finding of an illegal search. Fallon then turned to Malik's statements to Pacini and Sean.

"At some point during the night did your role change?"

"I'm not sure what you mean."

"I mean you started off helping out just as a friend, but at some point did you put your FBI hat on?"

"Yes, after Sean found the phone hidden in the defendant's house."

"And what did you do?"

"I interviewed the defendant."

"Did you read the defendant his Miranda rights before asking him questions?" Fallon asked.

"Yes. I remember because the defendant got angry about it. He said, 'I'm not like the poor dumb black kids you're used to dealing with,' and that he had nothing to hide."

A rumble filled the spectator section and the judge gave a glare that spanned the room.

"Did you ask the defendant when he'd last seen Abby?"

"Yes, he said they'd had a fight at dinner and Abby stormed out of the restaurant. He said he went after her and gave her a ride to the Supreme Court, where she liked to study. He said the last time he saw her was when he dropped her off at the curb in front of the building."

"What happened after you spoke to the defendant?"

"Some agents came to speak with him, and Mr. Serrat and I headed over to the Supreme Court."

"You thought Abby would still be at the court a day later?"

"No. But I thought it would be helpful to speak to officers from the court's police department and see if security camera footage showed Abby in the building."

"And you went to the court?"

"Yes."

"Did the officers show you any security footage?"

"Yes, footage showed Abby Serrat entering the court and walking to the library. There's no cameras in the library, so we couldn't see inside, just that she walked there."

"Was she alone?"

"At first, yes."

"You said that the defendant told you he didn't go inside the court that night, correct?"

"That's what he told us at his house. He said he dropped her off at the curb and that he went home."

"Did you see anything else on the surveillance footage?"

"About ten minutes after Ms. Serrat arrived at the court, the defendant entered the building."

"So, he'd lied to you?"

"Yes."

Sean looked over at Hellstrom expecting an objection, but Hellstrom just sat at counsel's table and gave an audible yawn.

"And you went to the library?"

"Yes."

Fallon waited a long beat before the next question. "And what happened in the library?"

The courtroom was still. Not a sound.

"We found Abby Serrat." Pacini let out a long sigh. "Her body was shoved into a bookshelf. Her face was covered in blood. It was obvious"—Pacini paused a moment—"she was gone. Mr. Serrat fought past the court's officers to get to his daughter. We had to subdue him until he collapsed from shock."

Fallon let the image hang there. Sean wasn't sure how long, but it seemed like forever.

"Nothing further."

CHAPTER 71

Blake Hellstrom took his time. He stood slowly, buttoned his jacket, and gave Frank Pacini an extended glare. "Deputy Director Pacini, how long have you been in the FBI?"

"Twenty-five years." If the goal was to downplay Pacini's role as a federal agent, he wasn't doing the prosecution any favors. He wore a crisp white shirt, spoke in clipped agent-speak, and sat up straight—he looked every bit the quintessential G-Man.

"And when Mr. Serrat phoned you that night, he called you because of your law enforcement expertise, not because you two were such good friends, right?"

"I'd say a little of both. We were certainly friendly, and our daughters were friends. He didn't know what to do."

"You went to his daughter's apartment in the middle of the night?"

"Correct."

"And when you got there, what did you find?"

"Someone had broken in. The place had been torn up pretty good."

"Were you concerned for Ms. Serrat at that point?"

"When Mr. Serrat first called, I thought he might be overreacting. Girls in their twenties sometimes go away for a weekend and don't tell their parents. But the apartment changed things for me."

"And you called in some agents?"

"Yes."

"And you had Abby's phone tracked?"

"Yes."

"So, even before you ever got to my client's home you were acting like an agent, isn't that right, Deputy Director?"

"I already said, I went as a friend."

"Is it typical when you go on a social visit with friends to call for backup?"

A titter from the gallery. A glare from the judge. Hellstrom didn't wait for a response. "When you arrived at my client's home did you tell him you were with the FBI?"

"I don't remember, maybe."

"So, you've called in your men and had them processing Ms. Serrat's apartment like a crime scene, you had the government trace her phone, yet when you arrived at Mr. Montgomery's home for the search you somehow didn't have your government hat on? Is that your position?"

Fallon started to stand, but the judge darted her a look.

Pacini didn't flinch. "I'm not a lawyer. But I'm telling you what was in my mind, and I was there as a friend. And it wouldn't have mattered either way, since your client gave us clear consent for the search."

"Says you, Deputy Director, says you."

No reaction from Pacini.

"Tell me, did the FBI ever connect my client to the break-in at Ms. Serrat's home?"

"No."

"Has the FBI looked for *any* suspects in Ms. Serrat's murder other than Malik?"

Sean and Emily leaned in at this, but Fallon stood ready to object.

Before Fallon got out a word, Judge Chin said, "Not the time or place, Mr. Hellstrom, move on."

"About the phone that was found in Mr. Montgomery's home," Hellstrom said. "Are you aware that all the data was wiped from the phone?"

"Yes."

"Wouldn't it require some computer expertise to wipe a phone that way?"

"I'm not assigned to the investigation, but, based on my general understanding, I assume it would require some experience with software. But that's hardly uncommon with the younger generation, and the Internet has instructions available."

Hellstrom paused. He seemed to be debating whether to ask his next question. "You say you gave Mr. Montgomery his Miranda rights before speaking to him, is that right?"

"Yes, I did. I distinctly remember because he was insulted by it."

"It's routine to have suspects sign a Miranda waiver before questioning them, isn't it? The FBI even uses a standardized form, right?"

"This wasn't a planned interview, and I—"

"It's routine to have a form signed before an interview, correct?"

"Yes."

"And there's no signed form here, correct?"

"That's right, but as I said—"

"You mentioned the camera footage at the Supreme Court," Hellstrom interrupted.

"Yes."

"It showed Malik entering the building?"

"Yes."

"What did it show after he entered the building?"

Pacini paused. He looked at Hellstrom and said, "It didn't show anything. The rest of the footage went blank."

"Blank? What do you mean?"

"I mean the screen went blank. I understand they believe someone erased it." Pacini looked toward Malik Montgomery as he said the last part.

Hellstrom slowly turned his head following the imaginary dotted line from Pacini's eyes to his client. "So, Malik Montgomery, a Georgetown Law graduate, a Rhodes Scholar, a Supreme Court law clerk, had the wherewithal to sneak into the Supreme Court police station, somehow access the video recording of the night Abby Serrat was murdered, and erase the video, yet he somehow deleted everything *except* the footage incriminating himself? He took Abby Serrat's phone, wiped it clean, yet was foolish enough to hide the phone in his own home and leave the device on so it could be traced there? Is that what you think?"

They were similar to the points Hellstrom had made the day he visited Sean's office—questions that had rattled around in Sean's head since.

Before Pacini could answer the question, Hellstrom turned to the spectators in the courtroom and said, "I'm done with this witness."

CHAPTER 72

After some whispering between Fallon and her colleagues, she informed the judge that the prosecution had no further witnesses. She must have assumed that the word of a respected FBI official was enough. And it probably was. It was unlikely the judge would throw out key evidence in a high-profile case absent compelling proof of government misconduct. So, with that, Judge Chin turned it over to Blake Hellstrom, who called Malik Montgomery to the stand, causing the spectator section to stir.

Malik was a handsome kid, which was always good for a defendant. An accused taking the stand, usually not so good. But Patti Fallon had correctly predicted that Hellstrom might take the risk. Sean turned and looked at the gallery and realized that Malik's testimony had nothing to do with suppressing evidence. Sure, Hellstrom wanted the phone, Malik's statements, and the surveillance video thrown out of the case. But eyeing the reporters taking notes, Sean understood that Malik's testimony wasn't about this motion at all. It was about the court of public opinion, adding fuel to the racial controversy over the prosecution.

Blake Hellstrom's suit jacket was tight over his belly and with a thumb and index finger he released the button. He stepped close to the witness box and gave his client a sympathetic nod. A fatherly gesture. "Malik, I want to ask you some questions about what happened the night the FBI and Mr. Serrat searched your home. But first, I have to ask: Did you murder Abby Serrat?"

Fallon stood, but before she got out a word, Malik definitively said, "No. I am one hundred percent innocent."

"Your Honor," Fallon said, a plea in her voice.

Judge Chin shot Hellstrom a look over the top of her glasses. "Don't try my patience, Mr. Hellstrom."

Hellstrom nodded, but his eyes didn't stray from his client. "Let's start with the search, tell the judge what happened."

Malik swallowed and turned his head slightly toward the judge, a doe-eyed gaze at Her Honor. He told her about his visitors in the middle of the night, that Pacini had shown his FBI badge, that Malik hadn't consented to the search.

"I felt compelled to let them in. I was kind of in shock and basically I just followed them around as they went room to room searching the place. I didn't want to be accused of obstruction of justice, so I just stayed out of the way."

Hellstrom nodded and started to ask his next question when Malik interrupted. "Besides, I had nothing to hide. I wanted to help." For the first time during the hearing, Sean thought Hellstrom's expression gave something away. Disapproval. His lips pressed tightly together and his eyes flashed for the briefest of moments. Malik had gone off script.

Hellstrom marched on. "And Mr. Serrat found his daughter's cell phone in your home?"

"Yes. Stuffed under a mattress in my spare bedroom. I told him that I had no idea how it got there."

"So, how do you think it got there?"

"Someone must have plant—"

"Your Honor," Patti Fallon spat. "This is beyond inappropriate, and Mr. Hellstrom knows it. He has no evidence that the phone was planted. And his motion doesn't argue the evidence was planted."

The judge pulled off her glasses and pinched the bridge of her nose. "Last warning, Mr. Hellstrom. One more time and . . ." she finished the thought with a hard look.

Hellstrom gave a quizzical expression as if he'd played no role in Malik's suggestion of evidence tampering. "I apologize, Your Honor. And let me say, we're not suggesting that the Deputy Director or Mr. Serrat planted the telephone." A pause. "We're suggesting the real killer did."

"*Your Honor!*" Fallon bellowed.

Before the judge could react, Hellstrom said, "I'll move on, Your Honor." He turned back to Malik. "After they found the phone, what happened?"

"Mr. Serrat got really upset. He pushed me against the wall and started threatening me. I said I hadn't seen Abby since the night before. Then the Deputy Director started questioning me."

"Did the Deputy Director read you your Miranda rights?"

"No."

A blatant lie. Sean couldn't help but shake his head.

Malik continued, "You have to understand, this was crazy. I had Sean Serrat, a legend in the Supreme Court Bar, getting physical with me and the Deputy Director of the FBI suggesting I did something to Abby. My head was spinning."

"What happened next?"

"Some other agents came to my house, and Mr. Serrat and the Deputy Director left. The agents took me to the FBI's field office for questioning. They kept me there all night."

"Did you agree to the questioning?"

"I went with them, if that's what you mean. I didn't feel like I had a choice."

"You heard Deputy Director Pacini mention that the video from the Supreme Court had been tampered with?"

Fallon broke in: "Your Honor, defendant's motion seeks to exclude the recording based on Fourth Amendment violations that allegedly took place at his home. Defendant's views about the tape itself are irrelevant."

Blake Hellstrom furrowed his brow. "Your Honor, it's true that we are claiming that the tape is a fruit of the poisonous tree. But the recording, as the government's own witness acknowledged, was altered. They seemed to suggest it was altered by my client, so

I think the court would benefit from hearing from him on this point."

"Overruled."

Hellstrom continued, "Did you alter the Supreme Court's surveillance video?"

"Of course not. I've never even been to the police office and certainly wouldn't have any idea how to delete something from their system."

"Do you know anyone else who had access to the building that night?"

"The Supreme Court building was filled with people the night Abby was killed. There was a reception for the Rex Lee awards."

"Could anyone else have access to the police office?"

"The building is like a small town with hundreds of employees, so any number of people could have gone there either the night Abby was killed or the next day before she was found."

"But the video shows you entering the building?"

"Yes. Abby had gotten upset at dinner and stormed out. I picked her up on the street and gave her a ride. After I dropped her at the Supreme Court, I wanted to talk to her some more about things, so I parked and went to the library."

"So why did you tell the Deputy Director otherwise?"

"I said no such thing."

Another lie. Sean's jaw clenched.

"Did you see Abby in the library?"

Another thoughtful look from Malik. "Yes."

The room filled with murmurs. The media had some new information. Malik Montgomery had just admitted to seeing Abby right before she was murdered. Emily tightened her grip on Sean's hand.

"Did you speak with her?"

"No."

"Why not?"

"I went into the library and the lights were out. I walked toward the stacks. I didn't see anyone but I thought I heard someone in the back of the Reading Room."

"And what happened?"

"I walked to the back where there's these two leather sofas. I didn't see Abby at first, but as I got closer I saw her."

"What did you see?"

At this, the courtroom seemed to freeze. The spectators made no sound and the lawyers were statues. Even the judge was still, her eyes fixed on Malik. Sean couldn't seem to exhale.

"She was with a man. They were on the couch. He was on top of her. I couldn't see who he was or anything but the back of him. But it was obvious. They were having sex."

CHAPTER 73

Judge Chin wacked her gavel at the ruckus that had erupted in the gallery. Patti Fallon was on her feet virtually yelling her objections as the U.S. marshals called for the spectator section to quiet.

"You two," Judge Chin's voice cut through the melee. She pointed her gavel at Hellstrom and then Fallon. "My chambers. *Now.*"

The lawyers sheepishly followed the judge through the door in the rear of the courtroom. The court reporter gathered her gear and trailed behind. The buzz in the room grew louder as reporters and spectators milled out. Cecilia barged a path for Sean and Emily to leave.

For their part, the Serrats played stoic, in part out of shock, in part to not give the media a reaction. They followed Cecilia to an anteroom Patti Fallon had reserved for them.

"I'll be right outside if you need anything," Cecilia said.

When the door clicked shut, Emily buried her head in Sean's neck and began sobbing. Sean tried to keep it together, if only for her. He was having a hard time absorbing everything, his mind and body overwhelmed with adrenaline and confusion over Malik's testimony. "We can go," he said at last, in a sort of fight-or-flight haze. "We don't have to listen to this."

"No." Emily was firm. She pulled away from him and dabbed her eyes with a tissue. She took a deep breath and collected herself. "We'll stay until the judge calls the hearing."

So they waited. A half hour, then an hour. All the while they replayed what they'd heard. Malik Montgomery now admitted to seeing their daughter moments before she was murdered. A belated truth or a desperate lie? It had to be a lie. Why else would he have waited to identify an alternative suspect? Abby's phone was found in his home. He'd lied about being at the scene. And he'd just lied under oath about being read his Miranda warning and his statements to Pacini.

But they couldn't shake the feeling that something didn't fit. Hellstrom was right. This was a smart kid. Why would he keep the phone after going through the trouble to wipe it clean? Why would he erase the surveillance footage except for the images showing him entering the building? And why kill Abby over the breakup of a relationship that everyone agreed wasn't serious? Sean had another surging thought. Malik's story about seeing Abby with another man in the library was consistent with two facts: First, Abby was seeing someone, a mystery man. Second, the draft e-mail arranged a rendezvous at the Supreme Court library the night she was murdered.

Cecilia popped her head in. "The judge will be back on the bench in five."

Sean and Emily stood.

Cecilia looked conflicted. "I have a client meeting this afternoon and was gonna leave, but I can stay if you—"

"No, you should go," Sean said. "We'll be okay."

"Are you sure?"

Sean took Emily by the hand. They laced fingers and both nodded.

"We'll be fine," Sean said. Truth be told, although Sean appreciated her support, he was happy to see Cecilia go. She was loud in the courtroom, whispering and sighing. And that was nothing compared to the scoffs or guffaws she'd made when Hellstrom said something she didn't like, catching the hard glare of the judge and even Patti Fallon.

Sean and Emily returned to the stiff wooden pews in Courtroom 4. Malik Montgomery came in next, accompanied by his father. Malik hugged his dad and shuffled through the swinging door. Malik's father gave Sean a quick glance and then looked away before returning to his front-row spot on the other side of the gallery. So many wounded parents. Emily and Sean. John Chadwick's mother. He'd heard that even Blake Hellstrom, Malik's lawyer, had lost a child. And now Malik's dad.

The room filled again, and Fallon and Hellstrom appeared from the door behind the bench. School children returning from the principal's office. Hellstrom in particular lacked his usual rumpled swagger.

The loud chime came again from the ceiling and all stood. Judge Chin took her seat and glowered at the two lawyers before her.

"Counsel, any more questions for your witness?" the judge said to Hellstrom. It was more of an accusation than a question.

"No, Your Honor. Nothing further."

Malik, who had returned to the witness chair, gave a confused look to his lawyer. Judge Chin's eyes locked on Fallon.

Fallon approached the witness box. Before Fallon began, the judge cautioned, "Let's make it quick."

Fallon nodded, lowering her eyes to a yellow legal pad. "When Mr. Serrat showed up at your door that night and told you Abby was missing, you just testified, and I quote, you 'wanted to help,' correct?"

"That's right."

"And you said—and I'm quoting you here—'you had nothing to hide' in your home, right?"

"Absolutely."

"So it would have been natural, in those circumstances, to let Mr. Serrat and Mr. Pacini look around your home, correct?"

As Malik contemplated how to respond, Fallon added, "You

would have *wanted to help,* including a search of your home. After all, you had *nothing to hide.*" It was a good question, one that seemed to have only one reasonable answer. One that could result in a government victory on the motion because if Malik had consented to the search there was no Fourth Amendment violation.

Malik raised his shoulders into a tiny shrug.

"And you have to agree—since you say you wanted to help and had nothing to hide—that all the circumstances indicate you *would have* consented if asked, isn't that right?"

"*Ob-jec-tion,*" Hellstrom said. He leaned back casually in his chair. "She's asking him to speculate."

Judge Chin frowned again. "Move on, counsel."

Fallon flipped the page on her legal pad and asked, "On the Miranda warning, you told Frank Pacini that you didn't need the warning like you were some dumb black kid, isn't that true?"

"Absolutely not. That's not something I would say."

"Let me ask you this. You say you wanted to help and had nothing to hide, so wouldn't you have voluntarily talked to Frank Pacini and Mr. Serrat if you'd been given the full Miranda warning?"

Malik thought. He touched his chin. "I suppose."

Fallon had a satisfied look. She had what she needed. "Let's talk about the video from the library."

"Tread lightly, counsel," the judge said.

"As a law clerk for the Supreme Court, it's fair to say that you were in the building late at night all the time, isn't that right?"

"Yes."

"Later than most court personnel?"

"That's correct."

"You ever explore the building? I mean, it's a historic place, didn't you ever scout around late at night?"

Malik pressed his lips together. "When I first started at the court, I suppose I did that. All of the clerks did. It's an interesting building, a lot of history."

"As a clerk, you had access to the chambers of the justices? And the police offices? You knew the security codes to most spaces in the building, right?"

"Yes, me and at least a hundred other people who work at the court."

Fallon seemed to ponder whether to ask the next question. She looked over to her hound-faced colleague, who nodded. Then: "Mr. Montgomery, I'm handing you what's been marked as Government Exhibit One and ask you to look at it." Fallon walked to Malik and handed him a sheet of paper. She then paced over to Hellstrom and slid a copy of the document across the defense table.

Sean noticed Hellstrom's wrinkled brow as he examined the document.

"Do you know what that is?" Fallon asked.

Hellstrom was already on his feet, but Fallon managed to sneak in her last question. "Isn't that an interview report from the Supreme Court Police showing that the day Abby was killed she'd alerted the police that a law clerk had been harassing her? Had threatened her?"

Before Malik said a word, Judge Chin said, "Don't answer that." She shook her head at Fallon: *You know better than this, Patti.* "I assume, Mr. Hellstrom, you're going to object to this as lacking foundation, hearsay, and completely irrelevant to this motion?" the judge asked.

Hellstrom gave a nod: *I should say so.*

"Sustained." The judge looked at Fallon. "And I take it that *you* have no more questions, Ms. Fallon?" Another question that answered itself.

Fallon opened her mouth to speak, but seeing the judge's expression, she simply nodded and sat slowly back down in her seat. An unceremonious end, but Sean assumed that Fallon had made the calculated decision that, like Hellstrom, she too should play to the media in the courtroom. To put some cold water on whatever flames Hellstrom had stoked.

There was more prattle from the gallery. Abby's visit to the police station the day she was murdered was truly damning for Malik. Sean wondered momentarily if it was true, thinking about how the police chief winked at him. But the chief wouldn't be so foolish as to fabricate evidence, would he?

CHAPTER 74

Judge Chin excused Malik Montgomery from the witness chair. "I'll take the motion to suppress under advisement and issue a decision shortly. Mr. Hellstrom, I understand you had one other matter you'd like to take up?"

Hellstrom stood. "Thank you, Your Honor. Yes, the defense requests that the court issue an order to allow the subpoena of records from Google concerning a Gmail account. The government recently advised us that Abby Serrat had an e-mail account that we had not been previously informed about. If you log on to the e-mail account, there are no sent or received messages. But there is one e-mail in the Drafts folder. The draft e-mail invited an unknown recipient to meet the drafter at the Supreme Court library on a Sunday, the same day Ms. Serrat was murdered. If I may approach the bench?"

Hellstrom was masterfully bringing the proceedings back to the question posed by Malik's testimony: Who was in the library with Abby? Hellstrom walked to the bench and handed the judge a sheet of paper.

"I've marked as Defense Exhibit One a copy of the draft e-mail printed from the Gmail account," Hellstrom said.

Judge Chin inspected the exhibit. Hellstrom continued, "It is a common practice, started by terrorists, that to avoid electronic detection or tracking of e-mails sent over the Internet, they will open an e-mail account, write an e-mail and place it in a draft folder, but never send it. The sender then gives the e-mail account login and password to the message's recipient. The recipient logs onto the e-mail account, reads the draft e-mail, then deletes it. This reduces the electronic footprint since the draft e-mail never transmits over the Internet and is erased after it is read."

Judge Chin eyed Hellstrom skeptically. "So you think Ms. Serrat was wise to the ways of al Qaeda?"

Hellstrom gave the judge a serious look. "It may not have been Ms. Serrat's idea—she could have been the recipient of the message. The sender could have just given her the e-mail account information and told her what to do. That's why we need information from Google."

"You know the statute places limits on subpoenaing e-mail service providers, and this seems like a fishing expedition. I just can't imagine any person not in law enforcement would know how to do—"

Before Judge Chin finished her sentence, Blake Hellstrom said, "With respect, Your Honor, this is not an unknown communication method. Teenagers use it. And the Supreme Court this term issued a decision that discussed the very practice I'm talking about here. The opinion in *United States v. Ahmed* spelled it out in detail."

Sean was pleased that Hellstrom was pursuing the e-mail, and that he'd mentioned the *Ahmed* decision, a case involving the constitutionality of the government's controversial surveillance program. Sean's good friend, Michael Freeman, the deputy solicitor general, had argued the case on behalf of the government. It was a five-four decision, with the minority submitting a vitriolic dissenting opinion. A dissent *The New York Times* had taken the rare step of reprinting in full.

And then Sean's blood turned cold.

The fragments all came together. A portrait of Abby's mystery boyfriend. Someone older, someone she admired. Someone she needed to protect, to keep their relationship a secret. Someone who knew how to send surreptitious messages through an e-mail account.

Sean got up to leave. Emily frowned as people in the gallery started looking at them. Even Hellstrom paused a beat.

"Where are you going?" Emily whispered.

Sean reached for her hand. She must have read it in his face because she let him virtually pull her out of her seat. Heads in the gallery snapped after them as Sean and Emily hurried out of the courtroom.

In the corridor of the Prettyman building, Emily turned toward her husband. "What's going on?" She looked into his eyes. "What's wrong?"

"I know who was with Abby in the library that night."

CHAPTER 75

Sean charged into the Supreme Court, the wind whooshing into the entryway doors. It was the first time he'd been in the building since *Before*.

The ground floor still gleamed with white marble, John Marshall still sat stoically in bronze, the eyes on the portraits of past justices still seemed to follow as you walked by. Sean headed to the elevator and waited. He kept his head down. The court was a friendly place, a community of people who cared about the institution and one another, and he didn't want to have to engage in obligatory small talk or condolences. The elevator door opened and he had a rush of emotion, recalling the last time he'd glided up to the library that dark night. Today, though, the attendant was present. Esther was an elderly black woman who'd spent the better part of her life working in the seven-by-five-foot paneled box, crouched on a stool pushing buttons for people. Sean was surprised when Esther didn't say anything, but lifted herself up from the stool, gave him a hug, and returned to her station. It was one of the most genuine responses he'd received to Abby's death.

The elevator doors opened and Sean stepped into the library. He paused a beat, bracing himself, before he crossed the hall to the librarian stations. He fought off the image of his daughter's twisted and lifeless body, stuffed away in the shelf. He needed to stay sharp.

The library staff fluttered around, whispering and staring, until one of the librarians approached and asked Sean if he needed assistance.

Sean asked for the location of the court's most recent opinions from the term. It would be too soon for the opinions to be in the bound *U.S. Reports,* Sean knew. The opinions would still be in the small booklets printed by the court. And sure enough, the librarian led Sean into the Reading Room to a cache of booklets stacked on a shelf near the front of the room. She averted her gaze from the back, which had a scrim that hung from the vaulted ceilings cordoning off the scene of the crime. Sean wasn't sure whether it was sealed off by the investigators or whether it was now a construction area. Sean presumed that the court's curator would order a fresh redesign of the back of the library as soon as possible, to prevent the staff at One First Street from having to imagine the grisly events.

"Here they are," the librarian said.

Sean thanked her and she scurried off. He sorted through the opinions until he found it: *United States v. Ahmed.* The case Blake Hellstrom identified in his argument to Judge Chin. He flipped to the back and found the dissenting opinion. Dissents are authored by a single justice and other justices join the opinion. He found the name and his rage boiled to the surface.

CHAPTER 76

Sean approached the Supreme Court officer stationed at the north corridor that separated the Great Hall from chambers. The officer was a young guy who wore a blue blazer and radio clipped to his belt. His eyes widened a trace at the sight of Sean.

"I have an appointment."

The officer gave him a concerned look. "Mr. Serrat, I'm sorry, I wasn't told that they were expecting visitors." He fumbled for his radio. "I'll need to call . . ."

Sean gave the man a long stare. "If you think you need to clear it, please, call Carl." He'd been in D.C. long enough to know the power of the name-drop.

The officer washed a hand over his face, seeming to deliberate what would be worse, breaching protocol and letting Sean through or getting taken to task by Police Chief Martinez for daring to question a respected figure at the court, one whose daughter had been murdered on their watch. He lowered his radio and moved aside, gesturing with his arm for Sean to pass through the bronze trellis.

The secretary in chambers looked equally surprised at Sean's visit. She asked him to take a seat in the reception area, picked up the telephone, and spoke softly into the receiver. The large doors to chambers were closed, but Sean could hear the whispers of the law clerks in the adjoining offices.

Sean's mobile buzzed and he clicked open a text. It was from Emily:

> Call me as soon as you're done. Jon gave me a ride home. I love you.

The intercom on the receptionist's desk buzzed and she picked up the phone, listened, and placed it back in the cradle.

"He'll see you now."

Sean took a deep breath and opened one of the impressive mahogany doors. He walked down a corridor lined with shelves filled with old law books and into an ornate office. Oriental rugs covered the floor, and a settee and two wing chairs were placed in front of a massive fireplace. Out the window, a spectacular view of the Capitol dome. Sean recalled from his own clerkship days that the space had once been home to Justice Kagan, though she had gone with modern décor. The only modern item here was a gold football helmet placed prominently in a display cabinet.

Justice Carr, wearing a white dress shirt with the top button undone and his tie loosened, greeted Sean as he entered chambers. Carr's shirtsleeves were rolled up, showing muscular forearms.

"Sean, what a pleasant surprise." He stuck out his hand.

Sean let it hang there.

The justice let his hand fall slowly. Less confident, he said, "To what do I owe the pleasure?" He gestured for Sean to take a seat in front of the fireplace, but Sean stood.

"*United States v. Ahmed*," Sean said.

Carr returned Sean's stare with a confused squint of the eyes.

"Your dissent," Sean added.

Justice Carr held his stare at first, but looked away. Then, a half-hearted, "I don't understand."

"Neither did I until I saw your draft e-mail message to my daughter."

"I don't under—"

"*Don't,*" Sean said through gritted teeth. He glared at Justice

Carr until the man averted his eyes again. "Do you know how I got here today?"

Justice Carr's gaze lifted, he shook his head.

"I took a rickshaw. You know, one of those bike contraptions. Mine was operated by the brother of one of Abby's friends. A friend who lives in Adams Morgan on Kalorama Road, an address I think you're familiar with."

Justice Carr's eyes flashed, but he didn't say anything. He walked to his large wooden desk, which was stacked with briefs— the blue, red, gray, and green little booklets Sean had spent nearly his entire adult life reading and writing. There were two phones on the desk, one red with no buttons, the panic phone, the other an ordinary office phone. The justice eyed them both, then pushed a button on the ordinary phone. A voice bellowed from the speaker. "Can I get you something, Justice Carr?"

"Yes, Kathryn. It's been an exceptionally long week. I'd like you to tell the law clerks to take the rest of the day off."

"You'd like me to send them home?" the voice said from the speaker. Tentative, like perhaps she had misunderstood.

"Yes. They need a break."

A pause. "Yes, sir."

"And Kathryn," Justice Carr added, "why don't you take the rest of the day off, too." It was more of a command than a request.

"Of course, sir."

When the phone beeped off, Justice Carr's eyes turned again to Sean, who was now standing in front of the desk. A long silence fell between them. Then, the confession: "I loved her."

Sean took it in. *"Loved,"* he finally spat back.

"Believe what you want, but we were in love." There was a rehearsed quality to it, acting, Sean thought.

"You loved her so much," Sean said, "that you immediately came forward after she was killed to tell the police what you knew."

"It wasn't that simple."

"Actually, it was." Sean's pulse was hammering now. "Unless you had something to do with it."

Carr's expression hardened. "Never."

"Then, who?"

"You know who—they've arrested him. Malik killed Abby."

Sean gave a sharp shake of the head.

Carr continued, "I saw her that night, she was scared. It had to be Malik."

"So you admit to being in the library?" Sean's mind jumped to Malik's testimony: *She was with a man . . . They were having sex.*

"I met her there, yes," Carr said. "But she was alive when I left. I swear to you."

"What did she say? What was she scared of?"

"She wouldn't tell me. She just said she needed to speak with you. We heard the library's elevator and she told me to go. It was Malik. I left through the hidden staircase in the back. I wouldn't have left her if I knew he would . . ." Carr's voice trailed off.

"If you left, how do you know it was Malik?"

"Who else would it be? He was on the surveillance video. He was angry . . ."

"What about Mason James?" Sean knew that the senator had been out of town that night, but he wanted to see Carr's reaction.

The justice shook his head in dismissal. "James is a corrupt viper, but he didn't have any reason to hurt Abby."

"How do you know that?"

"Because I know." Carr looked down again. "They were following her after she visited that guy at the prison and must have seen us together. James's security man said if she backed off and kept quiet about whatever she'd learned about James, they'd do the same about her relationship with me. She agreed, so they had no reason to hurt her."

"Then why did you meet with them at the Shakespeare library?"

That seemed to send a jolt through Carr. "They wanted my support for James's nomination. They threatened to expose my relationship with Abby unless I helped."

"Or they knew you were involved in her death."

"You're wrong."

"So you're either a murderer or a coward who left her alone with a killer?"

At this, Carr's tone grew emotional. "You don't think I wish I would have stayed? You don't think I wish I could've saved her?"

"I don't need to know what you *think*. All I *know* is that you are the last person who was with my daughter before she was killed. You didn't go to the police after her murder. And you had a motive to kill her. To save your precious job."

"No!" Carr pounded his desk with a closed fist. He was an imposing figure, someone who in a fit of anger could inflict a fatal head injury on a young woman with little effort.

"We're done here." Sean turned to leave and Justice Carr reached over the desk and grabbed his arm. Sean ripped it away and in a surge of fury swung his other arm wide and connected a fist on Justice Carr's jaw. The justice stumbled back. He clawed at the desk to prevent the fall, but managed only to bring down a pile of briefs onto the floor with him.

The justice slowly picked himself up. He gazed at Sean, then his eyes flicked to a gold letter opener that was at the edge of the desk.

"Everything okay in here?" a voice called out from the door. It was Carl Martinez. Someone must have heard the shouting and summoned him.

Sean turned to Martinez. "Everything's fine. I was just leaving." He turned back to Justice Carr and said, "It's over for you."

CHAPTER 77

But it wasn't over.

Sean sat at his dining room table amid the remnants of Thai take-out: empty cardboard boxes and plastic containers of red curry with chicken. Jack's glass of milk was smeared with handprints and kernels of white rice. The sound of the boys playing video games floated up from the basement.

Emily surveyed the wreckage. "I really need to start cooking for us again."

"I think we all feel bad enough," Sean deadpanned.

A faint smile crossed Emily's lips. There was a knock at the front door.

"Frank's here."

The three converged in the living room. Frank Pacini sat on the couch, Sean and Emily in the chairs across from him. Each held a cup of coffee. Pacini reached for a coaster and set down his mug. "What a day," Pacini said. "I think we won the motion to suppress. But, between us, I'm starting to question the government's case."

"We are too, which is why I invited you over." Sean told him about his confrontation with Justice Carr, that the justice admitted to having a relationship with Abby and to seeing her the night she was murdered.

"How did you find out about them?" Pacini asked.

"Today in court. It was the Gmail account. When Blake Hell-strom mentioned the court's decision in *Ahmed,* I remembered it was Justice Carr who wrote the dissent, spelling out how terrorists use draft e-mails to communicate. We knew from Abby's friend that she was seeing someone and that she was keeping his identity a se-cret. Before I confronted him, though, I wanted to make sure. The brother of Abby's friend had seen her with an older man. I showed the kid a photo, and he recognized Carr."

Pacini rubbed his chin. "So, what's it mean? You think Carr murdered Abby?"

"I don't know. He had motive—he told me that someone knew about their relationship." Sean left out that Senator James was blackmailing Justice Carr. The senator still had the evidence on Ryan. "And Carr admits he was at the library that night and he didn't come forward after her murder."

"He's married, though, so that could explain his silence, right? And his job . . ."

Sean nodded. "He's got life tenure, but if the affair went pub-lic, he'd face insurmountable pressure to resign. What I can't figure out is something he said about that night. He said that he heard the elevator and got out of the library quickly through a back stair-well. But Malik Montgomery's testimony is inconsistent with that. Malik said that he saw Abby and a man together on the library's couch. If Justice Carr and Abby heard the elevator—which has gotta be at least a couple hundred feet from the back of the library— they wouldn't have been on the couch by the time Malik came upon them. But Malik testified that he saw them without them knowing it."

"Someone's obviously lying."

Emily weighed in: "Or, there was a third person in the library that night. Malik crept in and saw Abby and Justice Carr without them realizing it and left, then a third person took the elevator up there. Carr and Abby heard it and Carr took off, leaving Abby and the person there alone."

Before Pacini responded, Ryan came into the living room.

"Yes, sweetie," Emily said.

"Jack and I were watching TV and there was a breaking news story."

"Yeah?" Sean said.

"It says there's police cars at a Supreme Court justice's house. The justice, the man we met at the court that day, has gone missing or something."

CHAPTER 78

"Thanks for letting me come," Sean said from the passenger seat of Pacini's car. Pacini had contacted the Supreme Court Police and learned that Justice Carr's detail had put out an alert that the justice was missing.

"No problem." Pacini kept his eyes on the road ahead of him. "But you need to let me do all the talking."

Pacini drove past several parked news vans and pulled up to an officer manning a sawhorse that blocked the street. Pacini flashed his credentials and the officer nodded, then waved him through. In front of Justice Carr's home were three black SUVs and a black sedan, the Supreme Court Police and an FBI team. The justice's home was a turn-of-the-century mansion in Cleveland Park. Sean followed Pacini up the porch steps. The curtain was open, and Sean could see into the place. Two men in suits sat at a formal dining table speaking to an elegant woman in her late thirties. Her hair was pulled back, and her sleeveless black dress revealed the arms of a woman who spent substantial time at the gym.

A young agent met Pacini at the door. "Justice Carr's detail got concerned when he didn't show up at home after work. His wife said they were scheduled to appear at a speaking engagement at seven o'clock, and he isn't answering his cell phone. There's a GPS tracker on the justice's phone and his car, but neither are giving off a signal. He also has an implanted device."

"The implant isn't working?" Pacini asked. "That doesn't make sense."

Sean looked at Pacini, not understanding.

"High-level officials are often given an option to have a GPS chip implanted under their skin in case of abduction. It's not invasive, and is activated only in extreme emergencies."

"Who would know about that?"

"Only Carr and his police detail." Pacini turned back to the young agent. "His detail, weren't they with him when he left work?"

"No, apparently he rarely uses them. His wife said that Carr isn't usually recognized, and he thinks the security detail only draws attention to him. His wife said they typically use the detail only for the justice's public appearances, and on those occasions the detail picks him up at the house."

Pacini looked at Sean as if to confirm.

Sean nodded, "That's pretty common for the justices. Most don't want to have officers hovering around."

Pacini peered inside at Carr's wife. She smiled at something one of the agents said. "She doesn't look too worried."

The agent shrugged. "She said she and Carr have been separated for about a year. They have an agreement that she'd attend events with him until they finalized the split and went public. In the past few months he's been slipping away; she presumed he was seeing someone. But his security detail got concerned because it was unlike him to miss a speaking event. And his GPS isn't giving a signal . . ."

Inside the house one of the agents stood abruptly, talking on his phone. The young agent at the door pressed a finger on his earpiece.

"What's going on?" Pacini said.

"They found the justice's car. It's at Union Station."

CHAPTER 79

Light poured out from under the triumphal arches at Union Station and the moon washed a pale glow over the long white granite façade. Pacini and Sean steered around the grand front of the building to the entrance of the parking garage, a drab seven-tiered structure filled with thousands of vehicles. They bounced over the speed bumps and spiraled to the top floor where two agents maintained a perimeter. The car came to a quick stop and Pacini jumped out.

Sean followed after him and watched Pacini speak to an agent. Several other agents hovered around a silver BMW sedan. The top floor of the garage wasn't covered, and stars twinkled in the cloudless sky. Sean breathed in the nighttime air. Police Chief Martinez, who'd interrupted Sean's confrontation with Justice Carr, stalked over to Pacini and pulled him aside. He had a concerned look on his face and he kept glancing over at Sean. Pacini was shaking his head and then came back over.

"The chief wondered where you were tonight," he said.

Sean nodded. It was understandable given Sean's encounter with Justice Carr. It didn't take a seasoned cop to know that the guy last seen in a hostile argument with the missing person was a good place to start the investigation.

"I said you had the misfortune of being with me," Pacini said. "Either way, stay close."

"Is that his car?" Sean asked, pointing to the BMW.

"Yeah. They want to get some techs here before we search."

"May I?" Sean said, cocking his head toward the vehicle.

"You can look, just do not, under any circumstances, touch."

Sean stepped closer to the BMW, Pacini at his side. The trunk was open, but the interior of the car remained locked. The cops probably didn't want to wait to open the trunk in case Justice Carr was inside. Sean crouched and looked intently inside the luxury sedan. He felt an ache at the sight of a pendant and chain that sat on top of a piece of paper on the passenger seat.

"Frank, I think that's Abby's necklace." Sean reached for the door handle, but Pacini caught him by the wrist.

"We need to wait, Sean."

Sean paced the garage, his thoughts a jumble, as Pacini and the agents made small talk. Martinez continued to flick hard gazes in Sean's direction.

Finally the crime scene techs arrived, and the lead tech snapped on latex gloves as she spoke to the police chief. She then unlocked the car's doors with a key fob, possibly a spare provided by Justice Carr's wife. The tech leaned inside the vehicle, not touching any part of the interior, and eased back out. In her right hand was a pair of what looked like large tweezers. Clamped in them was a piece of paper. She put the paper in a clear plastic bag. She performed the same maneuver with the necklace.

Holding the corner of the bag, the tech brought it to Police Chief Martinez. He signaled for Pacini to come over and Sean followed after. The chief held the plastic bag by the corner up at eye level. In sloppy handwriting were three sentences:

Forgive me for what I've done.
I loved Abby.
It was an accident.

The note was spattered with tiny speckles of what looked like blood.

CHAPTER 80

One month later

Late July in Washington was swamp hot, and Sean began to sweat the moment he stepped out of his front door. The air was filled with the sounds of summer. A lawn mower buzzed in the distance, kids playing outside. Standing on the porch, Sean pulled at the collar of his dress shirt to air himself out. Even with no tie, the suit was steaming. He adjusted the strap on the briefcase slung over his shoulder.

Ryan and Jack were in the front yard tossing a football. Jack launched the ball awkwardly to his big brother, but it fell short, and Ryan had to stumble forward to catch it. Ryan still wasn't himself. He was quieter and had been moping around, so it felt good to see him outside, playing with his little brother.

"Nice catch," Sean said. Ryan tossed the ball to Sean, who caught it one-handed. "You boys are up early."

"Mom was tired of us sleeping in," Ryan said.

"Go long," Sean said, cocking the ball back in his arm. Jack ran and spread open his arms, eyes shut, as the ball flew over his head and bounced about the yard.

"Daddy, Daddy," Jack said.

"Yes, sir," Sean said as he skipped down the front steps.

"Wanna hear a joke?"

"Of course."

"What did the beaver say when he ran into the wall?"

"What?"

"Daaamn."

Sean forced a laugh and walked the brick path to his SUV, parked curbside. As Sean opened the front gate, a dark sedan pulled up. Sean's body tensed at the sight of the man who climbed out of the vehicle. Sean turned to his sons.

"Why don't you boys go inside."

Ryan's face was tight. Anxious. He seemed to understand immediately and launched Jack over his shoulder and carried him inside.

On the street, now leaning on the hood of the SUV, was Detective Whiteside, the Montgomery County homicide detective working the Billy Brice, aka Chipotle Man, case.

Sean decided not to engage. No upside to it.

"Do you mind getting off my car?" he said. The vehicle tweeted when the doors unlocked. The detective didn't budge.

"I'd like to have a short word with you, Mr. Serrat, if you would?"

"If this is about your wild theories, I have nothing to say to you."

The detective frowned and then said, "How's the nomination going?" It was an awkward change of subject. Or was it an implied threat? Sean's nomination to replace Justice Carr was front-page news. The media was lapping up the poetic justice of it all: a member of the Supreme Court missing and accused of murdering a young woman, the victim's father nominated to replace him. You couldn't make this shit up.

"The nomination is going fine," Sean said. "I'm actually late for a meeting, so if you don't mind . . ."

Whiteside stepped away from the SUV. Sean opened the rear door and threw his briefcase inside. He walked around to the driver side and swung open the door.

"You're not helping him, you know," the detective said.

Sean stopped before getting into the SUV. "Helping who?"

"Your son," the detective said. "It's going to haunt him for the rest of his life if you just pretend it didn't happen. He's going to go through life thinking he's a killer."

Better that than the alternative. "Let me worry about my son, okay?"

"I believe it was self-defense. Or he was defending you. He's a young man and no one has an interest in locking him up."

"You seem to have an interest in making allegations that could hurt my son more than anything he's ever done. I've told you, if you have questions, talk to my lawyer." Sean stared him down. "If you want to make a name for yourself, you're going to have to find another case."

"Oh, I already know that, Mr. Serrat."

At this Sean paused.

The detective added, "It seems the State's Attorney has decided to close the Billy Brice case. Funny, right as he's about to seek support in his campaign for governor, he and my boss decide for the first time that closure rates don't matter. They weren't too subtle about what would happen to my job, either."

"Just as well, detective, you were wasting your time."

Whiteside shook his head: *You know better.*

"So you came here just to tell me that?"

"No, I came here to see if you'd do what's right for your son. Come clean, get him some help, tell the truth. Stomping on someone's throat is not something that's easy to forget."

The last part hovered in the humid air. Sean examined Whiteside, caught off guard by the comment. "His throat? I thought it was a blow to the head? The news said . . ."

Now the detective's eyes narrowed and he looked at Sean as if he suddenly had doubts himself. "Someone clocked Billy Brice, but that's not what killed him. We withheld the full cause of death from the media. It helps weed out the nut jobs. Brice died of a crushed larynx."

The detective's words cut loose a ten-thousand-pound weight anchored to Sean's neck since that night on the football field. Ryan hadn't killed Billy Brice. Someone must have stomped Brice while he was out cold on the field. Who? Probably the only other person there that night. The person who'd tromped through the trees to find the steel rod containing Ryan's prints. The person who'd taken the photos of Ryan. Sebastian Finkle. But why? Just to get some dirt on the Serrats? Or maybe Brice had seen Finkle following Sean, and the man didn't want any witnesses. Sean thought back to the day he'd hidden in Finkle's closet. *No violence this time,* the senator had said to his lover. Whatever the reason, all that mattered was that Ryan had not delivered the fatal blow.

The detective kept talking, but Sean didn't hear any of it. He just slipped into the SUV and pulled from the curb. In the rearview mirror he saw the detective, hands on his hips, watching him drive away.

CHAPTER 81

Sean coasted down Rock Creek Parkway to the final murder board the administration had scheduled to help him prepare for his Supreme Court confirmation hearing next week. The air-conditioner blew cold in his face, but he still felt warm and flushed. He was driving on autopilot, a muddle of thoughts still vaulting about in his brain.

Sean and Emily had a deal with the Devil. The Serrats would stay quiet about Mason James, and James would stay quiet about the Serrats, including that spring night on the football field of Bethesda–Chevy Chase High School. The deal with James wasn't easy. By keeping James's secrets, Sean had to watch in horror as the Senate confirmed James's nomination to the high court and he became Chief Justice James. Not since Justice James McReynolds, a dreadful man and a proud anti-Semite who would get up and leave when a Jewish justice entered the room, had a more despicable human graced a black robe at the Supreme Court. Soon, Sean would have to see Chief Justice James on a regular basis. They would be brethren.

Sean and Emily had considered going to Detective Whiteside, having Sean turn himself in. On Cecilia's advice, they'd even hired the best criminal defense lawyer in the country—none other than Blake Hellstrom—to guide them through the morass. And Sean had told Hellstrom everything. Even seen-it-all Hellstrom was taken aback. He was looking into whether and how Sean could make retribution for Japan. He never said so, but Sean assumed that Hellstrom also was trying to make sure the allegations about Japan would never come to light. But the main reason they'd hired Hellstrom was to see what could be done about Ryan because they all believed Ryan had delivered the fatal hit to Billy Brice. Hellstrom thought there would be a strong case for self-defense or defense of another. But coming forward about Brice—even if no criminal charges were ever filed against Ryan or Sean—would mean an investigation, one that could consume Ryan's high school years. And the media attention alone could forever eviscerate any hope of a normal childhood for Ryan or Jack. When Sean had asked Hellstrom what he should do, the lawyer had said, "Look at the fish," and pointed to a speckled brown trout mounted on Hellstrom's office wall. Under the fish's open mouth an inscription: IF I'D JUST KEPT MY MOUTH SHUT, I WOULDN'T BE HERE.

But if Ryan hadn't delivered the fatal blow to Billy Brice, didn't that change the equation? Sean wasn't sure. He needed to call Hellstrom. But first, there was someone else he needed to call.

CHAPTER 82

Sean wiped a tear from his cheek as he listened to Ryan's sobs from the SUV's overhead speakers.

"Are you sure it wasn't me?" his son said.

"It wasn't you. And it wasn't me. Someone wanted us to believe you did it."

"So, can we go to the police and tell them now?" Ryan asked. "Can we tell the truth?"

Sean swallowed. "Mom and I need to discuss what to do."

"Does she know? She didn't say anything . . ."

"She doesn't know. I just found out."

Ryan's voice broke, "Can I be the one who tells Mom?"

"Of course you can." Sean's eyes filled with more tears. The burden his sweet-hearted son had carried, yet fought so hard to conceal because he didn't want to pile on to the family's grief and worry, was lifted.

As Sean drove into the Georgetown Law parking lot, he saw two men holding cameras waiting for him. He slowed and said to Ryan, "I have to go, but we'll talk more this afternoon. I love you."

Sean pulled into a parking space and glanced at himself in the rearview mirror. His sunglasses concealed his red eyes, so he would look fine in any photos captured by the reporters. He wasn't sure how they knew he'd be here. Someone must have leaked that he would be at Georgetown for the murder boards. The media's interest in Sean had waned for a time, but his nomination to the high court put him back in the news cycle. It didn't help that every few weeks rumors surfaced that the FBI had a bead on former Justice Thaddeus Carr, who had eluded capture for a month now. Some speculated that he was living in Switzerland under an assumed name. Others thought he had jumped off the Eleventh Street Bridge and drifted into the Anacostia River, a hypothesis supported by the fact that the handwritten confession found in Carr's vehicle read like a suicide note. The spatters of his blood on the note—presumably a botched attempt to slash his own wrists—seemed to corroborate. But others speculated that the blood was from Carr removing the security GPS chip implanted under his skin. In the blogosphere, conspiracy theorists charged that the entire episode was part of a plot to change the makeup of the Supreme Court. So many questions remained.

Sean pulled the briefcase from the backseat and said hello as camera flashes went off. His handlers had advised that a nominee *must* act dignified at all times. Smile, say *no comment*, and move on. And that's what he did. Before entering the building, he called Blake Hellstrom's office and left him an urgent message.

Inside the Hotung building, he was met by a young lawyer holding an iPad like a clipboard. Sean's eyes darted about the room and after a moment he was back to the day he'd found Abby; he was at a function in this very space that day. Bile crept up his throat.

He walked into the moot courtroom. He'd been in this room many times when he was at the Justice Department. Georgetown's moot courtroom was designed to look like the courtroom in the Supreme Court. The bench was mahogany like the bench at One First Street, albeit a third the size. The red-rosette carpet matched the high court's. And the podium was the precise size and distance from the bench as the real thing. Everything aimed at making the practice argument sessions as real as possible for the advocates. Today, though, Sean wouldn't be questioned about a case, but rather interrogated about his background and judicial philosophy. Preparation for the Kabuki theater that was modern Supreme Court confirmation hearings. The art of giving the non-answer.

At the bench were six murder board participants assigned to play members of the Senate Judiciary Committee. At the last confirmation hearing for Mason James, the committee had taken it easy on the nominee, surprising everyone except for Sean and Emily—well, and the committee members James black-mailed. Without his own Sebastian Finkle to deliver dirt files to hostile committee members, Sean would have to prepare the old-fashioned way.

The spectator gallery was filled with administration handlers, justice department lawyers, and their respective entourages. Sean's old friend Professor Jonathan Tweed, who was charged with orga-nizing the murder boards, greeted him with a big smile.

After hellos and small talk, Tweed began the session. "Don't go easy on this guy," he said to the mock senators.

And they didn't. The questions were tough. Sean floundered as his mind meandered: From thoughts of Ryan to Mason James. From Billy Brice to Abby's last days. To Kenny Baldwin dying in the rain. He realized that he was like the man in Jack's joke, the man fired from the orange juice factory—unable to concentrate. Tweed was a good moderator and kept the proceedings moving along. But Sean wasn't performing well.

Seeming to sense Sean was struggling, Tweed called for a break. The room cleared. Sean assumed that Tweed had directed the others to leave so he could give a pep talk. Tweed sauntered over and put a hand on Sean's shoulder.

"You're doing great," Tweed said.

"No, I'm not."

Tweed didn't correct him. "You okay? You look tired."

"Yeah, I'm sorry I'm distracted. Maybe some coffee will help."

"Did you watch the RBG and Elena Kagan videos I e-mailed you?" Tweed asked. "Just do what they did and you'll be fine."

"I did. I'll do my best to emulate them. This is such a waste of time. Have the senators *ever* gotten answers that revealed the nominee's real views?"

"Yeah . . . Robert Bork," Tweed said, with a laugh.

Sean smiled. "You want to come over for dinner tonight?"

"I'd love to, but I have a bit of a drive. Staying at the lake house."

"The life of a law professor."

"Hey, you're going to be a Supreme Court justice. You know what John Roberts once said about the job: 'Only Supreme Court justices and schoolchildren are expected to and do take the entire summer off.'" Tweed grinned. "You got a little more prep in you?"

"I think so."

"Good, go get yourself some coffee."

Sean walked out of the moot courtroom. He nodded to the mock senators and other members of the team who brushed by, intent to get to Tweed when they saw Sean leave the room. Concerned, no doubt. The café just outside the moot courtroom was closed, but there was a table in the atrium set up with coffee and snacks.

He checked his phone. Two missed calls from Blake Hellstrom. Sean dialed the number, and Hellstrom picked up on the first ring.

"Sean, I'm glad you called, I was just about to call you myself. I have some news."

"Ryan didn't kill Brice," Sean blurted into the phone. He told Hellstrom what he'd learned from the detective, that Brice died not from a blow to the head but from a crushed larynx.

"If that's true, let's talk about coming forward. The State's Attorney will be receptive to helping, and I think they'll be open to a confidential immunity deal."

"I think that sounds right. Maybe we should—"

"Sean," Hellstrom interrupted. His voice had a hint of concern to it.

"Yeah?"

"I was actually calling about something else. My team has been looking into Japan. We found something unexpected."

CHAPTER 83

Sean's shoes clacked on the marble floor of the Supreme Court. Like every summer, the building was virtually a ghost town. Jon Tweed was right, only school children and justices take the summer off.

It was almost noon, and Sean lingered near the cafeteria on the ground floor. As expected, at twelve sharp, bodies began appearing from the offices. Lunchtime. Sean watched the door to the police office across the hall. His mind flashed to Abby visiting the office the day she was killed.

After a group of staffers left the office, Sean headed through the door. From his days as a law clerk he knew that only one receptionist would be left behind to cover during lunch.

"Can I help you?" The receptionist smiled, seeming to recognize Sean. He was a nominee to the high court now, a celebrity in the insular world.

"Hi. Is Police Chief Martinez in?"

"The chief is actually in the courtroom for the daily security check. Can I help you, Mr. Serrat?"

Sean forced a smile. He moved quickly past the receptionist to the chief's private office. "I left my phone in the office when I visited Carl yesterday. He told me I could stop by to pick it up."

The receptionist stood quickly, but Sean already had rushed by and into the chief's private office. He shut the door and locked it.

He scanned the room quickly. The receptionist was already tapping softly on the door.

"Excuse me. Mr. Serrat . . . Mr. Serrat . . ."

He didn't have much time.

The space was meticulously organized and tidy. The desktop had no papers or clutter. Just a nameplate, a fountain pen, and a small picture frame.

"Mr. Serrat . . ."

And then he saw it.

Sean swallowed hard. Blake Hellstrom was right. He scooped up the small picture frame and moved quickly to the door, turning the latch.

The receptionist stood there, looking flustered.

"I'm sorry, the door must have locked behind me. I don't see my phone. I'll go check with Carl."

The receptionist looked conflicted.

"You said he's in the courtroom, right?" Sean asked, nonchalant.

The woman exhaled, then straightened herself, the concern leaving her face.

"That's right."

"I'll go see him now."

In the courtroom, Sean marched down the center aisle toward two officers who were doing a sweep with a bomb-sniffing dog. Tight security even when The Nine were off in their summer homes or frolicking abroad on all-expense-paid teaching or speaking gigs.

"I'm looking for Police Chief Martinez," Sean said, not seeing Martinez in the gallery. His voice seemed to pinball around the twenty-four marble columns that encased the room.

"Sean," a voice called out. In the back of the room, behind the bench. The police chief stepped through the burgundy curtains that hung from the ceiling. He was standing at the center of the bench next to the chief justice's high-backed leather chair. Above him the famous clock, the one advocates were advised never to look up at during their oral arguments, hung from a steel cord.

Sean walked through the brass trellis to the bar-member section of the chamber. How many times had he been in this courtroom? Too many to count. But like everything else, the place didn't feel the same anymore. Not after his confrontation with Thaddeus Carr. Not after Abby. He suspected today would be the last time he'd ever step foot in this building. It would end where it all began. At One First Street.

The police chief nodded to the officers to give them some privacy, and they scuttled out with the dog.

Sean stepped up to the counsel table, which was less than ten feet from the elevated bench. Advocates were always surprised at how close the lectern was to the justices. The proximity, and that the bench was raised and the justices lorded down on you, was what first-timers seemed to remember the most. But today it wasn't the chief justice of the United States looking down at Sean with a black stare.

"What can I do for you?" Martinez walked the length of the bench and stepped down into the well. The two locked eyes.

"I know who you are," Sean finally said. Sean held up the picture frame he'd taken from the chief's desk, and displayed it to him. It was a photo of a teenage kid. The chief's son. Sean's boyhood friend.

Juan.

The chief gave a resigned nod. Then: "So you know who I am. Well, Sean, I know who you are too."

Sean held his gaze. Martinez navigated around the long counsel table and stood right next to him. He calmly reached for the picture frame, and took it from Sean. He examined the photo for a moment, then said, "I know that *you* are the man who killed a storekeeper in cold blood. That *you* let an innocent boy take the blame."

Another cold stare from the chief.

"But unlike my son," Martinez said, his tone still calm, "*you* got to live your life. A perfect little life with your perfect little career and perfect little family."

In other circumstances, Sean might pity the man. But rage was the only thing flowing through him right now. "I wasn't alone that night in Misawa," Sean said. "And I didn't know that Juan would kill himself, so don't you try to turn this on me."

"Kill himself?" He spit out the words like they were rotten food. "Don't you dare."

Sean didn't understand.

"They put him in the cell and those animals sexually assaulted him, six of them. And I don't care what the Japs said, he didn't hang himself. Those monsters strung him up like a dog." The chief's voice broke. "Because of *you*."

"What cell? What are you—"

"Don't you dare!" The chief eyes filled with tears and fury. "And you almost got away with it." He swallowed and seemed to plant himself more firmly.

Sean's thoughts were swirling. None of it fit with his narrative of events.

"All these years, I thought my Juan was a killer." Martinez's tone softened. "But then I learned the truth."

Sean stared at Martinez. "I don't—"

"Last year," Martinez interrupted, "one of my oldest friends became the Supreme Court's marshal and offered me the job as police chief. I didn't want to move to D.C. Plus I was thinking about retiring, so I was gonna turn it down." He stared off a moment into some middle distance. "But then Charles Baldwin got cancer and didn't want to die with the guilt of what you all did." The chief's eyes turned back to Sean. "And he told me everything."

Sean just stood there. Charles Baldwin? Kenny's dad.

"That's right, just like your father, Kenny's old man got what was coming to him for what he did. What you *all* did." The reference to Sean's father took some of the air out of him. And what did Kenny's father have to do with this? Sean tried, but couldn't picture Charles Baldwin's face. Nor did he recall ever meeting Juan's dad back then. They were just grown-ups at a time when such people were invisible to Sean.

"The famous General couldn't have his son go down for

murder. No, not precious Sean Serrat. They needed someone to pin it on."

Kenny once said that Sean's dad had hindered the investigation of the storekeeper's murder. But Martinez was suggesting something more sinister.

"That's not what happened." Sean heard the desperation in his own voice.

"Oh, it's true. Your father and Baldwin cooked it up. Got you safely out of the country, then got Kenny to point the finger at my Juan. Your father didn't think he could trust me because I was military police, so they blamed my son. Baldwin said your dad called it 'collateral damage.' Well, I showed Charles Baldwin what collateral damage was when I wrapped my hands around his throat. Cancer was too good for that man. I wanted my face to be the last thing he saw in this world. I only wish he got to see me blow his idiot son's head off."

Martinez swallowed hard, regaining control. "Those Japs took Juan away and put him in that cell." He broke into a sob. "I couldn't protect him. You all took my child."

"What about *my* child?" Sean shouted back at him. "She had nothing to do with this. She was an innocent."

The chief's eyes turned cold. "How's it feel, Serrat? How's it feel to have something you love taken from *you?*"

Sean lunged toward the chief, but stopped short when he saw the gun. It had a long barrel, a silencer, maybe. The chief gestured with the weapon for Sean to walk toward the marble columns along the wall. He marched him back toward the mahogany bench.

Sean stopped at the steps that led up to the nine spaces where the justices presided.

"Is that what this was all about? Ruining me? Killing me?" Sean said. "You didn't have to hurt Abby to do that."

"I actually wasn't planning on hurting her. Kenny was just supposed to tell her the truth about you. Let her see you for who you really are. But she was too smart for her own good. She found out who *I* was, put two and two together about Charles Baldwin's murder, something his own son was too stupid to figure out. And she threatened to expose *me* if I revealed your little secret."

Sean thought again about Abby's visit to the police office the day she was murdered. She hadn't been making a complaint against Malik, she was confronting Martinez. He'd killed Abby to cover his tracks. And so Sean would feel his pain. Martinez's involvement explained so much now: how the killer knew Abby was in the court that night, how he got into the library undetected, how the surveillance tape was erased. And the court's police chief undoubtedly had access to the home addresses and work schedules of the law clerks, so Martinez could easily have slipped over to Malik's house and planted Abby's phone. It explained why Abby's apartment was ransacked and her computer and notebooks taken. Martinez was looking for whatever Abby had uncovered that connected him to Japan and Charles Baldwin's murder.

Sean had a lump in his throat. Abby was trying to protect him. Whatever she believed about Japan, she still thought Sean was worth saving. He turned his head, eyeing Martinez. "You're not going to get away with it."

"Tell that to the Baldwins." The chief smirked. "Or to Justice Carr." Martinez pushed the gun's barrel into Sean's back, directing him through the curtains. Behind the bench, there was a medical gurney, presumably in the event of an emergency with one of the justices, and the place was a bit of a mess with some electronic cords and pads and pens strewn about. There was a large trash bin. Large enough to stuff a body in. He needed to stall.

"Why kill Justice Carr? He had nothing to do with any of this."

"Collateral damage," Martinez said, seeming to take pleasure in using the same phrase Sean's father had used about Juan. "Once they started to realize that Malik wasn't the one, it was only a matter of time before they started looking closer at everyone else."

Sean digested the words, rearranging the storyboard in his head. Finkle and Brice, Martinez and Kenny had been ships passing in the night, not knowing about one another. Their paths intersected only with Abby.

"Get in," Martinez said, pointing the gun at the trash bin.

Sean stepped toward the bin. He placed a hand on either side of it to allow him to climb inside. He imagined Martinez stuffing Carr in a similar trash can and wheeling him to Carr's BMW in the garage, forcing the justice to drive them out of the building, coercing him to write the incriminating note, cutting out the justice's GPS security chip, then disposing of his body and leaving the car at Union Station. Sean had a pang of guilt that it was his actions that led to Carr's murder.

No more.

In one fluid move, he lifted the heavy gray plastic container and whipped it around, connecting with Martinez's head. The gun went off with a quiet pop, and Sean ran through the curtains behind the bench.

There were more pops and stuffing poofed out of one of the justice's leather chairs. He heard the clank of metal on metal, bullets flying by and hitting the Kevlar lining of the mahogany bench, the shield to protect the justices from any attack. Sean dove over the bench to the black marble partition below.

He caught his breath, protected for a moment by the Kevlar. But then the police chief came soaring over the bench, gun still in hand. Sean darted under the counsel table. He rolled away just as there was a cracking sound and holes appeared through the tabletop. He felt a bite in his arm as he scrambled behind a marble column. He sat on the ground, back against the cool marble. He waited for officers to charge in, but the gunshots were faint and the chamber was largely soundproof.

Before he could stand up, Sean felt the wet thud of metal to the head. His face hit the carpet. In the haze, he turned his head and saw Martinez standing over him. He gave Sean a last, long look. Then he raised the barrel of the gun to Sean's forehead.

Sean managed a hard sweep at the chief's legs—giving it everything he had—knocking him to the ground. The gun flew out of the chief's hand, and Sean clawed on top of the man, his fists pummeling Martinez's face. He was yelling now, primal noises. He hit him again and again and again until his knuckles felt raw.

He would have crushed his skull but for an image that flittered through his head. A skinny Hispanic kid, crying, hugging his knees, in a vacant lot in Misawa, Japan. Juan.

Sean stopped hitting him. Martinez emitted a quiet moan, his face awash in red. Sean hung there, straddling the man, realizing that much of the blood was his own. There was the sound of a building alarm, footfalls and shouts, until he fell beside the man and things went dark.

EPILOGUE

The first Monday in October, the start of the Supreme Court's new term, came and went. Chief Justice Mason James was receiving high marks, though the *National Law Journal*'s Supreme Court correspondent Tony Mauro reported that behind the scenes the new justice was not popular with his brethren.

Sean had withdrawn his nomination. The official reason was to spend time with his family. That was true enough. But he also couldn't afford the scrutiny that went along with the job.

The public would never know why Carlos Martinez killed Abby or Justice Carr. He hung himself in his cell, a sad parallel given the death of his son. The media speculated that Martinez had been obsessed with a young woman and had killed Carr and framed Malik to cover his tracks. They never connected Martinez to the death of a petty criminal shot in the head outside a flophouse motel. No one asked Sean's opinion about it all. They just wanted it buried.

Sean looked about his office at Harrington & Caine. He was finally settling in. Framed photos of his family covered the place, as did Jack's artwork. Sean glanced at Jack's latest masterpiece drawn in colorful markers. It showed Sean, Emily, Ryan, and Jack walking outside, holding hands. All of them were smiling. Tiny smiles, but smiles nonetheless. Above them, a sun with a smiley face and a stick figure of Abby in the clouds, holding a leash and walking her dog, Lucy.

Sean swallowed hard. He would never know how her relationship with Justice Carr began. Nor would he understand it. But he believed, or wanted to believe, that they were genuinely in love. She'd backed off working on John Chadwick's case to protect Carr, and Carr had taken a big risk getting Abby's necklace back from Billy Brice, neither realizing that the real danger wasn't from Mason James or Sebastian Finkle or small-time drug dealer Brice. The real threat was hidden in plain sight at One First Street.

Sean glanced at a framed photo of Emily from *Before*. He doubted she'd ever look so happy again, but they were trying. They were in counseling and, like Jack's picture, their smiles were small, but he thought they would make it.

From the corner of his eye, Sean saw a familiar figure standing at the doorway. His assistant, Mable, knocked softly.

"Sean," she said. "Your guest is here."

Blake Hellstrom, looking as rumpled as ever, strolled into the office.

To Mable, Sean said, "It's Friday and getting late, you really should get home. Looks like more rain is coming."

Mable smiled and shut the door behind her.

Hellstrom removed his coat, and he and Sean considered one another. Finally, Sean said, "Remember the first time you came to my office?"

Hellstrom gave a knowing nod.

"How's he doing?" Sean asked.

"Malik? It's hard to wash off the stink of being charged with murder, even if you're proven innocent. But he'll be okay. Patti Fallon, to her credit—given the shit she got for prosecuting an innocent man—helped get him a job at Justice."

Sean nodded approvingly. "So, you wanted to come by," he said. "I take it you have some news?"

Hellstrom nodded and gestured for Sean to sit at the work-table next to the large rain-spattered window. Hellstrom pulled out some papers from his worn briefcase.

"Let's start with Japan," Hellstrom said. "The Japanese law experts I've spoken with don't think the events you've described would render you guilty of anything under Japanese law, other than being a dumb kid in the wrong place at the wrong time. That might be different under U.S. law, but since the incident happened outside the military base, Japanese law would apply."

The incident. The impersonal language of a criminal defense lawyer.

Hellstrom continued, "So, if this ever comes to light, there's no risk to you, at least legally."

"What if I come forward on my own?"

Hellstrom sighed. They'd been through this before. "It's unlikely they'd pursue it. Beyond the legal issues, it was a bit of a scandal back then when they put an American kid in a cell with some hard cases. Given what happened to Juan Martinez, they wouldn't want to dredge all that up again."

"Did you find Mr. Takahashi's family?"

"No. We had no better luck than you did. He and his wife ran the store together and they had no kids. Both are deceased with no living family, best we can tell, so there's no one to even try to compensate for the loss. Again, my advice is that there's nothing more to be done."

Sean made no response. He just stared out the window into the gloom.

Hellstrom remained quiet.

After a long moment Sean said, "Can I ask you something? It's personal, so I'll understand if you'd prefer not."

Hellstrom nodded.

"I understand that you lost a child?"

This time it was Hellstrom who shifted his gaze out the window. A hard swallow. "Tommy was sixteen . . ."

"Does it ever get better?" It was the same question Sean had asked Carl Martinez, who believed that peace came only through revenge.

Hellstrom thought awhile. "I can't say it ever gets 'better.' You don't recover. You cope. It used to be that Tommy was the first thing I'd think about when I woke up. Most days now I can make it until about noon."

Sean had hoped for a more optimistic answer. But he admired this wise old lawyer for stating the truth.

"Advice?" Sean asked.

"What I've learned is that everybody grieves differently, in their own way," Hellstrom said. "Some people are forever crippled in despair, some people bounce back faster than seems possible. All I know is that it's something that never leaves any of us. What I try to do is live my life in a way that I think would have made Tommy proud."

"I guess that's what I'm struggling with," Sean said. "Abby believed in justice, the rule of law, right and wrong. Wouldn't the right thing to do be coming forward about Japan?"

"I know you've lived with this thing for a long time, and you want to do something. But I can tell you from experience, sometimes there just isn't a clear right and wrong, a clear black and white, and I think your daughter understood that. It would be a mistake to come forward, Sean."

More silence fell between them. Hellstrom studied Sean for a moment, then sighed heavily. "Why do I get the feeling you're not gonna follow my advice?"

Sean gave a faint smile.

Hellstrom shook his head. "All right, let's move on to something we can agree on." His mouth curled into a mischievous smile. "I got a call from Detective Whiteside with the Montgomery County police. Based on your statement and Ryan's, they got a warrant and searched Sebastian Finkle's condo and his safe."

"Did they find the dirt files? Or photos of Brice or the metal bar to prove Finkle was at the football field that night?"

"Nope."

Sean met eyes with Hellstrom.

"The safe was cleared out. Nothing there."

"So why are you smiling?"

"Shoes."

Sean was puzzled.

"Finkle may have cleaned house of any incriminating files, but he didn't get rid of his size-eleven Prada sneakers. They were able to match them to marks left on Billy Brice's neck; he died after his throat was stomped on. I guess Finkle didn't want to throw out his five hundred dollar shoes."

Sean smiled. "What if he turns over the pole with Ryan's prints on it?"

"Covered in the immunity agreement. Our only contingency was that you and Ryan had to tell the truth, and you did. And, anyway, the only thing I think Sebastian Finkle will be turning over is his partner in crime."

"You think he'll roll over on Mason James?"

"I've found that it doesn't take long inside a cell for guys who wear five-hundred-dollar sneakers and who live in fancy condos to start thinking about how they can get out. And offering up evidence on the chief justice of the United States is probably one of the surest get-out-of-jail-early cards around."

"But if not?" Sean asked. "We can't just let James get away with what he's done."

That's when Hellstrom gestured to the papers on the worktable. "No. I have a contingency plan. Something I thought we might work on together."

Sean scanned the papers. They were motions challenging the conviction of John Chadwick, Mason James's college roommate.

"We can use the case to look into James's past." Hellstrom grinned again. "I doubt he killed those girls, but maybe we can connect James to Chadwick's beating at the prison or some of his other mischief. I thought we could finish the good work your daughter had started."

An image of Abby flashed in Sean's mind for the briefest of

moments. She was walking on the beach, hair blowing in the wind, waxing poetic about justice and the law.

"I think Abby would like that," Sean said. "I think she'd like that a lot."

ACKNOWLEDGMENTS

This book opens with a dedication to my children. I did this not only because I'm blessed to have such kind and remarkable kids, but also because the pages of *The Advocate's Daughter* are filled with things I've appropriated from their lives. It was only natural when writing about the Serrat family to turn to my everyday life for inspiration. But more so, I hope that years from now my children will read the book and understand that I saw them—that I heard them—and that they recognize the joy they brought to my life. From Em's sunrise escapes, to Jake's love of Guns N' Roses, to Aiden's jokes, to the loyalty they have to one another, my children are the heart of this novel. (My wife would be quick to point out, however, that all crimes and foibles of the Serrat clan are purely the work of their father's imagination.)

Speaking of my wife, Tracy, I've rewritten this part several times, but it still comes out sounding cliché, something all writers hate. But what the hell: Since I was sixteen, home to me has been wherever you are. I owe this novel, and everything else, to you. Everything.

Okay, enough of all that. There are many people I need to thank for their contributions to this book.

I'm fortunate to work with the best publishing team in the business. My literary agent, Lisa Erbach Vance, lived up to her reputation as a "super agent," providing exceptional representation and sage advice. It is also an honor and a privilege to work with my editors, Jaime Levine and Anne Brewer. Thanks also to Jennifer Letwack, Bill Warhop, and the rest of the St. Martin's Press team.

Special thanks also goes to my law firm, Arnold & Porter, which is filled with talented and supportive colleagues. Lisa Blatt, one of the best Supreme Court advocates of her generation (seriously, Google her), has been a loyal friend and supporter of my novels and legal career. I also must thank others in our top-flight Supreme Court practice group, including Reeves Anderson and Stanton Jones, who are my core beta readers in fiction—and everything else. So many other past and present lawyers and non-lawyers at the firm (and their significant others) also provided helpful information, feedback, or support: Brooke Anderson, Judy Bernstein-Gaeta, Annie Khalid Hussain, Dan Jacobson, Kathryne Lindsey, Chris Man, John Massaro, Evie Norwinski, James Rosenthal, Sheila Scheuerman, Mara Senn, Craig Stewart, and Rob Weiner.

Book clubs closely connected to the firm also deserve thanks. The Ladies of North Kenmore Street Book Club: Gayle Herbert, Joedy Cambridge, Denise Cormaney, MaryLynn Haase, Angela Huskey, Anna Manville, Marlene Regelski-RedDoor, Katherine Taylor, and Connie Young. Also thanks to Patty Donnelly's club, which includes Patty, Joanne Garlow, Cheryl Marsh, and Amanda Wingo.

I also must single out Debbie Carpenter—my longtime friend, legal assistant, and all around exceptional person.

Outside the firm, many other friends, including Dan Barnhizer, Robert Knowles, and Stacey Colino, provided helpful comments.

One of the great things about publishing novels is that it has given me the opportunity to branch out from the legal community into the world of writers. And so many writers have helped me along the way. I first must thank all my friends with the International Thriller Writers association. I encourage all current and aspiring thriller, suspense, and mystery writers to join ITW. From the moment I signed on, best-selling authors—too many to mention—went out of their way to support my work. During my time with the organization, I've served as Chair of the Debut Authors Committee, where I made several close friends (a rarity as you get older), including great writers Barry Lancet, Jenny Milchman, Ethan Cross, and ThrillerFest director Kimberley Howe. I then served as Awards Coordinator for ITW's annual book awards, and got to work with Carla Buckley, Joshua Corin, and Jeff Ayers. I then was the managing editor of ITW's *The Big Thrill* magazine, where I had a great time with my co-editors Barry Lancet and Dawn Ius, with endless support from ITW's leadership, including Liz Berry, M. J. Rose, and Janice Gable Bashman. At every turn, it seems, someone from ITW was there to help, from medical insights from D. P. Lyle, M.D., to advice about the publishing business from Alan Jacobson, to editorial feedback and many laughs from Barry Lancet (I've now mentioned Barry three times, to beat out the two nods he gave to me in his last book). And I cannot forget Shannon and John Raab, staunch ITW supporters and publishers of *Suspense Magazine,* who provided me many opportunities, and became good friends along the way.

Perhaps most remarkable, ITW's co-founder, best-selling author Gayle Lynds, took me under her wing. This book wouldn't have been published were it not for Gayle. She is a true writer's writer, and it is no surprise that the organization she co-founded carries forward her spirit of kindness, support, and mentorship. You're a rare and wonderful person, Gayle.

Last, but never least, thanks to readers. I love hearing from you, and I hope you'll drop me a line and let me know what you thought of *The Advocate's Daughter.*

ABOUT
AUTHENTICITY

The Advocate's Daughter is a work of fiction and the names, characters, places, and incidents portrayed are the product of the author's imagination or have been used fictitiously. Any resemblance to actual persons, living or dead, business establishments, events, or locales is entirely coincidental. (Forgive me, I've been a lawyer for twenty years.)

I'm often asked about whether some place or legal principle in my books is "real" or what inspired a specific scene, so I went through my research files to offer the following behind-the-scenes glimpse. Note, there are some spoilers, so wait to read this until you're done with the book.

There is a military base in Misawa, Japan, a place where I spent some unforgettable years of my youth. For dramatic purposes, I made the base and town dark and run-down. But in reality, it is a beautiful part of the world, the Japanese were kind and generous to us military brats, and I'll always hold a special place for Misawa and the friends I made there. I should add that my father, who spent a distinguished career in the military, bears no resemblance to "the General." (Sorry, Dad!)

I tried to capture the spirit of the Supreme Court community, though I had to take liberties since that crowd tends not to have many vices. It is true that Supreme Court justices are rarely recognized in public. Sadly, surveys show that more Americans can identify Judge Judy than a justice on the Supreme Court.

The scene at Georgetown University Law Center at the beginning of the book was inspired by an annual event held by the Law Center's Supreme Court Institute in which members of the Bar gather to celebrate the end of the term. Every year, the Institute, headed by Director Dori Bernstein and Professor Irv Gornstein, holds moot courts (practice arguments) for advocates appearing before the high court. It is a tremendous service to the advocates and the justices, and I'm proud to periodically serve as a moot judge. The 2012 event honored Justice Ruth Bader Ginsburg, an opera lover, and singers from the Washington National Opera serenaded the popular justice. It was beautiful and stuck with me, hence the scene.

Much of the information about the Supreme Court in *The Advocate's Daughter* was inspired by or derived from not only my law practice, but the great work of many esteemed journalists and commentators. I continue to draw from Jeffrey Toobin's fun, readable books about the court. (The prank Sean Serrat played on Professor Tweed about the fake call from the president was from a real event involving Chief Justice John Roberts from Toobin's *The Oath*. So was the "do-over" reference concerning Obama's botched oath of office.) And, like the rest of the world, I benefited from the coverage of the high court by the Supreme Court press corps, including Robert Barnes, Joan Biskupic, Marcia Coyle, Adam Liptak, Tony Mauro, David Savage, Nina Totenberg, and others. I'm always amazed at the quality and insights of their coverage, which often must be done under intense deadlines. And I cannot forget SCOTUSblog, everyone's go-to source for information on the high court.

I've been to all the places depicted in the book, and did my best to try to make them feel authentic. With respect to the Supreme Court Building, I'd encourage all readers who visit Washington to march up the forty-four marble front steps (you can no longer enter from the front doors for security reasons, but it's still an experience). And it's worth the wait in line to attend an oral argument. Not to be overly sentimental, but, for me, watching how our country resolves some of the biggest questions of the day in a civilized way, under the rule of law, without violence, dampens the cynicism that might otherwise sneak in from living in Washington.

The court's library is as majestic as I describe, though I made up the secret staircase, I'm sorry to say. I've been fortunate enough to step inside the conference room where the justices preside in secret, and did my best to describe it. And there is a basketball court on the top floor of the building—the real "highest court in the land," so goes the tired joke.

My scenes on the Hill I credit to the time my friend, and a senate chief of staff, Mike Sozan, has taken over the years to show me and my writer friends around, including the underground train and hideaway offices. And I'm lucky to know Brian Hook, the former special assistant to the president and assistant secretary of state, who is always a reliable source for Washington insights (and like me and Ryan, a connoisseur of eighties metal).

There is a Chipotle in Bethesda, Maryland, and Bethesda–Chevy Chase High School is a real school. Neither, of course, are frequented by a hapless, sketchy drug dealer. I hope they will forgive me.

Beyond the setting of the novel, the law school lecture Professor Tweed gives his students about James Callender will be familiar to law students I've taught over the years. The information on Callender, to the best of my ability, is accurate.

Some of the humor (or attempts at humor, anyway) in the novel come from real events. Like Ryan, my son Jake nearly fell asleep during a visit with a Supreme Court justice. And Jack's orange juice joke was taken from a funny article in *Salon* by Professor Jay Wexler about his time as a Supreme Court law clerk.

The speech Sean gives about his daughter on the front steps of his home was inspired in part by a high school commencement speech given by English teacher David McCullough, Jr., entitled

"You Are Not Special." I think the Serrats would share the same worldview as McCullough.

Capturing the grief of the characters was a challenge. I read several books about loss, but one that stayed with me was *When the Bough Breaks*, which contains many heartbreaking first-person narratives of grieving parents.

Many of the other insights about the court or Washington were the result of phone calls, meetings, and lunches with many serious people who took time to help me try to bring an air of authenticity to *The Advocate's Daughter*. All errors—purposeful or otherwise—are my own.